Acclaim for the authors of
STAY FOR CHRISTMAS

JUDITH STACY

"A fine writer with both polished style
and heartwarming sensitivity."
—bestselling author Pamela Morsi

"The characters and the story's touching sentiments
have a wonderfully warm appeal."
—*Romantic Times BOOKclub* on *The Hired Husband*

VICTORIA BYLIN

"[Bylin's] bad-boy western romances aren't
to be missed."
—*Romantic Times BOOKclub*

"Ms. Bylin is a growing talent in historical fiction
and her magic pen touches both your emotions
and your soul with each turn of the page."
—*Romance Reviews Today*

ELIZABETH LANE

"This credible, now-or-never romance moves
with reckless speed through a highly engrossing and
compact plot to the kind of happy ending we read
romances to enjoy."
—*Romantic Times BOOKclub* on *Wyoming Woman*

"Enjoyable and satisfying all round, *Bride on the Run* is
an excellent Western romance you won't want to miss!"
—*Romance Reviews Today*

JUDITH STACY

fell in love with the West while watching TV Westerns as a child in her rural Virginia home—one of the first in the community to have a television. This Wild West setting, with its strong men and resourceful women, remains one of her favorites.

Judith is married to her high school sweetheart. They have two daughters and live in Southern California.

VICTORIA BYLIN

has a collection of refrigerator magnets that mark the changes in her life. The oldest ones are from California. A native of Los Angeles, she graduated from UC Berkeley with a degree in history and went to work in the advertising industry. She soon met a wonderful man who charmed her into taking a ride on his motorcycle. That ride led to a trip down the wedding aisle, two sons, various pets and a move that landed Victoria and her family in northern Virginia.

Magnets from thirty states commemorate that journey and her new life on the East Coast. The most recent additions are from the Smithsonian National Museum of American History and a Chinese restaurant that delivers, a sure sign that Victoria is busy writing. Feel free to drop her an e-mail at VictoriaBylin@aol.com or visit her Web site at www.victoriabylin.com.

ELIZABETH LANE

has lived and traveled in many parts of the world, including Europe, Latin America and the Far East, but her heart remains in the American West, where she was born and raised. Her idea of heaven is hiking a mountain trail on a clear autumn day. She also enjoys music, animals and dancing.

You can learn more about Elizabeth by visiting her Web site at www.elizabethlaneauthor.com.

Stay for Christmas

JUDITH STACY
VICTORIA BYLIN
ELIZABETH LANE

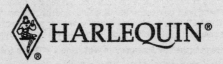

TORONTO • NEW YORK • LONDON
AMSTERDAM • PARIS • SYDNEY • HAMBURG
STOCKHOLM • ATHENS • TOKYO • MILAN • MADRID
PRAGUE • WARSAW • BUDAPEST • AUCKLAND

ISBN-13: 978-0-373-29419-0
ISBN-10:   0-373-29419-0

STAY FOR CHRISTMAS
Copyright © 2006 by Harlequin Books S.A.

The publisher acknowledges the copyright holders of the individual works as follows:

A PLACE TO BELONG
Copyright © 2006 by Dorothy Howell

A SON IS GIVEN
Copyright © 2006 by Vicki Scheibel

ANGELS IN THE SNOW
Copyright © 2006 by Elizabeth Lane

CONTENTS

A PLACE TO BELONG   9
Judith Stacy

A SON IS GIVEN   125
Victoria Bylin

ANGELS IN THE SNOW   213
Elizabeth Lane

A PLACE TO BELONG

Judith Stacy

Dear Reader,

Christmas is my favorite holiday of the year. The baking, the shopping, the decorating are all wonderful times for family togetherness. I love receiving greeting cards from old friends and distant relatives.

Throughout my husband's career in the U.S. Air Force, I worked extra hard to provide strong holiday traditions for my children. Now that my daughters are grown, they've added their own traditions, which have given our holiday an international feel in the past few years.

Now our bulging Christmas tree sparkles with ornaments from Harrods in England, glass shops in Rome, the Maya ruins in Mexico and handcrafted items from Iraq, Jordan and Kuwait.

Only our Christmas dinner remains unchanged. Turkey and all the trimmings, served on china used once a year. None of us would dream of changing that. Amid the hustle and bustle, the excitement of the holiday season, one thing remains at the center of our Christmas celebration: family. I hope you and your family will share the love and warmth that the holiday season brings.

Happy holidays!

Judith Stacy

Chapter One

Colorado
1887

She was going to hell.

Maybe.

Maggie Hudson hurried along the boardwalk feeling the winter chill on her cheeks, the knot of worry in her stomach—and the weight of the knowledge that she might very well go to hell.

Could a woman's soul be condemned to everlasting damnation for simply thinking unkind thoughts? Maggie wasn't sure—hoped it wasn't so. Because if it were, all the unsavory, unchristian, unladylike notions racing through her mind right now would surely condemn her to an eternity of fire and brimstone.

She picked up her pace. Around her the folks of Crystal Springs went about their business beneath the gloomy afternoon sky. Men in suits, miners with long beards, cowboys with guns on their hips. Women—some in calico and gingham, others in fine Eastern fashions—shepherded along their children, who were too young for school. Horses, wagons and carriages moved though the damp dirt of Main Street.

Maggie blended in with the other young women in town, in her gingham dress and the bonnet that covered her dark hair. Yet a woman her age—twenty—should have been trailing a child, or at the very least, walking with her husband.

Maggie was quite certain no one on the streets of Crystal Springs was surprised to see her alone.

Nor was she surprised to endure the looks of the towns-folk and feel the familiar sting of judgment, condemnation…pity. She knew what they were thinking.

Maggie forced the tension from her face, putting in place the neutral expression that had served her well these past months. The last thing she needed was to draw attention to herself. Especially now, when she'd finally been given the opportunity to redeem herself in the eyes of the town.

And she had so much to redeem herself for.

Maggie paused on the boardwalk, her gaze riveted on the jailhouse down the block.

Sheriff Jack Crawford. New in town, he'd been hired by the mayor only a few weeks ago. Maggie had never met him but she'd seen him around town. He'd been in Hudson's Mercantile, the general store her father owned, but Maggie had hidden in the stockroom each time she'd seen him approach; there was only so much even Maggie could take.

But there would be no hiding today. Jack Crawford stood in her way of finally making the long climb back toward self-respect. And Maggie wasn't about to let him do that.

She pulled in a big breath, lifted her chin and went inside the jailhouse.

Maggie was anxious to be out of the chilly breeze, yet it seemed no warmer in here. The few furnishings—desk, stove, gun racks—gave the room a cold, hard look. The stove in the corner put out little heat. The place smelled of gun oil and burned coffee. Off to the left, Maggie caught sight of the hallway that, she supposed, led to the cells.

The sheriff sat behind his desk across the room, feet propped up, reading the newspaper.

His gaze came up quickly, pinning Maggie in place. His feet hit the floor and he shot up from his chair so quickly it gave her a start. She gasped and froze. He froze, too. For a long moment the two of them just stood there, still as statues, staring at each other.

Finally, he took a single step forward.

"Afternoon," he said. "What can I do for you?"

Maggie kept staring. She knew that her mouth had sagged open but she couldn't seem to close it. Nor could she stop her knees from shaking or her mind from racing.

This was Sheriff Jack Crawford? She'd only seen him from a distance when, thanks to the cold, he'd had his jacket collar turned up and his hat pulled low. She hadn't realized he was…handsome.

Tall with wide straight shoulders, a head full of dark brown, slightly wavy hair and piercing blue eyes that were, quite possibly, responsible for the hammering of her heart.

Why had she not known how handsome he was? Why had she not realized it?

And why had she hidden in the stockroom every time he'd come to her father's mercantile?

He hung his thumb in his gun belt. "Can I help you?"

Maggie's senses snapped back, bringing with them a wave of embarrassment. Good gracious, what was she doing? Ogling a man—the sheriff, of all people—when her very future hung in the balance.

She cleared her throat. "I'm Maggie—"

"Hudson. I know who you are."

His tone was crisp and businesslike, cooling Maggie's feelings considerably.

Jack nodded toward the badge pinned to his pale blue shirt. "I make it my business to know everybody town."

She supposed that was a good quality in a lawman but it irritated Maggie slightly to think that he knew who she was. It alarmed her, too. What else did he already know about her?

Maggie exhaled slowly, composing herself. She nodded toward the hallway that led to the jail cells.

"I'm here to see Emmett Frazier," she said.

Jack's left eyebrow crept upward. "Are you a relative?"

"No."

"Is he your beau?"

Maggie cringed inwardly, thinking that most folks in Crystal Springs probably reckoned that being courted by the likes of Emmett Frazier was the best she'd ever do.

"I need to see him on church business," Maggie told him, making her voice sound as crisp as the sheriff's. "Church. It's the new building on the edge of town—"

"I know where the church is."

"Oh? I didn't realize that," Maggie said, arching her brows, "since no one has ever seen you there."

Jack shifted and Maggie glimpsed a flash of pink on his cheeks. An odd wave of satisfaction zipped through her, then evaporated when he crossed both arms across his chest and squared his shoulders.

"You can't just come in here asking to visit a prisoner," he told her. "I've got official business to attend to."

Maggie looked pointedly at the desk where he'd had his feet up, then at the newspaper he'd been reading and, finally, the rest of the room, empty but for the two of them.

"I can see you're terribly busy," she told him. "But I'm here on official business."

His eyebrows drew together. "What sort of business?"

"I'll have to see Emmett first. Otherwise, it would be an intrusion into your…busy schedule."

Jack stared at her for a long moment, his eyes narrowed, his jaw set. Maggie steeled herself, tried to keep calm when what she wanted to do was scream at him. Finally, he headed toward the hallway that held the jail cells.

Good gracious, what wide shoulders he had. The notion whipped through Maggie's mind. And a long back, too. His gun belt rode low on his hips, and his—

Jack glanced over his shoulder. Maggie jerked her gaze away, feigning interest in the gun racks, and determinedly held her gaze on them until she heard his footsteps disappear down the hallway. Heat rose in her cheeks.

A moment later she heard the deep rumble of his voice, then he stepped into the office. She started toward the cells, but he blocked her path.

Jack's gaze ran the length of her, head to toe, making her acutely aware of the dress she wore. For a desperate instant she wished to be wearing anything but the tired gingham gown. Oh, to look pretty—

"Have you got anything on you?" Jack asked, his eyes on her face now. "Gun? Knife? Any sort of weapon?"

So that's why he was looking at her. Maggie felt foolish, thinking otherwise. Her, of all people, wanting to look pretty.

Fighting off her embarrassment, Maggie told him, "As I said earlier, I'm here on church business. I don't know what sort of church you attended in the past, Mr. Crawford, but here in Crystal Springs we don't arm ourselves while doing the Lord's work."

"I'll keep that in mind, should I decide to attend church," he said, then led the way down the hall.

Three cells stood on the left. Emmett Frazier occupied the last one; the others were empty. Feeble sunlight filtered through tiny windows. The air was damp and cold.

Off to the right was another room. Maggie glanced inside. A bunk stood against the far wall, a single gray wool blanket spread across it. A pair of long johns peeked out from the open drawer of a bureau. There was a washstand surrounded by a razor, shaving mug, comb and brush. Trousers and shirts hung from a row of wall pegs. The stove was cold.

This was undoubtedly the most unappealing room she'd ever seen.

She gazed up at Jack. "Is this where you live?"

"It suits me just fine," Jack told her.

"But how could it?" Maggie asked, shaking her head.

"Do you want to see the prisoner or not?" he asked.

Jack didn't wait for an answer, just strode down the hallway leaving Maggie to follow.

"Keep away from the bars," he told her. "I'll be in the office."

Jack threw a glare at the prisoner so harsh it brought a deeper chill to the room, then left, leaving Maggie alone with Emmett Frazier.

He stood in the middle of the cell, head down, shoulders slumped. He was a big man, tall, with an unkempt beard and blond hair that hung to his shoulders. Fistfights and hard living made him appear older than his thirty years.

Maggie's heart sank. Here stood her redemption. Her salvation. Her only chance to get back in the good graces of Crystal Springs.

When Herb Foster from the feed-and-grain store had stopped by Hudson's Mercantile today and told her that Emmett had been arrested last night, she'd been frantic. Obviously, her worry had been well-founded.

She stepped closer to the bars. "Emmett Frazier, just look at you. What have you got to say for yourself?"

"I'm sorry, Miss Maggie. Powerful sorry," he said. "I went and did just exactly what I promised you I wouldn't."

"So it's true?" she asked. "You were out drinking last night? And fighting?"

"Yes, ma'am," Emmett admitted sorrowfully.

"You gave me your word," she reminded him. "You came to me and asked—begged—me for help."

He shook his shaggy head. "I know…I know…."

"You should be ashamed of yourself, Emmett," she told him. "Why, most people simply feel the presence of the Lord in their lives, but He actually spoke to you."

Emmett lifted his head, his bloodshot eyes mournful.

"I am ashamed, Miss Maggie. Truly, I am." He plastered his meaty palm against his chest. "But if you could give me another chance, I won't let you down. I swear I won't."

Maggie contemplated the gentle giant of a man standing before her. Emmett Frazier did odd jobs around town, mined a claim in the hills occasionally, worked on the surrounding cattle ranches when he needed money. He was a good man, usually. Quiet and kind. Yet his love of a good fistfight and a bottle of cheap whiskey had plagued his life for years.

But his day of reckoning had come earlier this week in the alley behind the Wild Cat Saloon, and sent him running to Maggie at the mercantile. God had spoken to him, he declared, and told him exactly what he should do to redeem himself for his life of excess and debauchery.

More than anyone in Crystal Springs, Maggie understood the need for redemption. By the end of their conversation Emmett had convinced her of her role in his salvation. She'd realized it would be her salvation, as well.

"All right," Maggie told him. "I'll take care of it."

"Thank you, Miss Maggie, thank you kindly."

"But you'd better not let me down again." She wagged her finger at him.

"I won't." He turned his palm toward her. "I swear, I won't let you down."

"Or yourself—or God."

"Yes, ma'am. I'll be good. I promise you—" Emmett pointed skyward "—and the good Lord above."

Maggie returned to the office and found Jack seated behind his desk, leafing through a stack of Wanted posters.

"You can let him out of jail now," she said.

Jack's gaze came up. "How's that?"

Maggie gestured to the ring of keys hanging by the rifle racks and said, "It's all right to let Emmett go."

"Is that so?"

"Yes, and hurry up, will you? I have to get back to the store." She'd been away for a while now and she shuddered to think what her father had done in her absence.

Jack leaned forward in his chair and rested his elbow on the desk. "In case you were confused by the bars on the cells, Miss Hudson, this is the jailhouse, and Emmett Frazier is a prisoner. He's not going anywhere."

Alarm zipped through Maggie. "But he has to be released. He's needed at the church."

Jack gave her a "so what?" shrug.

Her redemption, her salvation, flashed in her mind—along with Emmett's.

Maggie stomped over to the desk. "Emmett is sorry for what he did," she told him.

Jack just looked at her.

"This is for the church," she said, speaking each word clearly. "The church. You have to—"

"See, now there's where you're wrong." Jack came to his feet, towering over her, causing Maggie to lean her head back to see his face.

"Frazier is serving a thirty-day sentence for—"

"Thirty days!" Maggie's alarm turned to panic. She touched her fingertips to her forehead, then flung out her arm. "You can't keep Emmett here for thirty days. That's clear past Christmas."

"He was arrested and duly sentenced," Jack said calmly.

"You can't keep him here. You simply can't!"

Jack tapped his badge. "This says that I can."

"But you don't understand—"

"Then explain it to me," Jack told her. "What's so important about Frazier coming to church?"

Maggie seemed to transform right before his eyes. The warm blush disappeared from her cheeks. Her bright face dulled to a sick-room pallor. The shine vanished from her clear blue eyes. Her lips thinned to a taut line.

Jack's lawman instincts took over with a rush of impatience. What was wrong? He had to find out, fix it, make it right. That's what he did, all day, every day.

"What? What is it?" Jack demanded.

His harsh words sparked something in her—he wasn't sure what—but Maggie seemed to find her inner strength again. She squared her shoulders and pushed up her chin.

"I assure you, Sheriff Crawford, you haven't heard the last of this," she told him, then strode across the room toward the door.

Frustration and annoyance claimed Jack.

"Nor have you," he told her in the tone that had stopped hardened criminals in their tracks.

Maggie froze with her hand on the doorknob. She turned back and gave him a hard glare—or was it a dare?—then yanked the door open and marched outside, slamming it behind her.

Jack mumbled a curse. Concern, worry and something else that he couldn't name rolled through him as the vision of Maggie's colorless cheeks lingered in his mind.

What the hell had that been about? Jack pulled at his chin. He needed to find out.

Chapter Two

"**A**fternoon, Sheriff."

Ben Sheridan stepped into the jailhouse, closing the door with a thud and pulling Jack out of his reverie. He'd been looking out the window, so consumed by his thoughts that he hadn't seen his own deputy's approach.

How long had he been staring outside? Jack didn't know. He'd completely lost himself in the goings-on of Main Street.

Or maybe it was the sight of one particular woman.

Jack forced the vision of Maggie disappearing into Hudson's Mercantile from his mind and silently admonished himself for his lapse in judgment. He couldn't afford to let down his guard—no lawman could—for even a moment.

"I saw Maggie Hudson leaving here a few minutes ago," Ben said.

It had only been a few minutes? Jack was relieved.

"What did she want?" Ben asked, pouring himself a cup of coffee from the pot on the stove.

"Something about church business," Jack said, his gaze straying to Main Street again.

Ben walked over, sipping from his thick, white mug, and stared out the window, too.

Deputy Ben Sheridan was on the job when Jack arrived in Crystal Springs. He'd been hired by the mayor to insure some stability during the past few months when a succession of sheriffs had come and gone; the town's long-time sheriff had left unexpectedly. Though Jack was here now, the town council wanted Ben to stay on as deputy. Jack thought it a good idea, given the arrangement he had with the council.

He liked Ben. He was young—late twenties, Jack figured—and honest and hardworking. He'd lived in town for a while so he knew most everyone and shared the information without sounding superior. Jack appreciated that.

"Church business, huh?" Ben sighed thoughtfully. "I figured Maggie was here because of that pa of hers. Lord, that man's as ornery as a cross-eyed mule."

Jack couldn't argue the point. Already he'd been called to the Hudson's Mercantile more times than he could count.

"I'm going out on rounds." Jack took his coat and hat from the peg row beside the door and left the jail.

Folks on the boardwalk moved aside as he headed east, most offering him a smile or a respectful nod. Jack reminded himself to appear friendly, open, approachable.

Not an easy task for a man who'd spent most of his adult life hunting down, capturing and transporting some of the worst criminals known to man.

Jack's years as a U.S. Marshal had made him wary and suspicious, left him thinking the worst of most people. But it had kept him alive, too.

He wasn't sure he'd need many of those skills here in

Crystal Springs. The problems he'd handled so far ranged from a dispute over a checker game to fights at the saloon.

A quieter life, no doubt about it. And that's just what he'd wanted when he left the Marshal's Service.

Jack just wasn't sure he wanted that quieter life here in Crystal Springs. He'd know soon enough.

He paused on the boardwalk and eyed a freight wagon that ambled down Main Street. More than once, he'd wondered why the string of sheriffs who'd preceded him had decided to leave. Town too quiet? Pace too slow? Not enough to do?

Or maybe the place just hadn't felt like home to them.

A little knot jerked in Jack's belly, reminding him of the morning several months ago when he'd awakened in yet another strange hotel bed, in yet another strange town. He was there to pick up a prisoner. He'd done it dozens, maybe hundreds, of times in his career.

But this particular morning, Jack had stood at the window looking down on the busy street, unable to remember the name of the town. It startled him. Not because his memory momentarily failed him, but because this town was just like so many others he'd been to. And was just like all the others he would eventually pass through.

Who even knew he was in town? he'd wondered that morning, still staring out the hotel window. The sheriff, his boss at the Marshal's Service. That's all.

If he vanished off the earth, who would come to look for him? Who would even care? His folks were long dead and he heard from his sister back East only rarely. A couple of friends might wonder what had happened to him—eventually.

What evidence—aside from incarcerated prisoners—

was there that Jack had even been in this world? And what sort of legacy was that?

A long, endless succession of nameless towns and faceless townsfolk flashed in front of Jack that morning. His future.

He hadn't liked where he was headed so he quit the Marshal's Service and took another direction, looking for something better.

He wasn't sure he'd found it here in Crystal Springs.

But he was sure that he couldn't ignore the sudden jump of his heart as he realized that he'd come to a stop near Hudson's Mercantile. He squinted against the gray sky trying to see through the display windows.

Had someone walked past them? Was it a woman?

Was it Maggie?

Not once during his long career as a lawman could he remember anyone—certainly not an angel-faced woman like Maggie Hudson—marching into his jail and demanding the release of a prisoner. Even if it was for the church, as she'd claimed.

And what would the church want with the likes of Emmett Frazier? Jack thought it over but came up with nothing.

Another notion floated through his mind, this one more troubling. If Maggie was brazen enough to storm into his jail and demand Emmett's release, would she abandon her plan to secure his freedom just because Jack refused her?

He almost cringed as his mind played out the possibilities. How far would Maggie go to secure Emmett's release?

It hardly seemed likely, but what if a little slip of a thing like Maggie Hudson actually pulled off a jailbreak— right under his nose?

Jack considered going back to the jail, warning Ben to watch out for Maggie. But how would that look? A former U.S. Marshal locking down the jail under threat of a breakout by the daughter of the town's crazy merchant hell-bent on doing church work?

Jack knew he needed to find out what was behind the woman's insistence that Emmett be released from jail, and to do that he had to find out more about Maggie Hudson.

She'd threatened the town sheriff.

Maggie slapped her palm across her lips realizing she'd moaned aloud at the recollection. Had someone heard?

Her gaze darted across the mercantile. Two women—the store's only customers—stood near the windows looking at gray wool blankets heaped on a table. No sign of her father.

She turned back to the high rows of shelves along the store's west wall and the newly arrived crates of merchandise her father had ordered. She pulled another oil lantern from the packing straw and placed it on the shelf, trying to focus on her task, trying—yet failing—to keep thoughts of her scandalous behavior at the jail from her mind.

I assure you, Sheriff Crawford, you haven't heard the last of this.

Maggie cringed as she recalled the blatant threat she'd flung at him. She didn't know what had come over her.

And it hadn't ended there, of course.

Nor have you.

The sheriff's much more intimidating response had shattered her momentary bravado. She might have fallen to pieces right then and there had she not become so adept at hiding her true emotions these past months.

Maggie took the last lantern from the crate and placed it on the shelf. Twelve identical oil lamps, the last as plain and unappealing as the first. On the next shelf sat the two dozen hammers she'd already unpacked.

Nothing fancy or frilly at Hudson's Mercantile, her father had decreed. Crystal Springs was a town of hard-working people who needed the necessities of life, and it was up to his mercantile to provide them.

Maggie shook her head. She couldn't disagree with her father's assessment of the town, but still…

The bell over the door jingled. Maggie figured the two shoppers were leaving—empty-handed—and was surprised, instead, to see Sarah Patterson enter the store.

Sarah Burk, Maggie reminded herself. Only a few months ago Sarah had married Caleb Burk in the very first marriage ceremony to take place in the town's new church. Sarah was one of Maggie's true friends. They remained close, even after all that had happened.

Bess Patterson, Sarah's eccentric aunt, had given her blessing to Sarah and Caleb's union and urged the quick marriage. Some thought her actions conciliatory since the older woman had discouraged Caleb from courting her treasured niece. Others insisted the persnickety Bess Patterson simply wanted Sarah to be the first bride married in the church that Bess had donated most of the money to build.

"Just look at you." Maggie touched her palms to her cheeks. "Another new dress? It's beautiful."

Sarah smiled shyly. "Yes. Yes, it's…new."

Maggie took a quick turn around Sarah, admiring the dark green dress from all sides. It was an elegant costume, the skirt of lace flouncing, the top short-waisted. The collar was high, the sleeves turned back. Satin ribbon belted her waist and drew into a large bow at her bustle. A small hat festooned with matching bows sat at a jaunty angle.

"Another gift from Caleb?" Maggie asked. When Sarah nodded, she said, "That's two new dresses, this month alone. Did Kinsey make it for you in her new shop?"

"She does wonderful work," Sarah said.

Maggie couldn't agree more. Though Kinsey Mason had only recently opened the dress shop across the street from Hudson's Mercantile, thanks to the generosity of her new husband, she already had orders from many of the young women in Crystal Springs anxious to cast aside gingham and calico, and step out in the new Eastern fashions.

"How is Caleb?" Maggie asked.

Caleb had gone into partnership with Jared Mason, Kinsey's husband, in a construction business, and the two men quickly developed all the work they could handle. Caleb also owned part interest in MacAvoy's General Store, along with his mother, and spent many hours there, as well. And as if that weren't enough, both men were building houses for their wives on the edge of town. Maggie had watched their construction these past weeks.

"Caleb's busy. We're all busy," Sarah said with a tired smile. "Aunt Bess left this morning and she asked—"

"Miss Patterson left?" Maggie blurted out the words, causing Sarah to draw back a little. "Where did she go?"

"Maryland."

"Maryland?"

"She's visiting her cousin for Christmas," Sarah explained. "It was a spur-of-the-moment trip."

Maggie's stomach twisted into a painful knot. "So Miss Patterson won't be back until…after Christmas?"

"Is something wrong, Maggie?"

"It's just that, well, your aunt ordered some things for Christmas and she hasn't...she hasn't paid for them yet."

"Aunt Bess left me a long list of things to do for her while she's gone. I'll check," Sarah promised.

Maggie said a silent prayer that Bess Patterson had left instructions and hadn't simply forgotten the order. Because if she had—

"I knew it! I just knew it!"

Dabney Hudson burst through the door sending the little bell jangling madly. Thoughts of Bess Patterson and this looming calamity left Maggie's head. She braced herself as she always did when her father came into the store like this.

She gave Sarah a thin, apologetic smile and scooted around her.

"Papa, please, we have customers."

The redness in Dabney's cheeks crept upward until it spread across his bald pate and disappeared into the black tufts of hair that ringed his head. He planted himself in the center aisle and thrust out his arm.

"You're not going to believe what that woman is doing now!" he declared, jabbing his finger at MacAvoy's General Store across the street. "She's at it again!"

Maggie glanced at the two customers standing near the blanket display who'd turned to stare. "Please, Papa, lower your voice. We have shoppers—"

"I stock hammers and what happens? She stocks hammers! Only she stocks three different brands! And then— then—she undercuts my price by a full dime!"

The two women shopping by the blankets made a beeline for the door.

"Papa, please calm down," Maggie said.

Dabney paced back and forth, then swung around to Maggie again. "That Ida Burk is trying to put me out of business! Ruin me!"

Maggie glanced at Sarah, who'd come to see what the commotion as about, and her cheeks heated. Ida Burk was, after all, Sarah's new mother-in-law.

"Ruin me, that's what she's trying to do!" Dabney strode off toward the stockroom at the rear of the store.

"I'd better go," Sarah said softly.

Maggie turned to her. "Papa didn't mean—"

"I know," she said and gave her a compassionate nod.

"He's just upset about things. He wasn't like this…before." Maggie felt her cheeks burn hotter. "I'm so sorry."

Sarah took Maggie's hand and gave it a little squeeze. "It's all right. I understand. But I do have to go. The ladies are at the mayor's house already and I should have—"

Sarah stopped and her cheeks flushed. A dart of anguish pierced Maggie's chest as she realized she'd been excluded from yet another annual event in Crystal Springs.

"The ladies are making mittens and socks for the orphans' asylum Christmas, aren't they?" Maggie said softly.

"I told the mayor's wife you should be there, but…"

"It's fine." Maggie squared her shoulders. "The important thing is that the orphans get warm clothing."

"I'm sorry, Maggie. Truly I am."

Maggie could say nothing, do nothing, except watch Sarah leave the store. Her friend's words should have brought comfort to Maggie, but they didn't. They were another painful reminder of what her life had become these past few months.

And maybe an omen of what lay ahead?

Maggie's shoulders slumped at the thought of her newest problem.

What was she going to do now that Bess Patterson had left town?

Chapter Three

Saturday nights in Crystal Springs could get a little rowdy down at the Wild Cat Saloon, and some of the old men talking politics over breakfast at the White Dove Cafe might get stirred up expressing their opinions. But other than that, not much happened in the town.

So it struck Jack as odd that, as he stood outside the jailhouse in the closing darkness, he saw a man look back and forth, then duck into the alley alongside Hudson's.

Jack didn't recognize him, given the distance and the shadows that shrouded the town, and that was reason enough to see what he was up to. Jack headed toward the alley.

The streets were nearly empty now, the shops closed for the day. Lamplight burned in second-story windows as merchants and their families settled around the table to talk over their day and enjoy their evening meal.

Jack paused at the entrance of the alley and leaned around the corner in time to see the figure turn right and disappear behind the mercantile. Silent in the dirt, Jack hurried to the back corner and saw the man knock on the rear door of Hudson's. The stranger bounced on his toes, glanced around nervously then knocked again.

The door opened and a slice of light illuminated the alley and the man's face. Herb Foster from the feed-and-grain store. Jack's eyebrows drew together. What was Foster doing sneaking around the alley at this time of night?

The door opened a little wider and Maggie Hudson stepped into view, holding up a lantern. She spoke quietly, Herb took another look around then she waved impatiently and he followed her into the store. The door closed behind them.

What the hell?

Jack eased into the shadows on the building across the alley. The mercantile was closed for the night and he'd seen Dabney cradling a bottle of whiskey at the Wild Cat just a few minutes ago. So what was going on here?

Five minutes passed, then ten. He turned up the collar of his jacket and waited.

The alley that backed the businesses on Main Street was a wide dirt trail. On the other side stood rows of barns, storage buildings, outhouses and animal pens. Jack's gaze traveled down the alleyway, the length of Main Street. No one else was out on this cold night.

The layout of the buildings that housed the town's businesses was much the same. Each had an exterior staircase that led from the alley up to a landing and the entrance to the second-floor living quarters. Inside each building was a second stairway, usually in the stockroom, that also led upstairs, giving the merchants access to their home from both inside and out.

Jack leaned his head back and studied the upstairs of the mercantile. One window glowed with lamplight.

A knot of hot suspicion gathered in his chest.

A few minutes later the rear door opened and Herb Foster stepped outside, talking to Maggie as she stood in the doorway. They exchanged a few words, amicably it seemed, then Herb hurried away.

Maggie glanced around, squinting into the darkness. Jack stepped deeper into the shadows and watched until Maggie ducked inside and pulled the door closed.

What was Miss Church Business up to? Jack wondered. Having a man slip in the rear door of the mercantile after dark, when the place was closed and her father was gone?

The wind picked up and the cold stung Jack's ears as he silently debated the possible reasons behind what he'd just witnessed. He prided himself on being an excellent judge of character, and he'd pegged Maggie as a decent woman right from the start. Surely, something perfectly innocent was going on inside the mercantile. Surely…

Nathan Gannon, the senior express agent from the stage depot, strode down the alley and knocked briskly on Hudson's back door. Jack watched as, once more, Maggie answered, glanced around, then gestured Nathan inside.

Both Nathan Gannon and Herb Foster were older men with gray hair, wives and children. Respectable businessmen. Well off. Pillars of the community.

Maybe—just maybe—Jack had judged the folks of Crystal Springs all wrong. Maybe more was going on in this quiet little town than he'd realized. And maybe Maggie wasn't the sort of person he'd thought she was.

The hot swell of emotion deepened in Jack's chest.

Ten minutes crept by, then fifteen, then twenty. What the hell was going on inside? His ears strained but all he heard was the wind. He glanced at the lighted window on the second floor. No shadows moved past it.

Finally, the door opened and Nathan stepped outside. He turned back to Maggie and held out several bills. She took the money and shoved it into her skirt pocket.

Jack's blood ran cold, chilling him worse than the winter wind that whipped through the alley. He wouldn't wait in the shadows another minute.

As soon as Nathan disappeared toward Main Street, Jack strode to the rear door of the mercantile and pounded his fist against it. Immediately, it swung open and Maggie's big blue eyes gazed up at him. Recognition—and surprise—registered in her face.

"Oh." She gulped. "Sheriff Crawford…"

Jack's anger pivoted in a different direction now.

"What the hell are you doing opening the door this late at night?" he demanded.

"You knocked," Maggie told him simply.

"You didn't know who it was. I could have been some-one trying to hurt you, or rob you—or kill you."

"I wouldn't think a murderer would knock."

Further irritated now because she was making so much sense, Jack pushed his way inside and pulled the door closed.

Lanterns hung around the stockroom, sending lively shadows dancing across the towers of wooden crates. They were everywhere, stacked at odd angles, piled atop each other, some reaching nearly to the ceiling. The staircase that led to the upstairs living quarters stood on the left, the curtained doorway to the mercantile on the right.

"I want to know what's going on," he told her, nodding toward the back door. "What were those two men doing here?"

Maggie felt her cheeks color. "You—you saw them?"

"Damn right I did, and I want to know why they were here," Jack said.

The last thing—the very last thing—Maggie intended to do was give the sheriff an explanation of what was going on in the back of her father's mercantile.

She pressed her lips together and drew herself up, hoping to present a picture of indignation.

"I hardly think it's any of your concern, sheriff."

"You were at the jail this afternoon acting suspicious and demanding the release of a known criminal," Jack said. "Now you're hiding something. I want to know what it is."

With some effort, Maggie held her chin up while her mind whirled frantically. She had to tell him something.

"It's business," she declared. "What could be wrong with my conducting business?"

Jack's eyebrows drew together and he leaned a little closer. "It depends on what sort of business you and those men are conducting in your back room, this late at night."

Jack's subtle innuendo, the knowing tone in his voice, swept through Maggie. Business? Men? Alone in her back room? Whatever did he mean? What was wrong with—

Breath left Maggie in a sickly wheeze. She touched her hand to her throat.

"You don't think that I—that we—that I—"

Jack's eyebrow crept up and the horrid realization of exactly what he suspected crashed down on Maggie.

He thought she was…entertaining…men. That she was a floozy, a fallen woman, a soiled dove.

The same thing the entire town had whispered about for months.

"No…"

Maggie mumbled the word in a strangled whisper and turned away, her head spinning. She'd lived with these suspicions for so long, had even come to tolerate them. But now, now when her redemption was in sight, when she'd begun to think she could overcome all of them, here she stood accused again.

Heat swept up her neck and over her face. Her breath came in short puffs and the room swayed.

"Whoa…hang on…"

Jack's words intruded on her cacophony of thoughts, distant and faint. Big warm arms encircled her shoulders.

She was going to faint. The realization stunned Maggie, then alarmed her. She was going to faint, right here in her stockroom, in the arms of the handsome sheriff, who earlier today had suggested Emmett Frazier was her beau and had just accused her of being the lowest, most common of women.

Good gracious, what would the townsfolk say to that?

"Leave me alone." Maggie batted at his arms. She simply was not going to faint.

"Come sit down." He held her firmly in his arms.

"No…" Maggie pushed at him but to no avail. He lifted her into his arms and laid her atop a big wooden crate. His face appeared through the swirling fog that threatened to overtake her as he leaned down.

"Lie here. I'll get the doctor," he told her.

"No…"

"I'll be right—"

She couldn't have this situation become public knowledge. With every ounce of her strength, Maggie grabbed the front of his coat with both hands and yanked him down until they were nose-to-nose.

"No! You will not get the doctor!"

His eyes rounded and Maggie suspected that she'd genuinely startled him, but she held on.

"All right, fine." Jack's expression softened. "I won't go anywhere."

He closed his hands around hers. Warmth seeped into her fists and radiated up both arms. They gazed into each other's eyes.

"I swear I won't," Jack said, then grinned. "I'd swear on the Bible but since I haven't found my way to the church yet I don't think that would convince you."

Warmth pooled inside Maggie now, heating her from within.

Gently, Jack worked his thumbs under her palms and unfolded her fingers from the fabric of his coat. He held on for a few seconds, gazing down at her. Her mind cleared, bringing on the realization of her circumstances.

Maggie pulled her hands from his grasp and tried to roll off the crate. Jack eased her down again, but not before she saw the printing on the side of her makeshift bed.

She moaned and closed her eyes. Great, the most handsome man she'd met in her life was tending to her and here she lay on a crate of men's long johns, facing the prospect of explaining why she really wasn't a prostitute.

"Take it slow," he said softly, then sat on the edge of the crate beside her.

Maggie felt the brush of his hip against her thigh and her eyes popped open again.

"Do you really think I'm a…a lady of the evening?"

"You have to admit your behavior was suspicious."

"Only to you."

"And half the town, if they'd seen you."

"Don't remind me." Maggie shoved herself up, forcing Jack to his feet. She swung her legs over the edge of the crate and shook her head. "Well, at least you said it to my face, rather than whisper behind my back like everyone else."

"What are you talking about?"

Maggie rose, steady on her feet now, the very unpleasant reminder of what she'd been through these past months renewing her strength.

At least this time she had a legitimate explanation for her behavior.

She drew herself up. "So, you want to know what those men and I were doing back here alone? Fine. I'll show you."

Maggie marched to the largest stack of wooden crates piled haphazardly against the wall, gathered her skirt and began to climb.

"Hey," Jack called, following her. "Get down from there. You're going to fall."

She glanced back and saw Jack following her up the crates. The climb wasn't as dangerous as it looked. She'd deliberately arranged the crates so that they appeared to teeter and lean, but actually formed a staircase to the top of the stack—provided one knew where to climb.

But this time her legs felt unsteady. Maggie couldn't imagine why. She'd made this many times but now her knees wobbled. And the stockroom had gotten awfully hot.

Her near-fainting spell, Maggie decided. What else could it be?

She pushed on until she reached the uppermost crates,

high above the floor. Jack stopped on the crate below her, putting them on eye level.

And what lovely eyes he had, Maggie realized. Deep blue, like the sky on a spring morning. Beautiful eyes—when he wasn't frowning, as he was doing right now.

Maggie remembered herself. "I'll show you my secret, but you have to swear not to tell anyone."

Jack's gaze hardened. "You're kidding, right?"

She knew she'd get no promise from him, but she huffed irritably, just to show him that his actions didn't suit her, and lifted the top from one of the crates.

"Congratulations, Sheriff," she said. "You've cracked Crystal Springs' most notorious secret. Christmas gifts."

Jack poked at the packing straw. "Why aren't these things out in the store? Why are they hidden back here?"

Maggie sighed heavily, hoping Jack would get the idea that further explanation didn't suit her. He didn't seem to notice.

"Because these are lovely, thoughtful things—actual gifts," Maggie said. "Jeweled mirror sets, kid gloves, silk handkerchiefs, pipes, books. All sorts of items. Papa won't allow them to be stocked in his mercantile."

Jack nodded. "He carries basic necessities."

"Exactly," Maggie agreed, a little surprised that Jack had noticed the stock on the shelves of the mercantile. "Take hammers, for example, and the dozen lanterns I unpacked today. We've got a whole tableful of ugly blankets. And just last week I stocked three dozen white aprons—plain white aprons no one in town will want."

"You should be used to this by now."

"It wasn't always like this. Up until a few months ago Papa was reasonable about the merchandise we carried."

"So what changed?"

Maggie's gaze swung to Jack. Was he being deliberately hurtful? Did he take some perverse pleasure in asking her to retell the awful circumstances of the past few months?

But Jack just looked at her, waiting, and she realized that no, he didn't know what had happened.

Still, she wasn't going to tell the story again.

Maggie waved her hand, gesturing to the crates piled high around her. "So, this is my big secret. I ordered these things without Papa knowing it and hid them up here. He has a bad knee and can't climb up the crates. Then I sell them to the townsfolk quietly—or I did until you came along—and slip the money into the till."

"And you meet your customers back here after your pa is gone," Jack concluded.

"Everyone keeps it from Papa because if he finds out, he'll return everything I bought—and no one will have a chance to purchase a special gift for a loved one," Maggie said. "It isn't a hard secret to keep. Papa isn't all that friendly with the townsfolk, if you've noticed."

Jack nodded and she appreciated that he didn't remind her of all the times he'd been to the mercantile to settle a dispute her father had started.

Jack gestured to the many crates piled around them. "This looks like a lot of stuff to sell by Christmas."

"Bess Patterson ordered most of it—"

"She left town."

"Miss Patterson's niece is handling her affairs while she's away," Maggie explained, trying to sound confident that the whole matter would be taken care of quickly and easily. If not, and Maggie got stuck with the big order—

"Any more customers coming by tonight?" Jack asked.

She glanced toward the door. She wasn't expecting anyone but she never knew when her father might come home. She didn't want him to find her there with Jack.

He seemed to read her thoughts as he latched on to her elbow and they climbed down the crates. Maggie's knees seemed to wobble worse this time. When they got to the bottom crate, Jack stepped down, then circled her waist and lifted her to the floor.

They hung that way for a few seconds, her hands resting on his arms, his closed around her waist. Maggie lost herself in his gaze. Warmth seemed to radiate from his eyes, his arms, his chest—somewhere. It called to her, made her want to lean forward, snuggle against him, curl herself—

Jack's eyes narrowed and a frown pulled at his face. Maggie jerked away, freeing herself from him.

Good gracious, what was she doing? Holding on to him? Thinking such things? Why, she was acting like a fallen woman—the very thing he'd accused her of earlier.

Maggie headed for the back door, careful to keep her distance from him.

"You're not going to tell anyone about this, are you?" she asked.

"Sounds as if most of the town already knows about it," Jack said. "Everyone but your pa."

"I think of it as a community service." Maggie gave him a quick smile, but it did nothing to wipe the frown from his face. "Please, don't say anything about what I'm doing."

"I don't keep secrets," Jack said. "And I don't lie."

"Not even at Christmastime?" she asked hopefully.

Jack studied her for a long moment and she was sure she saw his mind working. Just when she thought she couldn't bear it another second, Jack nodded.

"I won't talk about it unless someone asks," Jack said. "But if anyone asks—including your pa—I'll tell them."

Maggie supposed that was the best she could hope for.

Jack opened the back room, letting in a gust of cold air, and making Maggie think her ordeal was over.

But then he turned back and leaned down a little.

"You've got a lot of secrets, Miss Hudson," he said. "And I don't think I've discovered them all yet."

Jack gave her a quick nod and closed the door.

Chapter Four

Thin. Not bony, though. Shapely. Yes, shapely. A good, solid handful. Two handfuls, actually.

Jack's palms warmed as he recalled last night in the mercantile stockroom when he'd placed both his hands on Maggie's waist and lifted her down from the crate.

Warm, soft flesh. Curves. He'd felt them, even through the armor of petticoats, corset, bustle and all the other trappings she wore. Womanly curves that—

Jack gave himself a mental shake, silently chastising himself for getting lost in thoughts of Maggie—again.

He stared out the jailhouse window at Main Street. Nearly noon, but few sun rays to prove it. Heavy clouds hung over the town. The jail was quiet. Emmett Frazier was snoring and Ben Sheridan was out making rounds, leaving Jack alone with his thoughts.

It wasn't as if he'd never touched a woman before. Jack shook his head, remembering last night again. He'd assisted a number of women, as a gentleman and in the line of duty. So why did he keep thinking about Maggie?

Her smell. Maybe that was it. A light and delicate scent

that seemed completely out of place with the determined fire in her eyes and the strength she'd shown when she'd grabbed his coat and yanked him down.

The image filled his mind of Maggie stretched out on the crate, her hair spilling around her, her rosebud lips parted ever so slightly, and Jack's blood warmed, bringing on predictable results. Thoughts of Maggie had kept him simmering all night and all morning.

He forced his gaze out the window again, to the chimney smoke from the shops along Main Street that blended into the gray-white sky. Snow on the way, probably. There'd been little of it so far this winter. Remnants of the last storm lay in frozen mounds along streets, a promise of more to come. Sooner, rather than later, surely.

In the past, Jack had spent many cold miserable days and nights on the trail of wanted men. Hunting them down. Hauling them to jail. Freezing rain, snow, wind.

But right now, staring out at Main Street, the thought of a cold night turned to something different. The vision of rolling under the covers, bedded down with Maggie, filled Jack's mind.

The jailhouse door burst open bringing in a gust of cold air along with Ben Sheridan. Jack mumbled a curse at himself for, once again, not watching the street diligently. A move like that could have cost him his life, back when he was a U.S. Marshal. It still could.

"Getting cold out there," Ben said, blowing into his hands and heading for the stove in the corner.

"Anything happening?" Jack asked.

"Things are quiet." Ben poured himself a cup of coffee from the pot on the stove. "Saw that Nelson boy in the alley behind Cochran's laundry."

Cecil Nelson, Jack recalled. A kid about fifteen whose mother, a widow, ran the Crystal Springs Hotel.

"Why wasn't he in school?" Jack asked.

Ben walked over to the window. "That's what I asked him. Got some nonsense from him, but no real answer."

Jack figured the boy was up to something—he'd had a guilty look on his face every time Jack had spoken to him—and Jack's mind conjured up everything from petty theft to bank robbery. But then he stopped himself, remembering that he was the sheriff of sleepy little Crystal Springs and was no longer dealing with hardened criminals.

"Mrs. Nelson ought to keep a tighter rein on that boy," Ben said and sipped his coffee. "But she's got her hands full running the hotel and looking after those daughters of hers. I reckon she's doing the best she can."

Jack drew in a breath. From vicious outlaws to truant boys. That was the life he'd chosen when he'd taken this job. Still…

"Any problems with the prisoner?" Ben asked.

"All he does is sleep."

"Frazier's pretty worthless, that's for damn sure," Ben said. "Makes me wonder why Miss Maggie was so anxious to have him released from jail. You told me she said it was for the church, but I don't see it. Not after what happened."

Jack felt the hair on his neck stand up. "Something happened? With Maggie?"

Ben paused, his coffee cup halfway to his lips. "Guess you didn't hear about that, huh? The whole town—"

The door opened and another gust of wind blew into the jailhouse. Nathan Gannon followed it in.

An unreasonable anger filled Jack at the sight of the

slight, graying man. He'd been in the stockroom alone with Maggie last night, had her attention all to himself, smelled that sweet scent of hers. Jack didn't like it, and really, he didn't know why. But it angered him, just the same. And so did the fact that Ben had just suggested that Maggie had yet another secret Jack didn't know about.

"We'll have us some snow pretty soon," Nathan predicted as he pulled an envelope from the pocket of his heavy coat and handed it to Jack. "Telegram for you, Sheriff."

Jack ripped it open and read the message, barely aware of the express agent's departure. His belly filled with the familiar cold, hard knot that he used to carry with him every day.

Jack folded the telegram and shoved it into his back pocket, then took his coat and headed out the door.

"Something wrong, Sheriff?" Ben asked.

"Nothing I can't handle." Jack closed the door behind him, hoping his words would prove true.

Jack Crawford had taken over too much of her life, Maggie thought again as she stepped out of the rear door of the mercantile and pulled her wrap around her. Already he knew her deepest secret, how she'd ordered merchandise behind her father's back, and sold it to folks around town.

None of it was any of his business, yet he'd insinuated himself into it. And, as if that weren't bad enough, he'd sworn to uncover all her secrets.

It was time she put an end to her involvement with Jack.

Maggie had thought of little else all night and all morning, and she'd searched her brain for a way to handle the situation. Finally, she'd come up with a perfect plan: she'd tell him the truth.

Most of it, anyway.

The wind blew in Maggie's face as she turned the corner into the alley and headed toward Main Street. Her papa was handling things in the store; not a big job, since they'd had only two customers all day. She'd offered an excuse to leave, one she doubted he'd even heard, grabbed her bundle from the stockroom and slipped out the back door.

The truth, or as much of it as Jack needed to know. Yes, Maggie decided, that would solve things.

Her spirits lifted at the possibility that her problems—one of them, anyway—would be solved, then plummeted when she caught sight of the White Dove Cafe across the street.

Through the big glass window she saw Vivian Fisher, the mayor's wife, and several other ladies seated together, sipping coffee, probably planning the next church social.

Maggie's steps slowed. At one time, not so long ago, she would have been sitting with the women. But not anymore. No one asked her to join them now.

Vera Lyle glanced outside and spotted Maggie. She froze, stunned at seeing her. Maggie pushed up her chin and kept walking, not wanting to see the looks on the other women's faces when they, too, turned to stare.

Under other circumstances receiving a telegram from an old friend would be welcomed. But the knot in Jack's stomach didn't fade, only grew tighter, as he thought about former U.S. Marshal McQuaid and the message he'd sent.

Jack left the express office, grateful for the blast of wind that stole his breath for a few seconds and jarred the troubling thoughts from his mind. The telegram he'd received from McQuaid had been intended for the sheriff of Crystal Springs; his old friend had no way of knowing that Jack himself held that job. The message indicated that

McQuaid was looking for him, and Jack had just tele-grammed back with the information.

Something was wrong. McQuaid wouldn't be looking for him otherwise. He and McQuaid had served together as U.S. Marshals. They'd become friends, or as good a friends as McQuaid allowed. He was a hard man with, Jack suspected, a hard past. But he never spoke of it, not even on long manhunts when conversation helped pass the time.

Jack headed down the boardwalk, hating that he'd have to wait to hear back from McQuaid to know what he wanted. Could be anything. Perhaps was nothing. Yet the knot in Jack's stomach didn't ease.

With a nod here and there, a considerate greeting, he passed the folks of Crystal Springs as they went about their lives. Jack's steps slowed as he passed in front of the Hudson's Mercantile and he gazed into the display windows. He'd seen Dabney Hudson leaving the express office earlier, just as Jack was entering. Now the man stood behind the counter hunched over a ledger. No sign of Maggie.

Where was she? Jack turned and caught a glimpse of a swish of skirt disappearing into the jailhouse.

Maggie.

He tensed as a half-dozen reasons popped into his mind—none of them good—for Maggie's visit to the jail. Jack hurried to the jailhouse and went inside. To his surprise, he saw Ben Sheridan seated behind the desk. No Maggie.

Ben shifted uncomfortably in the chair. "You, uh, you have a visitor, Sheriff."

His gaze swept the empty room. "Where?"

Ben got to his feet and ducked his gaze. "Miss Maggie, uh, she said she had something special for you and she went to your...your bedroom."

Heat swept through Jack as his gaze darted to the hallway that led to the cells and his room.

Ben cleared his throat. "I'll just go out on rounds for a while, Sheriff, and you can—"

"No, you won't. You're coming with me."

Jack led the way down the hallway and found Maggie in his bedroom, still wearing her wrap, standing near the washstand, eyeing the bed thoughtfully. He and Ben stopped in the doorway.

"What are you doing?" Jack demanded.

Maggie looked at them, her eyebrows drawn together in concentration, then gestured toward the bed. "I was just trying to decide which way would be best."

"What?" Jack asked.

"Positioning is important," Maggie explained. "There're several to choose from, but I don't want to force my selection on you. Which would you prefer?"

Jack's insides flamed and he glanced at Ben beside him. The deputy's eyes were wide and his cheeks glowed red.

"What the hell are you talking about?" Jack demanded.

Maggie gazed up at him as if he'd lost his mind. "The rug. I brought you a rug so your feet wouldn't get cold first thing out of bed in the mornings."

Jack looked at the floor and saw that a blue-and-burgundy braided rug lay beside his bed.

"Come out of there." Jack stepped into the room long enough to take her hand, and pulled her into the hallway.

"What's wrong?" Maggie asked, pointing behind her. "I thought you'd like a nice rug for you room. It was flawed. We couldn't sell it, but it's perfectly fine, otherwise."

Ben backed out of the way as Jack led Maggie through

the jail and out onto the boardwalk. The door slammed behind them and Maggie pulled out of his grasp.

"What's the matter with you?" she asked, looking up at him with those wide blue eyes of hers.

Jack gazed down at her, so heated from within that he wanted to throw off his coat to cool himself down.

"I brought you a gift," Maggie said, sounding exasperated. "I thought you'd appreciate it."

"That's it? That's the reason you came over here?"

"Well, there was something else," Maggie admitted, dipping her gaze.

Jack heated up again.

"It's about Emmett Frazier," she said.

Irritation, disappointment...*something* surged through Jack.

"That rug was the only bribe you intended to offer?" he asked.

"Of course. What else could there—?"

Maggie gasped and her cheeks turned pink, and Jack knew she'd figured out what he was getting at. But instead of turning away or lowering her lashes in embarrassment, Maggie drew herself up and glared at him.

Jack dropped back a step.

"Don't you ever insult me that way again, Sheriff. Do you hear me? Ever!"

Maggie whipped around and stomped away.

Chapter Five

How on earth did these embarrassing things keep happening to her?

Maggie shifted on the wooden bench and pulled her wrap closer around her. This spot outside the barn behind Herb Foster's feed-and-grain store offered much to attract Maggie, and she sought it often. A place of solitude, to think and, more lately, to dream.

Sheltered from the wind, Maggie gazed down the alley to the two houses that sat on adjoining lots at the edge of town. She'd watched their construction for weeks. White, with green shutters. Two beautiful homes.

Maggie's breath caught and tears pressed against her eyes. Beautiful homes for two young, growing families. She held her tears at bay, refusing to let them fall.

She knew the town had whispered about her for months. Ugly gossip about her. And perhaps, under the circumstances, she deserved it.

But she most certainly didn't deserve to be insulted to her face by the likes of Sheriff Jack Crawford. Especially when she was only trying to do something nice for him.

Maggie swiped at her eyes, not sure why Jack's insulting words had hurt worse than those whispered by the folks of Crystal Springs who were supposed to be her friends.

Was it because he was handsome that she wanted him to think well of her? Because he was the sheriff and, without knowing it, held her very future in his hand?

Or was it something else?

Drawing in a deep breath, Maggie tried to push the thought out of her head. None of it mattered, anyway, she told herself. She had real problems to deal with and they most certainly didn't include Jack Crawford's opinion of her.

Her heart sank a little as she couldn't shake the notion that Jack's opinion of her did, in fact, matter.

Maggie gazed at the distant houses again, an ache of longing filling her. She sighed slow and loud, feeling the envy deep within her.

"Mind some company?"

Jack's deep voice startled her. She turned to see him standing at the corner of the barn, feet spread wide as if to brace himself against a suspected attack. Despite the cold, he held his hat, turning it over in his hands, glancing back and forth between it and her.

Those deep blue eyes of his seemed to beam straight through her, as if he could see to her very soul. Maggie's heart rate picked up.

He didn't wait for her reply, just walked over.

"Whether it suits you or not," Jack said, "I'm sitting with you."

He lowered himself onto the bench beside her, still holding his hat. Maggie looked at him for a few seconds, then turned once more to the houses she'd so long admired.

Minutes passed with only wisps of the cold breeze passing them and the pale sun shining down.

"I come here quite often to look at the houses," Maggie said after a while. "They belong to—"

"I'm sorry."

Her heart rose in her throat and hung there. No one—not one single person—had said that to her.

Jack fiddled with his hat. "I'm sorry," he said again.

She thought she really would cry now.

"I, uh, I shouldn't have said those things to you. Insulted you that way." Jack cleared his throat. "I'm…I'm sorry."

No one, not one person in all of Crystal Springs, had told her they were sorry. For the things they'd whispered, the things they'd suspected, the things they'd said. Maggie had long dreamed that one day she'd hear those words, and now that she had, she could barely take them in. She just looked at Jack, unable to move.

He finally lifted his gaze and returned her stare. She saw sincerity in his face, true concern in his expression. It touched her heart as nothing had.

Then he slapped his hat down on the bench beside him and swung around to face her.

"Well, damn, you could say something," Jack declared. "It's not like I apologize to someone every day of the week. Hell, I don't even remember the last time I apologized to anybody for anything."

The warmth, the raw physical energy he exuded, filled Maggie, wound deep into her, bringing the most exquisite ache. Sheriff Jack Crawford seemed suddenly accessible. Human. Fascinating.

He pointedly stared at her, waiting for a reply. Maggie hesitated, unsure for a moment if she could really speak.

"You're sorry? Truly?"

Jack pressed his lips together, and for an instant she wasn't sure if he could really bring himself to say the words again. But then he gave her a nod.

"Yes, Maggie. I'm sorry."

"Thank you."

"You're welcome."

"Are you going to leave now?"

"Do you want me to?"

"No."

"Good. Because I intended to stay, anyway."

Jack sat back on the bench, a little closer this time. Maggie felt the heat of him seep into her. She fought to keep herself from leaning toward him.

"That's the Masons' house? And the Burks'?" he asked, pointing to the places still under construction.

Maggie sighed wistfully. "I've been here most every day since they started work on the houses, watching them being built. Oh, how wonderful for them to have such fine homes."

"You like the idea of having a big place to live?"

"I have a place to live. Our rooms over the mercantile are adequate." Maggie gestured to the house. "But these are real homes. Just the kind I've dreamed of all my life."

They were quiet for a few more minutes, then Jack said, "I don't believe anybody ever gave me a rug before."

"I didn't mean it as a bribe." Maggie turned to him and smiled. "But I figured it couldn't hurt."

"I'm not letting Emmett Frazier out of jail."

"I think you will," Maggie declared, "after I tell you the reason I need him released."

Jack studied her for a moment. "I'm listening."

She sat forward and turned to him, her heart rate picking up a little, trying to judge the look on his face.

Was he just indulging her because he'd insulted her earlier and wanted to make amends? Or would he honestly listen to what she had to say?

Jack was a fair man. Maggie knew that. And either way, she needed to tell him everything—most everything.

"Reverend Battenfield put me in charge of the Christmas Eve music program," she said. "It's the biggest event of the whole year. And he put me in charge of it. Me."

Jack tilted his head. "And this involves Frazier how?"

Maggie told him the story of how Emmett had come to her with the news that the Lord had spoken to him, and his desire to find salvation by participating in the Christmas program.

"Emmett has a beautiful singing voice," Maggie said. "It's just what I need to make this year's Christmas Eve service the biggest, the best, the most memorable ever."

Jack frowned as if trying to follow what she was saying.

"And the reason this year's service needs to be the biggest, the best, the most memorable is…what?" he asked.

"Because I want—I have—to do a good job." Maggie felt her hope building with every word. "Don't you see? This is my chance. My one chance to—"

Maggie pressed her lips together. She'd intended to tell Jack the truth about Emmett Frazier's fine singing voice and her desperate need to have him in the Christmas Eve service. But that's all of the truth she'd planned to share with Jack. Now she'd gone too far, though. Said too much.

She looked at Jack, at the intent expression on his face. She'd never get away with not telling him the whole story now.

Maggie slumped against the barn, not sure she could bare to relate what had happened—to Jack, of all people. She'd wanted him to think well of her.

Another foolish thought on her part?

Maggie sat up, forcing herself to face Jack. What would he think of her after hearing this story? The same as the rest of the town had thought? The prospect caused Maggie's heart to ache but she pressed on.

"The church burned down several months ago. I'm sure you heard that around town," she began. "But, obviously, no one told you the reason why."

Jack shrugged. "I never thought much about it."

"Then you're the only one in town who hasn't." Maggie drew herself up, making herself continue. "My mother became…involved…with the minister—the minister we had at the time, not Reverend Battenfield, of course—and, during an afternoon tryst, they knocked over a lantern and burned the church down."

Jack just looked at her, stunned.

Maggie froze. What was he thinking? Terrible thoughts of her? Shameful things? Was he repulsed by her now?

Jack burst out laughing. He rocked forward and slapped his hand against his knee.

Maggie's mouth flew open. "It's not funny! Stop laughing! How dare you—!"

She whacked him on his shoulder with her open palm, horrified and enraged.

"Stop that! It was awful!" She swatted at him over and over. "The church was in flames! The whole town came running! And here was my mother and the minister, stark naked, dashing from the building!"

Jack threw his head back, howling louder.

"Stop it!" Maggie cried. She grabbed his arm and shook. "It was the worst day of my life! It was—"

"Funny," Jack managed to say.

"No, it wasn't! It was—"

Maggie looked at him, at the tears in his eyes, heard the big gusts of laughter rumbling from him and, for the first time ever, her hurt and humiliation turned into something else. She burst out laughing, too. And how good it felt. She hadn't laughed in so long. And to be laughing with Jack…

Finally, the two of them pulled themselves together, swiping at their eyes, sniffing.

"Well, I can understand how upsetting that must have been for you," Jack said, then snickered again. "But, after knowing your pa, I can't say I blame the woman."

"It was humiliating. But that wasn't the worst of it," Maggie said. "Afterward, everyone in town started whispering about me. Wondering if my morals were as loose as my mother's. It was all anyone talked about."

Jack coughed, finally getting himself under control. "I know Crystal Springs is a small town, but surely there was more gossip going around than you and your morals."

"Well, yes," Maggie admitted. "Our old sheriff left town suddenly because of a problem with his wife. And Mr. Mason arrived with a mysterious past, looking a great deal like Kinsey's little boy Sam, which caused a few heads to turn. There was Dixie, the woman with the most disreputable reputation, besides my mother, but she moved to Texas."

"With all that going on, why do you think the town is still talking about you?"

"Because those situations are all resolved. I'm still here, and the new church is a constant reminder of what happened."

"I guess your ma and the minister left town?"

"What else could they do?"

"And that left you and your pa to face the wrath of the townsfolk, the embarrassment, the scorn," Jack said.

"It's really taken a toll on Papa. He's not the same man he was."

"Tough on you, too," Jack said. "Dealing with your pa on top of everything else."

Maggie sat forward. "So, you see, this is my chance to get back in the town's good graces. I'm going to put on the best Christmas Eve service anyone has ever seen. Emmett will sing and everyone will love his beautiful voice, and they'll see what an upstanding Christian woman I am. Everyone will have something new to talk about when they're at the church."

Jack considered her words for a moment. "Makes sense."

Maggie's heart soared. "So you understand? You'll help? You'll let Emmett out of jail?"

"No." Jack shook his head. "I can't let him out of jail. Like I already told you, Frazier has to serve his sentence. That's all there is to it."

"No, it's not," Maggie declared, sitting upright. "You're the sheriff. You can exercise some discretion."

"I'm not letting Frazier out of jail," Jack said simply.

His calm, his resolve, angered Maggie. She shot to her feet. "You're just being stubborn."

Jack gazed at her, his jaw set, his lips sealed.

Aggravated beyond belief, Maggie stomped away. She'd only gotten a step or two before Jack appeared beside her.

"I'll walk you back to the mercantile," he told her.

Maggie's irritation doubled, causing her to walk faster.

"I just told you everyone in town talks about my morals.

I certainly don't want to be seen being escorted by the town sheriff. How would that look?"

Jack caught her hand, spinning her toward him. "And how would it look if the town sheriff let a pretty woman walk unescorted?"

Once again, she wondered if she'd heard him correctly. "Did you say I was…pretty?"

Jack stepped closer, still holding her hand. "I did."

She felt herself melt inside. From the heat of his fingers around her palm, the warmth radiating from him.

"I think you're very pretty." He traced his thumb over her hand and grinned. "A little stubborn, too."

"One of my faults, I'm afraid," she murmured.

His grin reached his eyes now. "I like a little stubbornness in a woman."

All she could do was gaze up at Jack, lost in the blue of his eyes. They seemed to capture her, hold her, keep her in front of him—not that she wanted to go anywhere.

Then he stepped closer and leaned down. Maggie felt his hand settle on her shoulder, and his lips take hers. The most delicious warmth overcame her. She curled her fingers into the sleeve of his coat. To her horror, she heard herself moan. Then Jack groaned and her heart soared.

He ended their kiss but didn't pull too far away. He gazed at her, as if he too were reluctant to break the spell that held them together. Then, suddenly, he stepped back.

"We'd better get you back to your pa's store," he said.

They walked to Main Street. Maggie knew her cheeks were pink. Was it noticeable to everyone they passed?

She was relieved when they reached the mercantile but dismayed when Jack followed her inside. Her father came from behind the counter when he saw her.

"Where have you been?" he demanded.

Good gracious, could her father tell that she'd been kissing the sheriff in the alley?

"She was with me," Jack declared.

Dabney seemed not to hear his words as he shrugged into his coat. "You're going to handle things here for a while."

Jack's kiss and the fog it left her in dissipated as Maggie saw her papa cram his hat on and pick up a valise.

"Papa, what's happening? You're not leaving, are you?" she asked, feeling a little twinge of panic.

"For a while," Dabney barked, heading toward the door.

"But where are you going? Is someone sick or—"

"Nothing like that," Dabney grumbled.

"But, Papa, Christmas is coming up. You can't leave—"

"I'll be back in a few days," he told her, then gestured to the store. "You take care of things."

"But…"

Maggie's words died on her lips as her father disappeared out the door.

Chapter Six

"**Y**ou're not going to tell me what that's about, are you," Ben said, sounding a bit miffed.

Jack looked up from the telegram lying atop his desk, realizing that he'd been staring at it for a while. He folded the paper in half, same as he'd done with the first one he'd received several days ago, and shoved it into his shirt pocket.

"Just an old friend trying to track me down," he said.

Ben walked over to the desk. "Pardon me for saying so, Sheriff, but the look on your face every time you get a telegram tells me there's something else going on."

Jack supposed that was true. This second telegram Nathan Gannon had just delivered stated that McQuaid was on his way to Crystal Springs to see Jack. McQuaid wouldn't come all the way from Nevada for nothing.

Jack rose from his chair. "Until McQuaid gets here, I don't know that there's anything to worry about. I'll let you know."

Ben nodded, apparently accepting Jack's explanation. Jack shrugged into his coat and hat, and left the jail.

Darkness seemed in a hurry to settle over Crystal

Springs. Shadows claimed Main Street, and dimmed alleys and doorways. The town's few streetlamps and the lanterns in shops and homes glowed a warm yellow.

Signs of Christmas were there, too. The stores' display windows were accented with holly and evergreen boughs, wreaths hung on most every door in town.

There was a hustle and bustle that Jack hadn't seen in town before. More folks shopping, hurrying along with bundles and packages. Strangers in town. Ranchers, miners, farmers were showing up in Crystal Springs to sell their wares, to trade for, or buy outright, a gift for a loved one.

They brought trouble with them, too. More men drinking at the saloon. Jack had broken up more fights than usual, and he'd gotten reports of a number of thefts. He and Ben took turns making rounds more often now.

Jack walked along the boardwalk, looking into alleyways as he went, eyeing every person he passed. A chill not brought on by the winter air caused him to turn quickly and stare down the darkened alley that ran alongside the Crystal Springs Bath House and Laundry. A lone figure darted toward the rear of the building, keeping in the shadows. Jack went after him.

Halfway down the alley, Jack knew whom he followed. Cecil Nelson, the young truant Ben Sheridan had recently caught in the same alley.

Jack grabbed the boy's arm and jerked him around. Startled, his eyes widened, and even in the dark passageway, Jack saw the guilty look on his young face.

"What are you doing sneaking around the alley this time of night?" Jack demanded.

"Nothing," he declared, the word coming out in a squeak.

Jack hauled him to the boardwalk and, under the light of a streetlamp, planted him against the building.

The boy didn't have a father, just a recently widowed mother and a bunch of sisters. Jack decided it was time the boy dealt with a man. He eased closer, effectively pinning Cecil against the wall, and leaned down a little.

"When I ask you a question, boy, I expect an answer," Jack said.

Cecil pressed himself back against the wall and gulped.

"Well, Sheriff, I was, uh, I was going over to the stage depot for my ma. She wanted me to check on something. That's all. I—I was just taking a shortcut through the alley. I swear."

Jack didn't believe him. Everything about his demeanor told him the boy was lying. But his story made sense.

He stepped back. "Don't be roaming through the alleys after dark."

"Yes, sir." Cecil nodded quickly, causing his brown bangs to bounce up and down. "Can I go now?"

Jack gave him another hard look, then nodded. The boy took off down the street toward the hotel. He waited, watching until Cecil dashed through the front door of the Crystal Springs Hotel.

"Hell…" Jack sighed long and loud, wondering, not for the first time, what his life had turned into since he took the job of sheriff.

Just to prove he hadn't lost his edge, Jack headed down the alley in the direction Cecil had been going. At the back corner of the laundry and bath house he saw nothing. Then he spotted a young girl at the second-floor window. Becky Cochran. Fifteen years old, blond, very pretty. When she saw Jack, she ducked away.

So that was the big attraction in the alley.

Jack mumbled under his breath and headed toward Main Street again. He stopped, gaze drawn to Hudson's Mercantile.

He didn't like Maggie working alone in the store now, since her pa had run off. It wasn't good for her to be by herself, especially with so many strangers in town.

Jack stood there for a while, the image of Maggie filling his mind and, somehow, filling the rest of him, too. He remembered the way she felt when he held her in his arms, when he smelled her delicate scent, when he kissed her.

He probably shouldn't have done that, Jack decided. Maggie was worried about her reputation—rightly so— and he would have made things worse if someone had walked up and caught them together like that. Maybe he should apologize.

Jack silently debated the possibility. He didn't like apologizing for things. But it was different with Maggie.

With her, everything was different.

Jack crossed the street and went inside Hudson's Mercantile. The store was empty, save for Maggie at the counter, a shawl around her shoulders, studying a tablet.

She looked up when the little bell jangled and Jack figured she expected a customer as she forced a smile into place. Recognition registered and a genuine smile took its place. Jack's chest swelled.

"You're open late," he said.

She pulled her shawl closer around her shoulders and stepped out from behind the counter. A blue dress today, Jack noted. Dark blue, like her eyes.

"I didn't realize it had gotten so late," she said.

"Busy day?" he asked, walking a little closer.

She shrugged. "Some new customers in town for the day. Probably just passing through or here for a special shopping trip. Not the sort of folks we'll see again for a while."

Jack just looked at her, thinking how pretty she looked in the light from the lanterns that hung on the walls. A few strands of her dark hair curled at her ears. For some reason, he wanted to wind his finger around them.

Then he realized he was staring.

"Quiet in here," he said, just to have something to say.

Maggie gave him a weak smile. "You can tell Papa isn't here."

Something in her tone alerted Jack to perhaps an inner thought. "You miss your pa?" he asked.

She gave him another tired smile. "Harsh and difficult as he was, Papa was a lot of company. He always had something to talk about, even if he was simply railing against sweet Miss Ida and MacAvoy's across the street. Truthfully, I hadn't expected I'd miss him so much."

Lonely and alone. How many days and nights had Jack spent feeling those same things?

Maggie tightened her shawl around her and clutched it together with her fist. "Papa's been my most reliable company these last few months. After what happened with Mama at the church…"

"You don't want to spend much time with your friends and the other folks in town?" Jack asked.

"I don't have much choice. I'm not included in the women's church and charity activities, as I once was," Maggie said. Then she straightened her shoulders and gave Jack a thin smile. "But maybe it's for the best. It was diffi-cult walking into a room and having everyone suddenly stop talking, and look at me the way they did. And who knows? Maybe I deserved their scorn after what happened."

"The hell you did," Jack said, the words coming out more harshly than he'd intended. He made an effort to soften his voice. "Your mama did what she did for her own reasons. It's no reflection on you."

"I wish the rest of the town felt the way you do."

"I guess you miss her, though. She was your ma, after all."

Maggie shrugged. "We weren't close. I was a chore for her. I don't think she was ever happy with a child. Or a husband, either, given the way things turned out."

Jack walked closer, unable to maintain any distance from her. "That must have hurt you."

Maggie thought for a moment. "It made me determined. Determined never to be the sort of woman, wife or mother she was."

"Determined, huh? Is that another word for 'stubborn'?" Jack asked.

She must have realized he was teasing because she tilted her head playfully. "Oh, Sheriff Crawford, you don't know the half of it."

Jack shared her smile. The minutes stretched by until they both realized at the same moment that they were alone in the quiet store, just looking at each other.

"It's cold in here," he said, just to break the silence.

Maggie gestured to the stove in the center of the store. "I ran out of wood and I didn't want to leave the store unattended," she said. "Papa usually sees to things like that. I'll bring more in once I lock up."

"I'll take care of it," Jack told her, glad to have something to do. He headed toward the rear of the store.

"I can manage," she assured him.

Jack stopped. "It's dark outside."

She looked slightly offended. "I'm not afraid of the dark."

"What about spiders? Mice?"

Maggie cringed.

"Lots of those in the woodshed, especially after dark," Jack pointed out.

"Well, Sheriff, you are the one with the gun."

"Don't believe I've ever shot a spider before."

"I'll brace myself for gunplay," Maggie said.

Jack grinned and headed once more toward the rear of the store. "Lock up."

He went through the stockroom and across the alley to the woodshed, gathered an armload of logs and went back inside. Maggie had locked the front door, pulled down the window shades and was counting money in the till. The nightly accounting didn't take long, Jack noticed, and by the time he'd filled the wood box she'd finished her work.

They spent another long moment looking at each other. Jack knew he should leave. It was the right thing to do. But he couldn't bring himself to head for the door.

Besides, he hadn't apologized for kissing her yet.

"I'll get you some firewood for upstairs, too," he offered. Not waiting for her response, he retraced his route to the woodshed. But this time, instead of coming back into the mercantile, he climbed the back steps to the second floor and found Maggie waiting at the door for him.

Warmth and the delicious smell of roasting meat greeted him as he stepped inside. A lantern burned low on the table, casting everything in a welcoming light.

The large room held the cookstove, cupboards and the table, and the area adjacent to it was the parlor with a settee, two rockers and shelves of books. Off to the left was a short hallway that, he figured, led to the bedrooms.

Jack dumped the fire logs into the wood box beside the cookstove and brushed his sleeves. Maggie had already hung her shawl beside the door and put on an apron. He liked the way it tied tight around her waist.

"Nice place. Looks like a real home," he said. "I'm surprised, after what you said about your mama."

"Mama wasn't very interested in the place." Maggie glanced around with pride, then went to the oven. "I put in a roast earlier this afternoon. I thought Papa might come home so I wanted to have supper ready, just in case."

She opened the oven and peered inside, then used a folded towel to pull out the pan of beef and vegetables.

"Looks good, doesn't it?" she asked.

Jack's gaze lingered on her backside, his attention drawn there when she bent over at the oven. "Sure does."

She looked back at him and he forced his gaze to her face.

"Hungry? There's plenty," she said.

"You bet," he said, and shrugged out of his coat and hat.

Maggie started to set the table but Jack stepped up behind her and reached over her head into the cupboard for the plates. Her scent washed over him. He saw her hair curling softly against her neck. The long line of her back. The curve of her hips. They seemed to call to him, somehow. If he leaned forward, just a little, he could—

"Coffee?" She looked back at him, her blue eyes wide.

"Uh, yeah, sure."

Jack took the plates and turned away, only to nearly collide with her again. He sat the plates aside. Supper, good as it smelled and looked, was the furthest thing from his mind right now.

"I had a reason for coming here tonight," Jack told her.

Concern drew Maggie's eyebrows together as she sat the coffee cups aside. She was pretty even when she looked worried.

Jack decided he'd better get on with it. If he lingered much longer, well…

"I came to apologize," he told her.

"For what?"

"For doing this."

Jack kissed her. He put his mouth over hers and his arms around her and kissed her. Long and slow. Soft and easy. Carefully. Then her lips relaxed and moved delicately against his. He felt his knees weaken and pulled away.

Maggie gazed up at him, her lips moist, her eyes sparkling.

"Your apology for a kiss was another kiss?" she asked, her voice a little breathless.

"Yeah. Can I apologize for this second one?"

"Oh, my…"

Jack kissed her again. His mouth glided over hers, urging her gently. She parted her lips and he groaned. Her breath caught. Her fingers wound into his shirt. Jack deepened their kiss and she swayed against him.

He could so easily have lost himself to her right then. Given in to what he really wanted to do, what his body urged him to do. But when he pulled away and looked deep into Maggie's eyes, he knew that once wouldn't be enough.

Jack backed away. "I…I have to go."

She looked confused. "Did I do something—"

"No," he told her quickly. "You did everything right. Too right. So I'd better go."

Pink flashed across her already heated cheeks and Jack knew she understood what he meant. She was inexperienced—her kisses told him so—but innocence didn't mean ignorance.

He got his coat and hat but didn't put on either. He carried plenty of warmth with him already.

"Good night," he said and opened the door.

"Good night," she answered.

He lingered for a few seconds, then forced himself out the door.

"Be sure to lock up," he told her.

She nodded and closed the door behind him.

Jack pounded down the stairs. Cecil Nelson popped into his head. The boy sneaking through the alley was suddenly very understandable.

Chapter Seven

Redemption. Finally.

Maggie's emotions swelled as she headed for the church, market basket in her arm and salvation within sight.

Her day had been long and lonely at the mercantile, with little to do but dust the already spotless shelves, watch out the window for potential customers and think.

The glow returned to the pit of her stomach once more as she recalled last night and Jack's kiss. She'd thought of little else. He seemed to saturate her parched senses, bring her alive, somehow, with the touch of his lips.

The church came into view and Maggie forced thoughts of Jack and his kiss out of her mind. Tonight was the first rehearsal for the Christmas Eve service. Her first effort in the long-awaited chance to show the town what a fine Christian woman she was and, at long last, give everyone something else to talk about.

She was ready.

Maggie touched the checkered cloth over her market basket as she crossed the churchyard, confirming yet again that she'd brought everything. She'd written out the program for the ten-member choir, Miss Marshall, who played the piano, and the young people who would portray Mary, Joseph, the angel, shepherds and wise men.

She'd made a list for herself, too, reminders of all the things she needed to check on, including the costumes. Everything had to be made new, since the ones they'd used in previous years had been burned along with the old church.

The church windows glowed with light as Maggie climbed the steps and went inside. The reverend, seated in the last pew reading, gave her a warm smile. "You go ahead with the rehearsal. Don't mind me."

While Maggie sat at the front of the church going over her lists, her "Mary" and "Joseph," Cecil Nelson and Becky Cochran, arrived. Maggie hadn't asked the young people who would portray the nativity to attend tonight's rehearsal. She wanted the choir to practice first.

"We thought you might need some help with things," Cecil offered. He glanced at Becky and she nodded, too. "So is it all right with you if we stay?"

"Of course," Maggie said, pleased to have volunteers she hadn't counted on. "Why don't you two get the hymn books?"

Cecil smiled broadly as he and Becky hurried away. A few minutes later, several members of the choir arrived.

"Where is everyone else?" Maggie asked, looking past them toward the door.

Miss Peyton, the schoolmarm, spoke up. "Dora's got sick children, and Mr. Townsend's busy at the restaurant."

"Ida Burk's open late on account of all the shoppers in town," Chester Livingston said.

Vera Lyle, a robust, gray-haired woman, said, "Everyone's pretty busy, you know—"

"Don't soft-pedal things," Charlie, her husband, insisted. "Truth is, there's no need for rehearsal. We've been singing these same Christmas songs all our lives."

"But we're doing things differently this year," Maggie told them. "I've planned—"

"Christmas is Christmas," Charlie complained. "That's all there is to it."

"Don't sound like such a grump," Vera told him.

"It's cold outside." Charlie waved his hand toward the rest of the choir. "We ought to be warm at home right now, not here practicing songs we could sing in our sleep."

"But this year our program is going to be different," Maggie said, fighting down a wave of panic. "This year—"

"Maggie?" Miss Marshall, the church's stoop-shouldered pianist, made her way down the aisle. "My rheumatism is bothering me, dear. I don't think I can play tonight."

"That settles it," Charlie Lyle declared. "Rehearsal's cancelled."

"No, wait," Maggie said.

Vera gave her an apologetic smile. "We'll try again later in the week, maybe." She headed down the aisle with her husband and the other choir members.

"Wait…"

No one stopped, but Maggie spotted Sarah Burk at the rear of the group and called to her. She turned back.

"How are things going with the costumes?" Maggie asked, trying not to sound desperate.

Sarah's eyebrows drew together. "Costumes?"

"For the nativity," Maggie said, her stomach twisting into a knot. "You said you'd take care of them."

"I did?"

"Weeks ago. Remember?"

"I've been so busy with the new house and everything. I suppose I forgot," Sarah said. "Goodness, you need all those costumes? I don't think there's time."

"There has to be," Maggie insisted.

"Oh, by the way. I looked through Aunt Bess's things and she didn't leave me any money for the things you say she ordered. Sorry."

Breath left Maggie in a sickly wheeze as Sarah hurried out of the church. No money from Bess Patterson for all the things she ordered? And no costumes? A choir that refused to rehearse? Would the children in the pageant also refuse—

Mary and Joseph.

Maggie whirled. Where were Cecil and Becky?

She walked past the altar and into the alcove containing the storage cabinets, and froze in her tracks at the sight of the two young people in the dark corner, kissing.

Becky squealed and jerked away, then ran past Maggie. Cecil, a little slower to respond, stared at her for a moment, then hurried after Becky.

Maggie's cheeks burned and her heart pounded. An ugly image flashed in her thoughts. She was responsible for what went on at the rehearsals. What would people say if they learned that these two young people were kissing at the church while Maggie was supposed to be supervising them?

She pressed her palm to her forehead and staggered out of the alcove. Her mind whirling, she gathered her wrap and market basket and headed down the aisle. Reverend Battenfield rose from the last pew, stopping her.

"I'm disappointed at how rehearsal turned out," he said.

Heat roared up Maggie's neck and covered her face.

"Do you think you'll be able to get the program ready?" he asked. He'd said it kindly, but the doubt was evident in his tone.

"I'm sure that I can," she told him, hoping that the fires of Hell wouldn't blaze up and consume her for the lie she'd just told.

The reverend smiled weakly. "Fine, then. Good night."

Maggie murmured a goodbye and dashed out of the church, never more anxious in her life to get away from somewhere. Her knees weakened and she might have plopped down on the church steps if Reverend Battenfield hadn't come out of the door just then. Maggie couldn't face him again.

She hurried away from the church and through town, grateful for the darkness, the late hour, the empty streets. She rushed past the streetlamps and glowing windows, praying no one saw her. If they stopped her, she'd burst into tears and never quit.

Her Christmas Eve program was doomed. No one wanted to hear about the special service she'd planned. The costumes weren't even being worked on. Reverend Battenfield was questioning her ability. The choir didn't want to sing, Emmett was stuck in jail and Cecil and Becky would once again make her the talk of the town if word of what they were doing ever got out. And what on earth was she going to do with all those decorations she'd ordered for Bess Patterson?

Absolutely nothing was going right.

She wanted to cry. She wanted to get home, lock herself inside and cry. Tears welled at the thought.

But there would be no one waiting to comfort her. She'd

be all alone. Maggie pressed her lips together and hurried faster down the boardwalk...then stopped suddenly.

The jailhouse. Inside was Jack.

Emotion tightened her throat.

How she wished she could go to him. He had that big, strong chest, and how nice it would be to lay her head against it. And maybe he'd put his arms around her, hold her so she'd feel secure and safe—for just a few minutes.

But he didn't want her there, probably. Or maybe he did. Maggie didn't know.

Rooted to the spot on the boardwalk, she thought of how Jack had said nothing, hinted at nothing that would allow her to go to him. All he'd done was kiss her.

Was that reason enough to go to him? Did those few acts allow her to run into his arms?

Shouldn't she know this? She'd let him kiss her—she'd kissed him back. Yet she didn't know if it meant anything.

She was a failure at this, too, it seemed.

Overcome, Maggie plopped down on the boardwalk, buried her face in her hands and cried.

She'd barely gotten into her second wrenching sob when footsteps and a shout interrupted her. Then Jack was kneeling before her, firing questions, gripping her hands.

She swallowed hard and blinked away her blurry vision.

"Are you hurt? Did someone do something to you? Maggie, talk to me. What happened?"

She realized then that he thought she was injured, or had been attacked.

"Answer me, Maggie. Are you all right?"

"No, I'm not all right! I'm sitting in the middle of the boardwalk, at night, with no wrap on, it's wintertime and I'm crying! Of course, I'm not all right!"

Jack eased the pressure of his hands around hers but didn't seem relieved in any way.

"What are you doing out here like this? I saw you from the jail and thought—hell, I don't know what I thought, but you scared me half to death," he told her.

"Oh! I'm so sorry if the occasion of my entire life falling to pieces inconvenienced you! I'd think those kisses I shared with you would allow me a little consideration!"

Maggie jerked away from him and scrambled to her feet. He sprang up in front of her and she saw him draw in a big breath, struggling to calm himself.

"Tell me what happened. What's wrong?" he asked.

"Everything," she declared. "My Christmas program is a failure, the reverend hates me, the whole town is going to turn against me even worse than before when they find out what Mary and Joseph were doing and—and—"

Jack moved closer. "And what?"

She couldn't bring herself to actually say aloud that she was saddled with Bess Patterson's Christmas decorations.

"And I don't know how things could get any worse!" Maggie declared.

"Well…" Jack eased back. His gaze bounced to the ground, then the sky, then to her. "Well, uh, I ran into Gannon from the express office a while ago. He was looking for you. You got a telegram."

Maggie held her breath. "Papa? Is he all right?"

"He's all right," Jack said, and shifted uncomfortably. Then he straightened his shoulders and looked into her eyes. "Your pa's not coming home for Christmas."

The words hit her like a spike of freezing wind. She heaved a ragged breath and just stared at Jack.

If she looked at him hard enough, long enough,

maybe he'd take back his words. Maybe they wouldn't be true. Maybe her papa would come home and she wouldn't be alone...

Maggie burst into fresh tears.

Jack's arms came around her and pulled her against his chest, and Maggie sobbed harder. She'd never felt such strength before. His chest was firm yet more welcoming than the softest pillow she'd ever laid her head on.

He let her cry for a while, then fished his handkerchief from his pocket and put it into her hand.

"It's freezing out here," he said quietly. "We need to get you inside."

He picked up her wrap and draped it around her shoulders, then took her market basket in one hand and her in the other, and urged her along. At the rear of the mercantile they climbed to the second floor and went inside.

Jack guided her to one of the chairs at the table and lit the lantern.

"Tell me what happened at the church," he said, as he added wood to the cookstove and lit it.

"I hardly know where to start."

"How about starting at the part that won't make you cry?" he suggested, as he shrugged out of his coat and hat.

He grinned at her and Maggie couldn't help but laugh a little, enough to take the sharp edge off her emotions.

"Well, to begin with, my Christmas Eve program is a failure—what are you doing?"

Jack turned back from the cupboard. "Fixing something to eat."

"I'm not hungry."

"I am." He raised an eyebrow at her. "I seem to recall that I gave you a few kisses. That ought to entitle me to a meal."

Maggie blushed and giggled softly, then told him what had happened at the church while he heated the roast and vegetables that had been left from the night before. When Maggie finished her story, they ate at the table together. The conversation changed to gossip and news from town, and Maggie appreciated the respite from her own problems.

"Did Papa say why he wasn't coming home?" she asked.

Jack hesitated, then said, "He's with your ma. She must have sent for him. I guess that's why he left town in such a hurry."

Maggie thought about it for a moment. "She's the only thing who could get him to leave the store. He loves her desperately. The incident at the church wasn't the first time something like that happened. We always moved around a lot. I suppose I know why now. Does that make sense?"

"You mean that a man could love a woman that much? No matter what?" Jack shrugged. "I never thought about it."

When they'd washed and dried their supper dishes, Jack looked as if he didn't want to go, to leave her alone.

Or was that just wishful thinking on her part?

"So what are you going to do about your Christmas Eve program?" he asked, pulling on his coat.

"I'll figure out something," Maggie said, though, really, she didn't have any idea how it could be salvaged.

"I can go talk to the choir members, explain things," Jack offered. "Or, if you want, I could lock them up, hold them in jail until they agree to rehearse."

Maggie's eyes rounded in horror and she was about to protest when she saw the tiny hint of teasing in Jack's eyes.

"I just may take you up on your offer," she said with a grin, then remembered another problem she'd faced tonight. "I should talk to Becky's mother. Maybe Cecil's, too."

"I'll handle Cecil," Jack said, pulling on his Stetson.

"What are you going to do?" Maggie asked. "And don't even joke about throwing that boy in jail."

"Don't worry. I'll take care of it."

Something about the hard look in his eye and the determined jut of his jaw told Maggie that she didn't have to worry about this. And what a nice feeling that was.

Jack put his hand on the doorknob. "Are you going to be all right? I'll stay longer, if you want."

With all her heart, Maggie wished she could ask him to stay, but it wasn't right. And it certainly wasn't proper.

"Promise me you won't cry after I'm gone," he said.

"I promise," she said. "I feel better now. Really."

There was no reason to stay, but Jack lingered. They spent a long moment looking at each other, then he left.

Maggie threw the lock and pulled back the curtain at the window. She listened as his footsteps pounded down the stairs, then saw him in the alley. He turned back and waved, and her heart thudded a little harder as he disappeared into the shadows. Some piece of her went along with him.

She could have stood there half the night, watching the spot where she'd last seen him, feeling the glow inside her. But she didn't have time. Not for tears, or thoughts of Jack, or disappointment about being alone on Christmas.

She had to figure out how to salvage her Christmas Eve program.

Chapter Eight

The boy was hiding from him. Jack was sure of it.

Mid-morning and the streets of Crystal Springs bustled with shoppers, wagons, horses and carriages. Jack took his usual route down the boardwalk, his gaze sweeping from one side of the street to the other. More strangers in town as Christmas drew nearer. More problems to deal with.

The one he'd wanted to handle today had proved the most elusive. Cecil Nelson wasn't in school or at the hotel his ma owned. Most likely the boy was avoiding him.

But maybe Jack wasn't looking all that hard.

A pang of guilt rolled through Jack as he crossed the street. He intended to give Cecil a stern talking-to about kissing Becky Cochran in the church during choir rehearsal. But every time he imagined lecturing the boy on his conduct, the image of Maggie popped into his mind.

How could he fuss at Cecil for kissing Becky when kissing Maggie—and doing a lot more than that—had been all Jack could think of lately?

Just to prove to himself that he was really trying, Jack walked down the alley next to the Crystal Springs Laundry and Bath House. No sign of Becky or Cecil. He headed back to Main Street.

Of course, kissing Maggie, and doing other things, hadn't been the only thing on Jack's mind. He'd been surprised when he'd walked into her place over the mercantile. Neat and clean, he'd expected. But it was more than that. It was warm and welcoming, inviting. Not just a place to eat and sleep after a long day, but a real home.

And Maggie had done that herself. With no help and, probably, little training from the woman who was her mother.

As he walked, Jack thought about how Dabney Hudson had run off to be with his wife. Yet instead of anger, an odd sensation filled him, causing a fullness in his chest.

What would it be like to love a woman like that? After what she'd done, the hurt and humiliation she'd caused, Dabney had forsaken everything—his daughter, his business—and gone to her.

Jack headed back to the jailhouse. Something was different when he walked inside and he knew immediately what it was.

Maggie. Her scent was in the air.

Ben glanced up from his seat at the desk. "Miss Hudson's here to see the prisoner. And you."

Jack ignored the knowing grin on his deputy's face as he hung up his coat and hat and walked back to the cells.

Maggie looked as bright and as welcoming as a morning sunrise as she stood at the cell, talking to Emmett. She made the whole place smell good.

"Good morning, Sheriff," she said and turned a smile his way. "Could I speak with you for a bit?"

That strange glow was back in the pit of Jack's stomach. He'd agree to most anything if she'd just keep smiling.

Maggie spoke quietly to Emmett. He nodded and ambled to the cot in the rear of the cell.

"Who's minding the store?" Jack asked.

"I decided to open a little late this morning. I had errands to run." She paused, looking pleased with herself, and said, "I took the liberty of bringing you something."

Jack followed the wave of her hand into his bedroom. A blue quilt lay atop his bed and two pictures hung on the wall, all blending nicely with the rug she'd brought him earlier.

He didn't know how to tell her that a quilt was the last thing he needed. He was uncomfortably warm in the room, thanks to her leaving him taut with desire every night.

"Do you like it?" she asked, smiling sweetly up at him.

He'd like it better if she were under those covers with him, but since he couldn't say so, he simply thanked her.

Then something else dawned on him.

"Let's go outside," he said.

Jack grabbed his coat and hat as they walked through the office, then escorted Maggie down the boardwalk to the corner next to the alley. The air was cold. Maggie's cheeks flushed from the chill but Jack hardly felt it.

"I'm not letting Frazier out of jail," he said.

Maggie gasped. "Why, Sheriff, do you really think I'd stoop to bringing you gifts—"

"I'm not letting Frazier out of jail."

Her pretense crumbled. "Please, Jack, you have to. The way things are going, Emmett may be the only person in the entire program."

"No."

"I've explained this to you before. This could be my only chance to gain favor with the town."

"Look, Maggie, people are either going to like you, or they aren't. No church program is going to change that."

"Yes, it will," she insisted. She drew herself up and squared her shoulders. "I'm tired of feeling bad, being upset, worrying about what the town thinks of me. This Christmas Eve program is my chance to prove who I really am, and I'm going to make it happen. Somehow."

God, how he wanted her.

She was angry and determined, and her nose flared just a little and, if he could, he'd pull her under that new quilt right this minute. The air around Jack heated and it was all he could do not to go to her.

"Won't you please reconsider?" Maggie asked.

He wished he had another choice, a different way of handling the problem. But the law was the law and he was there to enforce it. He didn't get to pick and choose when it suited him.

"I can't let Frazier out of jail," he said softly. "I'm sorry, Maggie, I wish I could. But it's not right and I won't do it."

"Releasing Emmett could work in your favor, too," she pointed out. "Everyone will think very highly of you when they learn that you let him out of jail for the betterment of our Christmas program. You're new in town and you've got a long future ahead of you here."

A chill swept over Jack that had nothing to do with the cold breeze or the snow still lining the edge of the board-walk. It showed in his expression, he realized, because Maggie reacted to it. Her sweet little smile vanished and her eyes widened.

"What is it?" Her words weren't a question as much as a demand.

Jack hesitated. He'd told no one about the agreement he'd made with Mayor Fisher when he took this job in Crystal Springs. They'd both decided it wouldn't do Jack, or the town, any good if the truth became public.

But he couldn't keep it from Maggie, no matter how much it hurt to say the words—something he'd never anticipated when he'd signed on as town sheriff.

"Truth is," Jack said quietly, "I told the mayor when I took this job that it was only for a few weeks. A month or so, at most."

Maggie just stared at him. She didn't blink or even seem to draw a breath.

"I didn't know if I'd like the job—or the town," Jack explained. "When I left the Marshal's Service I decided I'd try a few places, see how I liked them."

"You're…you're leaving?" She whispered the words.

"I've got another job waiting for me up north. And if I don't like that town, and I don't like being the town sheriff, I'm going back to the Marshal's Service," Jack told her. "That's my plan, anyway."

A miserable minute crawled by as Jack watched the expression change on Maggie's face. It reminded him of the first time she'd come to the jail, demanding Frazier's release, then wilting right before his eyes when he'd asked her why.

But this time, the pain he saw in her face seemed to cut deeper, hold her in a tighter grasp. And this time, Jack felt the ache in his own chest.

"Look, Maggie—"

"Well, then," she said, drawing herself up and gulping down a big breath. "Good luck to you, Sheriff, in whatever you do."

She turned crisply and walked away, part of him wanting to go after her, another part wondering what he'd say when he caught her.

How could she have been so foolish? So stupid? How could she have thought—

Maggie huddled deeper inside her wrap as she hurried away from the jail, humiliation, hurt and anguish boiling inside her.

How could she have thought—even for a moment—that a handsome, kind, caring man like Jack Crawford would be interested in her? The entire town had whispered and gossiped about her. They'd suggested all sorts of things about what type of woman she was. Decent people snubbed her and her friends had turned away.

And yet, for some ridiculous reason, she'd thought Jack cared about her. Her. She'd let him kiss her. She'd let him hold her, comfort her. She'd told him her worst secrets, her deepest secrets, her most treasured secrets.

And all along he'd intended to leave.

She'd been but a passing fancy for him. Or a charity case because he'd felt sorry for her.

How could she have thought—even for a moment—that she might have a home of her own, like those being built on the edge of town…with Jack?

She should have known. She should have known.

Maggie's chest ached and tears burned her eyes. She pushed on down the boardwalk toward the mercantile. Back to her solitude.

The other shops along Main Street were already open and doing a brisk business. No one seemed to notice that

Hudson's was still closed. Not one single person waited at the door or peered through the window.

This morning, Maggie was glad. She didn't know how she'd face anyone right now. Still, her pa wouldn't have liked that she'd opened the store late today.

Maggie gulped hard, forcing down her emotions, as she drew the key from her handbag and unlocked the front door. It was small comfort that, since her pa wasn't there, she could run her errands and open late if she wanted, and be alone with her humiliation.

The store was silent as Maggie stepped inside and closed the door behind her. The jangle of the little bell rang hollow in the big room. She pulled her cloak closer around herself against the chill.

Jack floated through her mind but she pushed him away. No sense in remembering. No sense in rehashing the hurt.

He'd never said he loved her, or cared for her. He'd kissed her, but she'd let him. He'd never said he intended to stay in Crystal Springs…or with her.

So, it seemed, she only had herself to blame for this bit of misery in her life. For most everything else—the church burning, her mother's conduct, her father's foul moods— she'd been but a bystander, a hapless victim painted with the brush of another's misconduct.

But this time, it was all her doing.

Maggie forced down her emotions and looked around the store. Her prison? Her sanctuary? She wasn't sure which.

All she knew for certain was that every ounce of her being ached and she could easily have collapsed onto the floor and cried the entire day.

Her gaze settled on the crates of merchandise her father had left her to unpack and shelve. Her heart ached anew at the thought of what awful items might be inside the crates. Maggie didn't know if she could bear to look at them.

So maybe she just wouldn't do it.

The idea stung Maggie and she stopped dead in her tracks.

Not shelve the merchandise? Not do as her papa had told her?

Why not?

A sense of freedom—and daring—coasted through Maggie, overwhelming the ache, the hurt, the humiliation.

Maybe she wouldn't shelve the merchandise. Maybe she'd leave it in the crates. After all, her father wasn't there. He'd left her in charge. And she could do whatever she wanted.

Whatever she wanted.

Maggie turned in a circle, the idea making her feel light of spirit, suddenly alive. She could present the store's merchandise any way she wanted. There was no one to tell her she couldn't. No one to admonish her or belittle her ideas.

She could do anything she chose—until after Christmas, anyway.

Joy filled Maggie and its energy pushed her into action. She locked the door, tossed off her cloak and headed for the stockroom.

Some time later, she heard a fist pounding on the rear door.

"Come in," she called from her perch among the crates high above the stockroom.

The door opened and Jack strode in, Cecil trailing behind him. Maggie's breath caught. She hadn't expected to see Jack so soon—if at all. He'd hurt her—hurt her badly—and she mumbled a curse directed at herself for thinking instantly of how handsome he was.

Maggie brushed an errant strand of hair from her face,

reminding herself that Jack had done nothing wrong. He hadn't deceived her, or misrepresented himself to her in any way. Luckily, her joy in her new decision about the mercantile carried her emotions.

Jack shouted her name again.

"Up here," she called.

Maggie knew she must look a sight. She'd spent hours going through crates, sorting and moving things around. Her forehead was damp and packing straw clung to her.

"Jack, I had the most wonderful idea." She gathered her skirt and started down the stacks of crates.

"Hold on," Jack told her, and climbed up to meet her while Cecil lingered near the door. He stopped in front of her, as if he weren't sure what sort of reception he'd get.

"I saw your shop closed all day and I was worried about you," he said. "And I told you I don't like you back here on these crates. You're liable to fall and hurt yourself."

Maggie paused on the crate that put them at eye level, telling herself that his words were nothing more than that of a concerned sheriff speaking to any citizen of the town.

She pushed on, anxious to share with him her grand idea. Despite everything, she knew Jack wouldn't discourage her or tell her not to try it.

"I'm putting all the Christmas gifts out in the store," she told him, the words rushing out. "Papa's gone and there's no one to tell me not to, so I'm displaying all of them. And I'm decorating the store. I'm using the things Bess Patterson ordered, most of them, anyway. It's going to be beautiful. A grand Christmas celebration."

Jack just looked at her as if this was the last thing he expected to hear from her. He took a minute, then nodded.

"Sounds like a good plan," he said. "Come down off these crates and tell me all about it."

"I have to get these things unpacked and onto the store shelves," she said, waving toward the mountain of crates. "I have so many things to do."

"I've got you some help," Jack said, and nodded at Cecil.

Jack reached for Maggie's arm to help her down the crates but she pulled away. Her emotions were still strong, and she knew her resolve to remain distant from him would likely crumple at his touch.

When they reached the floor, Jack said, "The boy's got something to say to you."

Cecil came forward. "I'm sorry, Miss Maggie, for what happened over at the church the other night. It was disrespectful and I shouldn't have done it. I'm sorry."

Cecil's gaze cut to Jack, and Maggie was sure he'd told the boy exactly what to say. Still, she appreciated it—from both of them.

"Cecil is going to work for you. You don't have to pay him. It's his way of making up for what he did," Jack explained, then turned to Cecil. "Isn't that right?"

"Yes, sir," he said.

"Get outside and bring in firewood," Jack told him. "Enough for the store and upstairs."

Cecil dashed out the door, seeming relieved to be away from Jack's hard glare.

"You need the help," Jack said, as if he'd anticipated Maggie's words. "And he needs to atone for taking advantage of things at church. The work will do him good, keep his mind off…things."

It seemed awkward standing alone with Jack, so near

to the place where he'd nearly kissed her. Maggie forced her mind to the matter at hand.

"What about his schooling, and helping his mother at the hotel?" she asked.

"It's all taken care of," Jack assured her.

Despite everything, Maggie smiled, pleased at the way he'd handled the situation. Not simply because she could use the help, but because he'd been fair in dealing with Cecil. An apology and a little hard work; a fitting punishment for what he'd done.

"Sheriff?" Ben Sheridan appeared in the doorway looking troubled. "You need to get to the jail. A stranger just showed up. He's big and mean, and he's looking for you."

Chapter Nine

"Jared McQuaid."

Jack recognized his old friend as soon as he stepped into the jailhouse. They shook hands and spent a while reliving their days together as U.S. Marshals before McQuaid asked Jack to show him around town.

"So you're a town sheriff now?" Jack asked.

"Little place called Stanford, Nevada," McQuaid said. "Not much different from your town."

"Quiet?"

"Too quiet, at first. Took some getting used to."

"How did you manage?"

"I had help." McQuaid grinned, the first grin Jack had seen on the man's face in all the time he'd known him. "I got married. Mattie is her name. She was a widow when we met, owned a nice restaurant in town. We've got a baby on the way. I'm hoping for a girl."

Jack offered congratulations, and saw the absolute joy in his friend's face.

"Truth is," McQuaid said, "I never thought I'd love a woman this much, or that I'd ever find a place to call home."

Jack had long suspected McQuaid had a troubled past and he saw hints of that in his eyes.

"Men like us don't quit the Marshal's Service for no reason," McQuaid said. "I figure you're here in this little town, looking for the same thing I was looking for."

"Not sure I'll find it," Jack admitted. "Here. Or anywhere."

"You will, if you keep your eyes open and pay attention."

"Sounds like the same advice you gave when we were trailing outlaws."

"Hunting is hunting," McQuaid said. His expression turned somber. "I came here to give you a warning. Trouble's headed your way. You remember Virgil Calhoun?"

Jack thought back over the many dozens of men he'd captured, transported, sent to trial and prison, searching his memory for Calhoun.

"About seven years ago. He robbed a half-dozen banks, wounded a sheriff and a couple of bystanders," McQuaid said. "He swore he'd get even with you when he got out."

"That could have been a lot of men," Jack said.

"One of the bystanders was a little girl."

That jolted Jack's memory, but his mental image of Calhoun was vague; there had been so many like him.

"I hunted him for weeks, finally brought him in," Jack said, nodding. "Yeah, I remember Calhoun."

McQuaid's expression hardened. "He was released from prison. Word is he's coming after you."

After two days—two long, hard days—Maggie had the mercantile ready for its Christmas opening.

She hurried down the stairs, the delightful scent of the sugar cookies she'd baked this morning wafting into the mercantile with her. She sat the tray on the counter and took another look around. A proud smile bloomed on her face. It was nothing like the store her father had left behind.

She hoped today's customers would share that same feeling. Maggie had kept the door locked and the shades drawn, and not let a soul inside. She'd put a sign in the window explaining the store would reopen today, hoping to pique the townsfolk's curiosity.

"Morning, Miss Maggie," Cecil greeted as he walked through the curtained doorway from the stockroom.

He'd been a great help these past two days. He'd lifted and carried, stocked shelves and had gone out past the edge of town to fetch the pine boughs, cedar and holly that she'd used to decorate the store. He'd even done a decent job of tying red ribbons in the greenery.

"You got customers waiting outside already," Cecil said. "I saw them just now when I walked over."

She gave the store a final check. Everywhere were displays of Christmas gifts. She'd even managed to turn some of her father's everyday stock into desirable gift items.

She'd cut red and green bell shapes from fabric scraps and sewn them onto the pockets of the plain white aprons, adding a tiny jingle bell at the bottom. She'd tied red bows around the chimneys of the plain lanterns her father had ordered, and wrapped the gray blankets with white yarn, adding a sprig of holly.

The display windows had come to life with all sorts of items. One she'd filled with toys. Jacks and dolls with fancy dresses. Kaleidoscopes, an army of pewter soldiers, wooden horses and a tiny tin kitchen set. Something to delight every child in town.

The other window held more gift items. For the ladies there were linen handkerchiefs, kid gloves, hair accessories, satin fans and silk parasols, jewelry. Gifts for the men included pipes, leather goods, inkstands and pocketknives.

With a flourish, Maggie pulled the door key from her skirt pocket and let in the half-dozen waiting customers.

"Thank you. Yes, thank you so much."

Maggie managed to keep a smile on her face as she walked her last customer for the night to the door, accepting their compliments on what a wonderful store she ran.

She locked the door, pulled down the shade and fell against it. Everything hurt. Feet, head, back. But she'd never been happier.

The store had been crowded all day, both with new folks she didn't know and many of the townsfolk. So crowded, at times, that she'd had to squeeze between customers and wait on several at a time. Thank goodness Cecil had been there. She didn't know how she could have managed without him. He'd gone home a few minutes ago, looking as worn out as she felt.

She pulled down the shades and blew out the lanterns, and went upstairs. The mercantile had to be restocked for tomorrow but she'd do that in the morning.

She'd just lit the lantern in the kitchen when a knock sounded on the door. She opened it to find Jack holding a market basket. Maggie's heart soared, but she immediately reined in her emotions. She could think of no one else in the world she'd rather share the end of this day with, yet reminded herself that the gesture meant nothing.

"Wasn't it wonderful, Jack? Did you see all those customers?" she asked, feeling a bit breathless.

He stepped inside and closed the door. "I kept an eye on the place all day. You had a crowd, all right."

She'd seen him several times on the boardwalk peering into the store and wished she could give him a wave, but didn't. No sense making a bigger fool of herself over him, and in front of her new customers to boot.

"I knew you'd be tired so I brought supper from the White Dove Cafe," Jack said, setting the basket on the sideboard.

She gasped. It was the sweetest, most thoughtful thing anyone had ever done for her. Yet why had he done it?

"Is this part of your official duties, Sheriff?" she asked.

He shook his head slowly. "No."

"Then why are you doing it?" Maggie asked. "It is the dearest gesture anyone has ever made before, but I'd like to know what's behind it."

"Are you asking me to declare my intentions?"

"You told me you were leaving, then you show up here tonight like this. I don't know what to think."

"Do you want me to stay in Crystal Springs?"

Maggie pulled up her shoulders. "I've already made quite a fool of myself over you, Jack. I wish you'd spare me further embarrassment."

He looked confused. "I've never kissed any other woman in town—not as an official duty, or otherwise."

That pleased her, but she didn't say so.

"You're leaving. You said so yourself," she told him. "What am I to think?"

Jack paused for a moment, then said, "I won't tell you something that isn't true, Maggie. I won't lie. I think you know that about me by now."

"Yes, that's true," she agreed.

"I don't know what the future holds for me," Jack said. "But the one thing I do know is that there's no place I'd rather be right now than here visiting with you tonight. If you'll allow it."

Maggie knew he was being honest, as always. He'd never lied, told her something that wasn't true or promised anything he couldn't deliver.

So maybe now, this moment, was enough. After all, he'd be gone soon, and wouldn't the memory of this evening together be a delightful one she could keep always?

"Fine, then. Let's have supper," she said.

"Go sit down and rest. I'll have everything ready in a few minutes."

Grateful, Maggie settled into a kitchen chair while Jack lit the logs in the adjoining parlor fireplace, then reheated the coffee and served the fried chicken, biscuits and vegetables he'd brought from the White Dove Cafe.

"So tell me all about your grand reopening," Jack said, as he took the seat next to her.

She ate and talked, telling him about the day. He listened and asked questions, seemed to enjoy every detail. Afterwards, they moved to the settee in front of the fire.

"My gracious," Maggie said with a small laugh. "I was so busy decorating the store I didn't even think about getting the Christmas tree for up here. I have to have one."

Jack smiled. "I think you've got enough to do already."

"Oh, that reminds me. Sarah Burk came by the store today. She's going to bring over the fabric for the Christmas nativity costumes. I told her I'd work on them. She's so busy with the new house, she doesn't have time."

They lapsed into a comfortable silence, watching the crackling fire. Sarah and Caleb were in Maggie's thoughts, along with the Masons, and the grand houses she'd watched them build on the edge of town. For so long she'd envied them, wished for a home as grand. But right now, sitting next to Jack brought her such peace, she couldn't imagine a house could do more.

She watched Jack as he studied the flickering flames and saw a flash of tenseness cross his face. She'd never seen that look before.

"You're thinking something right now. Something troubling," Maggie said. "What is it?"

He turned to her and shook his head quickly. "Nothing's wrong."

"Problems in town?" she asked. Though Crystal Springs was, generally, a quiet place, Jack's job as sheriff wasn't without some danger.

"Nothing for you to worry about," he said with an easy smile. "Nothing I can't handle."

A warm glow filled Maggie. She was certain there was nothing Jack couldn't handle.

"Tired?" he asked.

When she nodded, he offered his outstretched arm, but she hesitated.

"This is part of my official duties, ma'am," Jack told her with a little grin. "It's a new service I'm trying out tonight for the first time. Tell me what you think."

Maggie couldn't resist. She leaned against him, resting her head on his shoulder.

And what a fine shoulder it was, Maggie thought, relaxing against him. Solid, strong. Warm, too. The heat of his body melted into hers, making her tingle. She felt his jaw brush against her hair and looked up at him.

"I'm very much in favor of your new service, Sheriff," she whispered.

"Then you might like this one, too," he said.

Jack leaned down and kissed her.

Maggie gasped at the delight of it, his lips familiar to her now. He blended their mouths together, then drew her to him. His body was hard against her. His hand brushed her cheek, then traced the line of her jaw and neck. She gasped again when he cupped her breast. He moaned and deepened their kiss.

She could have stayed lost in the moment, in their intimate exchange, forever, but Jack broke their kiss. He held her, gazed into her eyes, struggling within himself, it seemed.

"I'd better go," Jack said. He sounded hoarse and none too sure of himself. More than enough reason to leave.

He fetched his coat and hat and opened the door. The cold wind blew in as he turned back and touched Maggie on the cheek.

"Good night," he said softly. He wanted to kiss her again. God, how he wanted to kiss her. But if he did, he might never leave.

"Good night," she said softly. "And thanks for supper."

Jack pounded down the wooden stairs to the alley, the gusting wind cooling him only a little. He stopped and looked back, making sure Maggie had closed the door. He saw her at the window and waved, then walked away quickly before he changed his mind and went back upstairs.

Halfway through the alley, a chill that had nothing to do with the wind stopped Jack in his tracks. He whirled and pulled his gun, searching the shadows. He sensed a presence but saw no one. Jack stood still, listening, then retraced his steps to the back of the store. He searched the outbuilding but saw nothing suspicious, yet that didn't relieve his sense of unease.

Upstairs, Maggie changed into her nightclothes and climbed into bed, the covers cold around her. Jack flew into her head. He was always so warm. Her bed would never be cold with him in it.

Maggie shot straight up. Good gracious, what was she thinking? Sharing a bed with Jack? Even after he'd told her he was leaving Crystal Springs, perhaps never to return?

She felt herself flush as the notion continued to wind through her. Certainly it was an unladylike thought. Sinful, even. But was it really wrong?

She lay back on the pillow and pulled the covers over her. Staring into the darkness she considered the notion again.

Jack. Strong, honest, fair. A good lawman. A good man. A good friend, too. The kind she could pour out her heart to, count on, depend on. The kind of man she'd gladly listen to, take care of, be there for.

Forever.

A wave of profound calm rolled through Maggie. A contentment she'd never experienced. She sighed in her quiet room. She'd fallen in love with Jack Crawford.

But would he ever return that love?

"My goodness, Maggie, what a wonderful job you've done here," Vera Lyle said.

Maggie smiled at the older woman as she stood across the counter from her, shaking her head in wonder. Maggie hadn't seen Vera since the night her husband Charlie had walked out of the church, taking the rest of the choir members with him and ruining her rehearsal.

Around them, customers moved through the store. In the corner, Cecil stood on a stool fetching items from a high shelf for two elderly women.

"Business is steady," Maggie said, proud that, after several days, customers were still coming in.

"And all these fancy decorations."

Vera pointed to the display that held many of the items Bess Patterson had ordered. Glass ornaments, some round or oblong, others shaped like cones, acorns, stars and balloons. Bright-colored Christmas-tree points for the tops of trees, silver-, gold- and copper-colored tinsel garland. Wax angels and Santa Claus figures.

"I have more," Maggie said. "I'm using them to decorate the church for the Christmas Eve program."

Vera's cheeks colored slightly and she ducked her head.

"I should apologize for Charlie's conduct the other night when you wanted to have rehearsal," she said. "He's such a cantankerous old coot sometimes."

"I understand," Maggie said. How could she not after dealing with her own father?

Vera gazed around the store again. "And you're going to decorate the church like this? For Christmas Eve? My goodness, but you really are planning something special."

"I'm working on the costumes," Maggie said. "In my spare time."

"Well, you certainly don't have much of that, now do you?" Vera thought for a moment. "I'll get some of the ladies over here to help out. You don't mind if we sew them here, do you? In the store? It's so festive here."

Maggie's heart soared for an instant, but she pulled back her emotions quickly. "That would be perfect. But, do you think the ladies would come?"

"Truth is I don't like some of what's been going on in town these past few months," Vera declared. "Just leave everything to me. And don't worry about rehearsals. I'll see to the choir. You just name the time."

A smile spread across Maggie's face. "Actually, I know the perfect time for a rehearsal—and the perfect place."

Singing? Was that singing he heard?

Jack picked up his pace as he wound his way down the crowded boardwalk. He'd had a busy morning. A fight had broken out at Foster's feed-and-grain store, about what, Jack had never figured out. He'd showed up at the MacAvoy General Store just as Ida Burk chased two boys with her broom, claiming they'd stolen a handful of peppermint sticks. And he must have listened to a dozen townsfolk who were angry, happy, fed up or excited about all the new people in town for the holidays.

All routine. Normal problems for the sheriff of a small town. Yet Jack couldn't shake the uneasy feeling that had come over him in the alley the other night when he'd left Maggie's.

And now he heard singing. Jack tilted his head. Coming from the jail…?

A group of people had gathered, listening to the strains of "Silent Night, Holy Night" floating out. Jack pushed his way through the crowd and went inside.

Ben sat at the desk, swaying his head to the music. "Choir practice," he said, and nodded toward the cells.

Jack stalked over to the hallway and saw about a dozen men and women gathered outside Emmett Frazier's cell, singing. Still confined, Frazier sang along with them. Maggie stood in front, studying a hymnal and directing them.

When the song ended, everyone turned to Jack. He

wagged his finger at Maggie. "Could I see you for a minute, Miss Hudson?"

She passed her hymnal to Miss Peyton and the choir struck up "O Little Town of Bethlehem."

"What's going on?" Jack asked when they were out of the hallway.

"The choir needs to rehearse and everyone had a few minutes to get together today. Vera Lyle arranged it," Maggie told him.

"But this is the jail. I can't have people—"

"How else are we going to practice with Emmett?"

Jack exhaled heavily. "Maggie, I told you I can't let Frazier—"

"I didn't ask you to let him out of jail, now did I?"

"Well, no," he admitted, though he didn't like it one bit that he had to.

"I have to finish rehearsal and get back to the store. Cecil is watching things and we're very busy today." Maggie gave him a quick smile and went back to the singers.

Jack blew out another heavy breath and trudged back into the office.

"Choir sounds good. Especially Frazier. Sure surprised me," Ben said, rising from the desk. "Would it be so awful to let him out of jail so he can sing on Christmas Eve? He made a deal with the Lord. It's his salvation."

"Frazier doesn't need to sing in church for salvation," Jack told him. "He can get salvation right here in jail, if he really wants it. He doesn't have to sing for it."

"Yeah, I know. But he does sound good. He'd make the first Christmas service in the new church something special."

"I've got bigger problems to think about than Emmett

Frazier," Jack said. He'd told Ben about Virgil Calhoun's recent release from prison and his threat to come after Jack.

"So releasing Frazier early would be one less thing to worry about, wouldn't it?" Ben asked.

Jack wasn't in the mood for such perfect logic. He went back outside without answering.

Breaking up the fight at the feed-and-grain store this morning and talking Ida Burk out of her broom had come easy to him—easier than it had since he'd arrived in Crystal Springs. Yet something about the town still didn't feel right to him.

Jack headed east, eyeing every rider on Main Street, watching everyone on the boardwalk. Since his old friend McQuaid had told him that Calhoun was headed his way, Jack had thought long and hard, dragging up old memories as he tried to recall every detail about the man. The most important remained elusive, though. Jack had only a vague recollection of what Calhoun looked like and, to make matters worse, that image was seven years old. Calhoun's time in prison had changed him, surely, in many ways, including his appearance. Jack hoped he'd still recognize him.

Had he gone soft? Jack wondered. Had the weeks away from his job as a U.S. Marshal taken away his edge? Or had he just grown accustomed to the relative peace and tranquility in his life here in Crystal Springs with Maggie?

Jack stopped at the edge of the boardwalk and gave himself a mental shake. There he went, turning everything back to Maggie again. Nearly his every thought started with her or circled back around to her. Seeing her, wanting her, lying awake at night thinking about her, imagining her in bed with him and the things the two of them could do.

He couldn't seem to control himself around her. The night after her grand opening he'd wanted to do the kind thing and take her some supper. But he'd ended up kissing her, then lying awake most of the night remembering the feel of her, the taste of her, the scent of her—

"Sheriff?"

Jack whipped around, his gun halfway out of the holster before he recognized Caleb Burk.

Burk stepped back. "I heard you were looking for me. Sorry, Sheriff, didn't mean to startle you."

"It's…it's all right," Jack said, shoving his gun into his holster again.

But it wasn't all right. He knew it wasn't. He'd gotten lost in thought again. Wasn't keeping his eyes open, wasn't paying attention.

He glanced at the crowded street. What if Virgil Calhoun had ridden into town just now?

Chapter Ten

∞

The night was still, with a quiet sort of cold that burned cheeks and ears. The clear sky twinkled with a blanket of stars scattered, it seemed, by a heavenly hand.

Jack's breath froze before him as he headed through town, his steps more anxious than they'd been in the past several days. He was on his way to see Maggie and he was in a hurry to get there.

He hadn't spoken to her in days. They'd both been too busy for more than a wave or a smile when he'd stopped by her store on his rounds to check on things.

Jack peered into the window of Hudson's Mercantile. The store was closed for business but full of people. Several women sat in chairs around the stove in the middle of the room, sewing. Their husbands were gathered nearby, talking earnestly. Cecil was busy restocking shelves.

Maggie saw him and the most beautiful smile bloomed on her face. Jack's heart rose in his throat.

"Come in," she said, opening the door for him. "We're finishing up the shepherds' robes—with a day to spare."

Warmth and the delicious scent of food struck Jack as

he came inside. The counter held plates of good things to eat that the women must have brought over in their last push to finish the costumes before tomorrow night's service.

Everyone called a greeting as he shrugged out of his coat and hat. Maggie fetched a plate piled high with food, then gave him a sweet smile before returning to her sewing.

Jack knew everyone and joined the men's conversation. He ate, stealing glances at Maggie as often as he dared.

Maybe Crystal Springs was starting to feel like home, after all, Jack thought. The mayor had asked him over for supper and, even though his wife's cooking had given him a bellyache, it was nice to be invited. Mrs. Townsend at the White Dove Cafe hadn't charged him for his dinner the other night. Just her way of saying "thank you" for making rounds so often, she'd told him. Most everyone in town called him by name now and had something nice to say when he passed.

Jack's attention drifted from Fred Hartwood's opinion on the possibility of snow in the next few days to Maggie sitting with the women. He'd never seen her look more happy or contented. Feeling at home, surely. And, of course, the satisfaction that her Christmas Eve program would take place tomorrow night, just as she'd planned.

Before long, the women announced that the last costume had been completed. They cleaned up, goodbyes were said and everyone left, except for Cecil, who was still stocking shelves. Jack lingered at the door.

"Can you believe it, Jack? Everything is going to be fine for the Christmas Eve program tomorrow," Maggie said, favoring him with a bright smile.

"So does that mean you don't need Frazier to sing?"

"Of course I do," she told him. "But you've told me dozens of times that you have no intention of...Jack?"

She must have seen something in his expression because her eyes narrowed, then widened when he couldn't mask a grin any longer.

"I'm letting Frazier out of jail tomorrow," he said.

Maggie threw herself at him, looping his neck with both arms and holding on tight. He stuck his nose in the curve of her neck for a sniff of her hair, then pulled away when he saw Cecil staring.

"But why?" she asked. "What made you change your mind?"

"Frazier's not violent. He's behaved himself in jail and served most of his sentence," Jack explained. "And, besides, it's Christmas. I'll release Frazier in the morning so he'll have time to get cleaned up before the service."

"Oh, Jack, this is wonderful," Maggie declared. "Now my Christmas Eve program is going to be perfect."

Jack basked in the glow of her smile, then was surprised when she rose on her toes and gave him a kiss on the cheek.

"Thank you, Jack. Thank you for everything."

"Lock up," he said. "I'll see you tomorrow."

Maggie closed the door and turned the key in the lock, enjoying the last glimpse of Jack as he walked away. She couldn't remember when she'd ever been happier in her life. The Christmas program she'd thought would be so terrible would surely turn out perfect, and so many other wonderful things had happened to her.

"I'm almost finished, Miss Maggie," Cecil called from the back of the store. "Just another crate to go."

Hudson's Mercantile, like all the other merchants in

town, would be open a half day tomorrow. Maggie wanted to be sure her shelves were still full.

"You're an angel, Cecil," she declared. "You've worked so hard. I don't know what I would have done without—"

A knock sounded on the door. She turned and saw a man with his hand against the glass panel, gazing inside.

"Doesn't he know we're closed?" Cecil complained. "Tell him to come back tomorrow."

Maggie had seen the man before. He'd been in the store several times over the past few days. He hadn't purchased anything, just looked around. Probably deciding how to spend his carefully saved funds, she guessed.

He looked like a miner, she thought, in dusty clothes and scuffed boots. He was tall, rangy, with shoulder-length hair and a unkempt beard, hollow eyes and a wrinkled face. It was impossible to guess his age.

"Now, Cecil, a good merchant never turns away a paying customer," Maggie said. She opened the door and stepped back. The man ambled inside.

"Can I help you find something?" Maggie asked.

He stood there for a moment, taking in the store, then pushed the door closed. Slowly, he turned to Maggie, his gaze hard and cold.

Alarm whispered through Maggie. She eased away from him. Quick as a snake, the man grabbed her arm and pulled her against him. She gasped and he squeezed her arm harder.

"Quiet now," he said, his breath foul against her cheek. "No reason to get upset, Miss Hudson. I'm just here to see an old friend. Boy!"

Cecil turned. He saw what was happening and froze.

"You get over to the jail," the man told him. "Tell Sheriff Jack Crawford that he's got a visitor. Tell him Virgil Calhoun is waiting for him."

The fire in the potbellied stove still burned warm, its occasional crackle the only sound in the mercantile. Maggie sat in a rocker, her hands clasped together to stave off their shaking. To her right, Virgil Calhoun sat rocking gently, a pistol resting on his lap.

He'd positioned their chairs so he could see both the front entry to the mercantile and the curtained doorway to the stockroom, then sent Cecil to fetch Jack, telling the boy to go straight to the jail and tell no one else. It probably had been only minutes ago; it seemed to Maggie as if hours had passed.

She laced her fingers, two versions of a prayer running through her mind. The first, that Jack would save her. The other, that he would stay away so Calhoun wouldn't kill him.

"Calhoun!"

Jack's voice bellowed from the stockroom. Tears welled in Maggie's eyes and she pressed her lips together to keep from crying out.

"I figured you'd sneak in the back way," Calhoun called. "Come on in, Crawford. Show yourself."

"Let her go!"

"I'm not even holding a gun on her," Calhoun said. He turned to Maggie. "Tell him."

She glanced at the gun in his lap and his hands resting on the rocker's armrests. He could snatch it up in a heartbeat, turn it on her or Jack.

"It's on his lap," Maggie called, not sure if that was helpful or not.

In the stockroom, Jack raised his pistol and eased

around the curtained doorway, taking in the mercantile in one big sweep. He glanced at Maggie only long enough to see she wasn't hurt, then focused his attention on Calhoun.

He'd seen this man around town a few times, but hadn't known it was Virgil Calhoun. Even though his recollections of the outlaw were vague, Jack would never have recognized him. Prison had aged him far beyond his years.

Yet that didn't make him any less dangerous.

Jack had sent Cecil to find Ben Sheridan and as many men as he could, but didn't know if they'd get here in time.

He pointed his gun at Calhoun. "Throw down your pistol."

"Well, look here. It's Sheriff Jack Crawford," Calhoun said, giving him a smile. "Come on in, Crawford. I'm sure you can't wait to hear what I have to say."

Jack moved into the doorway and came forward, his gaze steady on Calhoun. "I want you out of my town."

"In due time," Calhoun said. He looked hard at Jack, then shook his head. "I came here to kill you, Crawford. Thinking of you, planning how I'd end your life is about the only thing that got me through those long years in prison. But now, well, now I've changed my mind."

A tense silence hung in the mercantile. Jack didn't trust Calhoun, not for a second.

Calhoun grabbed his pistol and lurched from his chair, yanking Maggie up in front of him. Jack held his fire. He didn't dare shoot now.

Tears sprang into Maggie's eyes, her gaze imploring him to do something. Jack focused on Calhoun, blocking out Maggie, lest his inattention got them both killed.

"I've been around this little town of yours for a few days now," Calhoun said. "You've got yourself a nice place here. I've seen you and Miss Hudson together. So I decided there's no sense in killing you."

"Let her go, Calhoun."

"That wouldn't cause you too much suffering, now would it?" Calhoun said, then pressed the pistol barrel to Maggie's temple. "I decided to kill her instead."

She tried to pull away, but he jerked her against him.

"Doing away with her and leaving you to live out your life in misery, well, that's more of what I had in mind. Fitting, after the way you put me in prison for all those years."

"Don't be so sure of yourself, Calhoun," Jack told him. "You harm her and I'll kill you."

He shrugged indifferently. "She'll still be dead. Toss your gun aside, Crawford. Let's go out back."

Jack hesitated, calculating whether he could get a shot off—an accurate shot—and take out Calhoun here and now. He couldn't be sure of Maggie's safety, though. He laid his pistol on the floor.

"You first. Hands in the air," Calhoun said. "Go through the stockroom."

Jack raised his hands and looked at Maggie. "Remember what happened first time we were back there?"

"Shut up," Calhoun said. "Move."

Jack led the way through the curtained doorway into the stockroom, hoping Maggie understood what he'd tried to tell her, the reminder of how she'd fainted the first night they'd been in the stockroom together. He chanced a glance behind him and saw that Calhoun still held Maggie in front of him, the gun to her head. They wound their way through the stockroom until they reached the teetering mountain of crates. Jack knew it was now or never.

He whirled just as Maggie threw herself to the floor. Calhoun's gun came up. Jack grabbed his wrist. The pistol went off, firing into the ceiling. They struggled. Calhoun fell backward over a small crate. Jack went down with him. The gun went off again and both men went still.

The back door burst open and Ben Sheridan and three other men rushed inside, guns drawn. Maggie struggled to her feet, pressing her hand to her mouth, staring horrified at Jack and Calhoun together on the floor.

Then Jack moved. He pushed Calhoun away, revealing a growing bloodstain on the outlaw's chest.

"Jack!" Maggie burst into tears.

Jack rose and clasped her tight to his chest, and held her there while she cried.

Chapter Eleven

"He's—he's...gone?"

Maggie stared up at Ben Sheridan in the parlor of Charlie and Vera Lyle's home. Jack had brought her there last night, after the shooting, and the older couple had been more than anxious to take her in.

She'd hardly slept at all, her mind reliving the events of the night before. She'd finally drifted off around dawn. Over breakfast she'd decided not to go back to the mercantile this morning, as planned. If she missed some last-minute sales on this Christmas Eve, then so be it.

She expected Jack would come by this morning. Receiving this news from Ben was the last thing she imagined.

Ben nodded sorrowfully. "I'm sorry. He's gone."

"Emmett is—"

"Gone. Run off. Left town," Ben said. "I walked him over to the bath house after Sheriff Crawford released him this morning, but when I went back later to check on him, he wasn't there. Mrs. Cochran told me Frazier took off right after I left. She saw him heading out of town."

"Well, maybe he just wanted to walk a little?" Maggie said. "Maybe he came back and you just haven't seen him?"

Ben shook his head. "I've looked everywhere. Frazier's not in town. He left and he's not coming back."

"But what about his promise to God? His salvation? What about the service tonight?" Maggie asked.

Ben shook his head but didn't say anything and she supposed there was nothing he could say. Anyway, after what she'd been through the night before, the Christmas Eve music program didn't seem as important as it once had.

"Any word on Calhoun?" she asked.

"Doc says he'll probably make it," Ben reported.

Maggie drew up her courage. "And Jack?"

Ben glanced away. "I haven't seen the sheriff since first thing this morning. I don't know where he is."

He wasn't there.

From the alcove near the altar, Maggie peeked out at the congregation crowding into the sanctuary. The church looked festive, decorated with greenery, red bows and flickering candles. Maggie caught bits of conversation. Everyone, it seemed, commented on how beautiful the church looked, decked out in spectacular Christmas fashion. The townsfolk had been kind to her, as well, offering encouragement and comfort after her ordeal the night before.

Around her, the children were getting into their costumes, the older ones helping the little ones, and the choir was huddled together discussing who would sing Emmett Frazier's part tonight. Everything was as close to perfect as it could be.

Except Jack wasn't there yet. Maggie hadn't seen him all day. Neither had anyone else she'd asked.

Maybe this would be her worst Christmas, after all.

Three babies cried. Nathan Gannon had a coughing fit. Miss Marshall struck up "Joy To the World" when she was supposed to play "The First Noel," and one of the shepherds wet his pants.

But none of it mattered to Maggie after she saw Jack slip in and take a seat on the last pew halfway through the service.

Now, as everyone gathered in the fellowship hall for coffee and cake, Maggie said polite thank-yous as nearly all the townsfolk congratulated her on the service.

"Nice service. Even without Emmett Frazier," Jack said, suddenly appearing beside her.

"I'd wanted it to be perfect, but now…well, that hardly seems important," Maggie said.

"Families and kids. They're never perfect." Jack nodded toward the townsfolk gathered in groups, talking and laughing. "You've given everyone something grand to talk about. That should put an end to retelling the story of what happened at the old church."

"I don't care about any of that," Maggie said. "I was worried about you today. I thought maybe you'd—well, I didn't know what to think."

"I took a little ride outside of town," Jack told her. "I had some thinking to do."

"You should have told me about Virgil Calhoun looking for you," Maggie said, hearing a bit of anger in her voice.

"And you should stop opening your door to strangers," Jack shot back.

"I run a store. I can't question every person who steps through the doorway," she reminded him.

Jack pressed his lips together and looked away. A moment passed before he turned back.

"All I could think about since last night was how I'd put you in danger." Jack took a step closer. "If anything had happened to you…"

Maggie wanted to ask him more but couldn't quite bring herself to do so. She'd known all along that Jack didn't intend to stay in Crystal Springs. He had another job waiting for him up north. He may even go back to the Marshal's service. She'd considered that dealing with Virgil Calhoun last night had caused him to make up his mind. Now she wasn't sure…of anything.

Except that she would simply enjoy this evening with him. Now, while he was still here. While she could see him, talk to him, feel his strength.

It may have to last her a lifetime.

Maggie managed a smile. "Everyone has been so kind to me this evening. I feel as if I'm at home here again— finally."

Jack looked genuinely pleased for her. He touched his finger to her cheek and opened his mouth to speak, but Vivian Fisher, the mayor's wife, interrupted them.

"Maggie, we're planning a social for the New Year, and we just couldn't do that without your help," she declared. "I'll expect you at my house day after tomorrow with all the other ladies, to make plans. We're all counting on you."

Maggie nodded. "Of course, I'll be there."

"Good." She turned to Jack. "And look at you, Sheriff, standing here without a slice of cake or cup of coffee. Come on over here right now and have something."

"Yes, ma'am. I'll be right there."

Jack's gaze lingered on Maggie for a while, then he moved away from her toward the refreshment table. Maggie was immediately surrounded by a number of townspeople, telling her once again how much they enjoyed her music program.

When the evening ended, and everyone headed for home, the doors of the fellowship opened and a collective sigh went through the gathering. A gentle snowfall had begun.

Jack appeared beside Maggie, holding her cloak. "Can I walk you home?"

"I'd like that," she said.

With holiday well-wishes to everyone, they walked to the mercantile. Maggie held tight to Jack's arm, feeling his strength and warmth, and the love she had for him. No matter how things ended between them, she knew she'd always love Jack.

When she unlocked the door on the second floor, he eased inside ahead of her, helped her off with her cloak and hung it beside the door along with his coat and hat, then turned her to face the cookstove.

"Wait here for a minute. I've got a surprise for you."

Behind her, Maggie heard him light the logs in the fireplace, then felt his hands on her shoulders. She turned to see a small Christmas tree standing on the side table beside the rocker.

"Oh, Jack. I thought I wouldn't get a tree this year. How did you manage?"

"I had Cecil put it up here earlier today," Jack said. "I thought you might not like living here anymore, after what happened downstairs in the stockroom. I figured this would make things better for you."

Maggie supposed some women might never want to see the spot in the stockroom where an outlaw had nearly killed her and the man she loved. But for Maggie, that spot would always remind her of how Jack had saved her.

Jack took her hand and they crossed the room. "I told Cecil to bring some of the ornaments up here so we can decorate the tree together tonight."

Maggie gazed up at him, her heart overflowing. Yet she didn't dare believe this moment could be true.

"I think I'm entitled to a little more," she said softly.

His eyebrows drew together. "You want a bigger tree?"

"I want forever—or at least a good reason why I can't have it."

Jack paused and gazed at her for a long moment. Then he took her hand and led her to the settee. They sat down together. Still, he didn't speak for a long time, just watched the flames in the fireplace.

"After I'd been a Marshal for a while I lost count of how many outlaws I tracked down, how many I arrested, took to trial or to prison. Dozens, hundreds, I don't know for sure. Every one of them was mean as a rattler and would as soon kill me as look at me. But I was never scared. Never. Not one time." Jack looked down at Maggie. "Until last night."

Stunned, Maggie said, "You didn't look afraid—not for an instant. You were—"

"I wasn't afraid for myself. I was afraid that I'd lose you," Jack told her. "That ride I took out of town this morning was so I could think. About my life. About you."

Maggie braced herself, unsure of what he might say next. Yet she had to know.

"What did you decide?" she asked.

"I decided I'm not taking that sheriff's job up north. I'm not going back to the Marshal's Service, either. I'm staying here in Crystal Springs." Jack looked down at her again. "I decided, too, that I love you."

Maggie grinned. "You decided that?"

"Well, I guess I've known it for a while, I just didn't realize it, or something. Hell, I don't know." Jack shook his head, then drew a breath. "I guess this might be a good time to ask how you feel about me."

"I've known for a while now that I'm in love with you," Maggie told him.

Jack took her in his arms and she came willingly. They kissed, slow and easy, reveling in the joy of their newly professed love.

Jack deepened their kiss, claiming her lips with an urgency she hadn't felt before. Yet it didn't frighten her. Maggie kissed him harder. She pressed her palms against his chest. Such strength.

Jack's hands captured her face, then slid down to her shoulders and, finally, her breasts. Maggie gasped but didn't pull away. She felt the buttons on her dress open and his fingers slip inside. Feeling weak, she swayed against him.

He broke their kiss. In the glow of the firelight, she saw passion burning in his eyes and knew it was reflected in her own.

"I love you, Maggie," he whispered.

"I love you, too." She arched up to kiss him again but he pulled away.

"You know what we're getting ready to do here?" he asked. She nodded but he just looked at her. "You're sure?"

Maggie had never been more sure of anything in her

life. She loved this man. Loved him with all her heart. Nothing seemed more right to her.

Catching both his hands in hers, Maggie lifted them and planted a kiss on each. "I love you. And I'm sure."

Jack pulled the afghan off the settee and they settled on it in front of the fire. With exquisite slowness they discovered each other, finding their way through layers of clothing until they were naked.

Maggie moaned as new feelings claimed her. His hands were gentle, coaxing, bringing her pleasure she'd never imagined. He moved above her, claiming her body with his.

Maggie gasped and held fast to his wide shoulders. He kissed her, driving every thought from her head until all she could do was feel and respond to the rhythm of his body. One with him, an aching throb grew inside her, rising quick and full until it broke in pulsing waves. She grabbed a handful of his hair and cried out. Jack groaned and shuddered, locking her in his embrace.

Maggie came awake from a light sleep. Outside, snow drifted past the window. The fire still burned in the hearth but it was Jack's body wrapped around her that brought her warmth.

"Merry Christmas," he whispered against her ear.

He looked as if he'd been awake awhile, and she wondered how long he'd lain there, watching her sleep.

"You're beautiful," he said, caressing her cheek with his fingertips. "The best Christmas gift I ever had."

"Oh!" Maggie sat up. "I bought you a gift—a real gift."

"I like what I already got," Jack mused. "I don't know how you could top it."

She giggled and swatted at him.

"I'll be right back. It's in the bedroom. Now don't look," she insisted, struggling to wrap her petticoat around her as she got to her feet.

"Don't worry, I won't look," Jack called, with so much mischief in his voice she could almost feel his gaze on her backside.

She got the gift she'd wrapped special for him and brought it back to the parlor. Jack was stretched out on the afghan, the firelight sending shadows dancing over his big, naked body.

"Oh, my..." Maggie murmured as she fanned her face with her open palm and sat beside him again.

Jack pushed himself up on his elbow and took the small box she offered. "What's this?"

"Open it and see."

He ripped off the ribbon and paper and found a pocket-knife inside the box.

"It's a Hampstead and Rogers," Maggie told him with pride. "With a genuine pearl handle and four blades."

"A fine-looking knife," Jack said, turning it over in his hand, nodding his approval. "Don't think I've ever had one so nice. Thank you."

"You're welcome," she said, pleased with herself.

"I have something for you, too." Jack got to his feet and headed for his coat hanging beside the door. "I know you're looking at me," he said.

Maggie giggled, but couldn't make herself turn away.

He settled next to her on the afghan again and presented her with an envelope. Inside, Maggie found a piece of paper. She held it toward the fire and saw a drawing of a house as grand as those being built at the edge of town.

She shook her head. "I don't understand."

"I had Caleb Burk draw it for me—for us."

She gasped. "Us?"

"It started out that I wanted a place of my own to live. A real house, not just a room at the jail," Jack said. "But I couldn't imagine how a house could ever be a real home without you in it with me."

"Jack, are you—?"

"I'm asking you to marry me. Will you?"

"Yes!"

Maggie threw her arms around his neck. They kissed, then snuggled together and she turned again to the drawing of the house.

"We can really build this? For us?" she asked.

"I've never known a woman who deserved a real home more than you, Maggie."

She shook her head. "But your gift is so wonderful, so much bigger than the one I got for you."

Jack took her hand and pressed a kiss against it. "You've already given me the best gift I ever received. Love, happiness and, finally, a place I can call home."

* * * * *

A SON IS GIVEN

Victoria Bylin

Dear Reader,

The holidays are traditionally a time of joy. Families come together to celebrate. The carols lift our spirits. We eat sweet treats and feast on turkey. As one Christmas carol says, "It's the most wonderful time of the year." Our feelings run near the surface. What's beautiful is exquisite.

And what's hard is, unfortunately, sometimes harder. That's what Katherine Merritt experiences in *A Son Is Given*. Many of you will remember William and Katherine from *Of Men and Angels*. From the minute I finished that book, I've wanted to tell their story. Is there a better setting than Christmas for a tale about love and forgiveness? I don't think so.

This story is for everyone who's gone through a holiday that wasn't Norman Rockwell perfect. It's my hope that Kath's experience will bring you joy in spite of your hurts and a healing that goes to your heart.

Merry Christmas!

Victoria Bylin

To Al and Dorothy Scheibel, my wonderful in-laws, who have made Christmas special for so many years, and with love to Peggy, Kathy, Patti and the menagerie.

A special thank-you goes to Janice Peoples, a reader who gave me the idea for this story. Let's hear it for adjectives!

Chapter One

Denver, Colorado
December 1865

"Don't leave, Kath. I'm begging you."

Reverend William Merritt didn't know what more he could say to keep his wife from getting on tomorrow's stagecoach. It was all his fault—he knew that. Eight months ago he'd been a different man. He'd been drinking and they had argued. Hurrying to get away from him, Katherine had run from their bedroom and fallen down the stairs. She'd survived, but the baby she'd been carrying, a boy they had named William Jr., had been born two months early and had died.

William didn't blame his wife for leaving. But dear God in heaven, he wanted a second chance. He couldn't lose her. Not like this.

He watched as she lifted her underthings out of a dresser drawer. After the accident, he'd taken to sleeping in his study to keep from disturbing her as she recovered from the bruises and premature birth. An invitation to move back had never come.

As she put a camisole in the trunk, William felt a bolt of stark longing. At twenty-seven, Kath was five years younger than he was and even lovelier than the day they had met. Her dark hair was pinned up, but he knew what it looked like cascading down her back and over her bare shoulders. She was thin again, too thin if he told the truth. Her eyes, once as sparkling as new pennies from the Denver mint, were lifeless as she looked at him.

"It's settled, William. I want to be home for Christmas."

She meant her parents' mansion in Philadelphia. "But *this* is home, Kath. What happened was terrible, but I've changed. I haven't had a drink in—"

"Eight months and five days."

It wasn't the date of his sobriety that had seared her memory. It was the night of her fall down the stairs. He stepped toward her, his hand outstretched with the need to touch her. "Kath—"

"Don't," she ordered.

William lowered his arm. He wanted to fight for his wife, but how did a guilty man plead for his life? He'd already asked for forgiveness. The first time had been on his knees in front of God alone. The next fifty times had been in the presence of his wife.

Forgive me, Kath. It'll never happen again.

But no matter how many times he'd sworn to be a better man, she'd studied him with her sad brown eyes and turned her back. Looking at her now, William felt as close to hopeless as he'd ever been. Without Kath and Alexandra, their daughter, he had less than nothing. Still, he had to try to change her mind. Fearing it was a waste of breath, he made his voice deep.

"Kath," he said firmly. "I can't stop you from leaving and I don't blame you. But there's one thing I want before you go."

She gave him a hard look. "What's that?"

"A last Christmas with you and Alex." Their daughter was seven and the apple of her daddy's eye. "It's not a lot to ask."

She faced him with venom in her eyes. "Do you really think you have the right to ask me for anything? I'll never forget, William. Not ever."

He stayed silent because he couldn't say the same. A man couldn't forget what he didn't recall, and whiskey had stolen his memory. He vaguely remembered that they had been arguing and that he had followed her into the bedroom. She had tried to slam the door in his face, but he'd pushed it back. The next thing he remembered was seeing her at the bottom of the stairs with water and blood darkening her skirt.

Oh God, help me! William, get the doctor.

He'd been so inebriated that Alex had been the one to run three blocks through streets polluted with gambling and saloons to summon Dr. Hayden.

As the pastor of the biggest church in Denver, William had found himself in quite a predicament. Not only was Dr. Hayden the best physician in town, he was a member of their church and president of the board of elders. To his shame, William had told Kath he was fetching towels from the kitchen for the blood and water gushing from her womb. He'd gotten the towels, but he'd also gargled with vinegar to hide the smell of liquor.

What a fool he'd been. After Dr. Hayden had delivered the

baby, he'd sat William down in the kitchen with a pot of coffee and the empty bottle of whiskey he'd fished from the trash.

What's it worth to you, Reverend? Your calling? Your wife?

He hadn't mentioned the tiny baby clinging to life in his mother's arms, probably because he knew the boy was hours from death. Hayden had patted William on the shoulder and invited him to talk whenever he needed. Then he'd walked out the door, leaving William more alone than he'd ever been. He hadn't touched a drop of whiskey since that night and never would again.

His wife had shifted her attention from his face to the contents of her trunk.

"I've changed," William said to her back.

"It's too late."

"At least look at me."

After shaking her head, she answered in a passionless whisper, "I can't stand the sight of you."

As much as he wanted to clasp her shoulder and spin her around, he didn't do it. He hadn't touched her in eight months, not even a brush of their hands. Every time he'd come close, she'd stepped back and he'd honored her rebuke. He honored it now, though he wondered what she would do if he pulled her into his arms.

She made a show of opening the wardrobe and taking out all of her dresses except a gray traveling suit. William's heart plummeted. "Just twelve days, Kath. It's almost Christmas. Stay for Alex's sake if not mine."

He prayed for mercy as his wife took a final look around their bedroom. How many nights had they spent in the feather bed with the quilt she'd embroidered with roses? How many times had they made love late at night and again in the morning, hoping for children that hadn't been conceived? When she had missed her monthly, they had been over the moon. Tears pushed into William's eyes, but he wasn't ashamed. He cried every day for his son. So did Kath, but she hid the tears from him. When she grieved, she did it in private.

She was frowning at a lace doily on their nightstand, trying to decide whether to take it, when she turned abruptly to the dark window and rubbed her neck with both hands. "This is hard enough without listening to you beg."

"Twelve days, that's all." His voice grew stronger. "Have you told Alex yet?"

She shook her head. "No. I was hoping we could do it together."

"What about her things? Have you packed them?"

"They'll fit in a satchel."

William frowned. "What about her books? The collection of horses?"

"You'll have to ship them."

"No! Damn it, Kath. That's asking too much. I need you both."

She whirled away from the window and looked straight at him. Her eyes, dry and empty, found his moist ones. "It's settled," she insisted. "Alex and I are leaving tomorrow."

Please, God...

William wanted to hold her forever and kiss away her grief. But that wasn't possible. Every word he said only made her more determined. Helpless and close to defeated, he stood in front of the nightstand and the doily she'd made with her own hands. The last time he'd been in this room, their wedding picture had been on top of it.

"You're in my way," Kath said.

He stepped aside because he had no choice, watching as she opened the drawer and took out the missing picture frame. He knew every detail of the photograph by heart. It showed two youngsters who had eloped because his future father-in-law had seen past William's style to the lack of substance beneath his clerical collar. Now he was all substance with a lot less style.

With the picture dangling from her hand, Kath glared at him. "Don't get ideas. I'm bringing it for Alex. You're still her father."

"Then stay. Give me another chance." William wondered how far he could push without snapping the last thread between them. She hadn't mentioned divorce, an omission that gave him hope. '*Til death us do part...* He'd meant it and knew that she had, too.

But instead of looking into his eyes, she put the picture in the trunk. "You can write to her, of course. And you're welcome to visit us in Philadelphia."

"But, Kath—"

"The decision's made, William. I won't change my mind."

For the first time since the accident, William felt utterly defeated. When Kath said she'd do something, she did it. At a loss for words, he walked out of the room.

"Mommy? I don't feel good."

Kath jolted awake and saw her daughter standing at her bedside. In one motion, she sat up and put her hand on Alex's forehead. She'd been worried about the girl since yesterday when Emma, her best friend, had gone home from school with a cold.

Alex felt warm, but William had been up late and had

stoked the coal furnace just a few hours ago. Other than being flushed, she seemed fine.

Please, God. Don't let her be sick....

"Does your throat hurt?" Kath asked.

"It feels dry."

"How about your tummy?"

"I'm thirsty, but that's all."

Kath squeezed her daughter's hand. "Why don't you stay in my bed while I get a glass of water?"

"And a cloth for my head?"

"Sure."

Solemn and wide-eyed, Alex climbed into the feather bed and rested her head on the pillow. As Kath tucked in the sheet, she hoped the girl wouldn't ask about the trunk pushed against the wall. After William had left the room, she'd finished packing and closed the lid. Then she'd gone to bed and stared at the ceiling. Was she doing the right thing? They'd taken vows, but surely he'd broken them.

She had spent months making this decision. She'd endured her grief through the spring and the dry summer, but her sadness hadn't eased a bit. By September, she felt as barren as the cottonwoods. She'd prayed for God to take away the brittleness in her bones, but he hadn't. Instead of softening, her body had grown so stiff that her joints ached all the time.

Kath had tried her best to put the fall behind her, but she couldn't stop being angry with William. Every day she prayed to see her husband as a new man. But then she'd remember the terror of falling and the gush of water between her legs. Or she'd see a new baby at church with its squinty eyes and pink cheeks. Or she'd hear Alex singing to the rag doll Kath had made when she'd learned she was expecting.

Pushing back a wave of bitterness, she snatched up the pitcher next to her washbowl. "I'll be right back, honey."

"Okay, Mommy. Maybe you could read me a story. Or Papa could tell one about Christmas."

"I'll read to you when I come back," Kath said hurriedly. She had no desire to visit William in the study, where he was sleeping on an old divan. She'd hear him snoring in a low rumble that had once been a comfort to her. She'd ache to be held…but not by him.

As she went to the linen closet to retrieve a towel, her shoulders tensed with the memory of other towels. Shame on William for his drinking! That night…she felt the pain every time she walked down the stairs just as she was doing now. Only instead of falling, she had her hand on the railing. And instead of hurrying in a rage, she was calmly going to the kitchen to fill a pitcher at the pump.

As she worked the handle, she listened to the smooth glide of the metal parts. Before that night, it had squeaked every time she used it. She had often asked William to fix it, but he'd been too busy. Now he oiled it every Saturday. He was trying so hard, but she couldn't forget what had happened.

Not like William had… No, she corrected herself. He hadn't forgotten their son. He'd grieved, too. But somehow he'd turned that night into a tragic accident. From Kath's point of view, the disaster could have been avoided.

If he hadn't been drinking…

If he hadn't stumbled against her…

The marker on their son's grave said everything. She

had wanted a stone angel, but William had insisted on a plain white cross made out of wood. The first time she'd seen it, she had felt cheated. Somehow it forgave the unforgivable. Kath knew all about the gift of Christ's grace. She believed in it and needed it every day. But God help her, she couldn't pardon her husband for killing their son.

She worked the pump harder, faster, feeling tears build in her eyes. She had to get away from this house and the man whom she had once loved so deeply. But where did a woman go to escape her memories?

Blinking hard, she flashed on the first time she'd laid eyes on William Merritt. It had been a Saturday afternoon in April and the sun had been an orange ball low in the sky when he'd come galloping down the road. With his black cloak whipping behind him and his boots shiny in the stirrups, he'd resembled a highwayman on the run. Sensing danger, she had caught her breath and held it as he'd reined the horse to walk, turned and asked her for directions to a local boardinghouse.

His eyes…she'd never seen such an intense blue. He had stolen her breath and her heart with a single look.

Now she could hardly stand the sight of him.

Please, God. Let Alex be well enough to travel….

Kath lifted the pitcher, hurried up the stairs and walked into the bedroom where Alex was lying flat in the feather bed with her face turned to the door. Her brown eyes had a glassy sheen, and her cheeks were blotched with flaming roses.

"Now my throat hurts," she said. "I can hardly swallow."

Katherine managed a serene nod, but her insides were churning. A cold could turn into the croup, pneumonia, diphtheria… Alex was all she had left. She couldn't possibly get on a stagecoach with a sick child. Whether she liked it or not, she was stuck in Denver for Christmas.

Three knocks startled William out of a fitful sleep. He shot to his feet and looked at the open door to the study where he saw Katherine's silhouette against the gray hall. He'd taken to sleeping in his clothes, so he stood in front of her wearing trousers over his long johns.

"What's wrong?" he asked.

"It's Alex," she said, spitting the words. "She has a fever."

Terror ripped through his gut. Did parents with an only child worry more? He thought maybe they did. He couldn't bear to think about losing his little girl. Yet that's what he'd been doing since he'd left Kath packing the trunk—thinking and praying for a second chance.

He raked his hand through his hair. "How bad is it?"

"I think it's just a cold."

"But we don't really know."

"That's true."

"Kath, I know you want to leave, but—"

"Don't even say it." Her eyes snapped in the dim light. "I'm not about to put Alex at risk. If her fever's still high in the morning, we won't be leaving for Philadelphia until after Christmas."

She walked away as quickly as she'd appeared, leaving him staring at a hole in the wall. With his insides shaking, he dropped back on the sofa and bent his neck in prayer. "Lord, heal my little girl…but not tonight."

The way William saw things, he had twelve days to win his wife's heart. He just had to figure out how to do it.

Chapter Two

"Mommy? When are we going to decorate the house?"

Kath had been dreading that question ever since Alex's fever had broken. After two days in bed, the child was restless. The fever, though high for a full day, had dropped to normal, leaving her with a runny nose and a cough.

As grateful as she felt for Alex's recovery, Kath was dreading the next ten days. As a minister's wife, she felt obligated to keep up with the family traditions, which included a Christmas party after church next Sunday. She had a hundred things to do and not the slightest interest in any of them. Until this year, she had loved Christmas— the candles, the decorations, the songs and the love in the air. Her parents, having traveled in Europe, had brought home the tradition of a Christmas tree. It had been a novelty when Kath was young, but the custom had spread through the city. She had wonderful memories of visiting neighbors with baked goods and attending decorating parties with houses full of people.

She and William had brought the tradition to Denver. For the past ten years they had taken a sleigh to the foot-hills west of town, where they'd hunted for the best tree.

Kath tensed at the memory of that first Christmas. As a new bride, she had hung a single sprig of mistletoe just inside their bedroom door and William had taken full advantage. So had she....

Kath held in a sigh. Mistletoe was out of the question, but she had to put up a tree both for the Christmas party and her daughter. She smoothed Alex's hair off her forehead. "How about if we ask Papa to cut it down this year?"

"Can't we go with him?"

"No, honey. You still have a cold."

"But I'm almost better. See—I can breathe." The child gave a hearty sniff that only made her cough.

Kath hid a smile. "While Papa gets the tree, you and I can sort through the decorations."

"The things in the attic?"

"I'll get the trunk right now," she said.

As she stood, she heard William coming up the stairs. He stepped into the room and brushed his daughter's cheek with his knuckles. "How are you doing, Miss Merri?"

Kath thought her heart would burst. The nickname was just between Alex and William and a reminder of happier times.

"Papa, when can we get the tree?" the child asked.

"When you're all better."

Alex's eyes clouded. "But the best one might be gone."

That was a tradition Kath had started—hunting through the forest for the very best tree, even if it took hours. This year she'd send William and Alex alone. She simply didn't care.

William sat on the edge of the bed and squeezed his daughter's hand. "We can't go until you're all better, honey. That's the way it is."

Alex turned to Kath. "You and Papa could go without me."

"No," she said quickly. "I have to take care of you."

"You can ask Mrs. Howell to sit with me."

Kath frowned. "Alex—"

"She's right," William said. "The best tree might be gone."

The last thing Kath wanted to do was sit with her husband in a sleigh with the sun bright in her eyes. "I don't think it's wise."

"Why not?"

She sealed her lips but let the anger show in her eyes. "You know why."

Instead of backing down, William pushed to his feet and matched her stare with an intensity she hadn't seen in months. That look... It shot her back in time. She was seventeen again, sitting in church and daydreaming about her highwayman. To her utter shock, the object of her dreams had taken the pulpit and started to preach, breaking his rhythm only once—right after he'd clapped eyes on her.

A chill raced down Kath's spine. The young man in the pulpit was standing in their bedroom, looking at her with the same determination. "What I know," he said quietly, "is that Mrs. Howell loves Alex and she lives across the street. I'll walk over and ask her to stay."

"Yes!" cried Alex.

"But William—"

"Mama, you *have* to go. You *always* pick the tree."

As much as Kath wanted to argue, she knew that she'd lost the fight. She could have stared down William, but Alex's innocent eyes pulled at her heart. So did the sunshine pooling on the bed and a sudden yearning to feel it on her face. Shocked by that longing, she walked to the window where she saw casings of ice clinging to the barren trees. Backlit by the sun, the branches were exquisite.

Tears pressed into her eyes. She'd never be the same,

but that beauty beckoned to her just as it did every winter. "All right," she said without turning. "But only if Mrs. Howell is free."

"I'll ask her right now," William said.

For the first time in months, he sounded cheerful. Kath almost turned to look at him, but instead she listened as he gave Alex a peck on the forehead. "We'll be back soon, Miss Merri."

"With the best tree?"

"You bet."

He left the room, leaving Kath admiring the untouched snow. Last night's flurry had erased all signs of life, even the marks left by the birds that came for the crumbs she'd scattered near the porch. Feeding the birds was one of her favorite things to do, especially in the winter when a few crumbs meant the difference between life and death. Yesterday she had watched the sparrows with Alex and wondered again if she were doing the right thing by leaving. She loved Colorado and its rough edges. As a minister's wife, she'd been a partner in his work. Together they had made a difference.

Kath watched as William's shadow emerged from the eaves, followed by the flesh-and-blood man. He'd put on his coat, but he hadn't bothered to button it. Nor had he put on a hat. As he passed the empty branches, the sun turned his red hair into a halo of flame. How many times had she run her fingers through that thick mane? Unable to resist the fire, she'd touched it the first time they had kissed. On their wedding night she'd made another discovery. Her husband's chest had the same reddish curls and so did the rest of him.

Warmth spread from her belly to her heart, but then she remembered the baby and the spark faded to a cinder. Turning back into the room, she wished to God that she hadn't agreed to go with her husband to find a Christmas tree. They'd be sitting side by side in a cozy sleigh, under a quilt that had once graced their bed. She'd be assaulted by memories, both good and bad.

Of the two, the good ones were far more terrifying.

Some men were born with confidence and William was one of them. He simply didn't care what people thought. Growing up in the rough streets of Brooklyn did that to a boy, and he'd grown up faster than most.

He'd been fourteen years old when his father, a bricklayer, had died in a fall from a four-story house. With his mother and two young brothers in his care, William had done what was necessary to keep a roof over their heads. That had included stealing, a crime that had put him in the path of a minister named Alistair Whitley. William thanked God every day for that tough old bird who'd kicked his butt and saved his soul at the same time.

You're cocky, Merritt. But someday you're going to take on a fight that's bigger than you are.

That fight had come the day his son had died, and it wasn't over.

With Kath next to him in the sleigh, William let the team of horses set the pace as they headed west. His eyes stayed focused on the plain of snow sweeping along the foothills, but he was keenly aware of Kath sitting on the far side of the sleigh with her hands laced in her lap and eyes focused on the road. A year ago Alex would have been nestled between them and he'd have put his arm around them both.

If they had been alone, she would have snuggled against him, stroking his knee under the blanket.

"Are you warm enough?" he asked.

"I'm fine."

"We should be there in an hour or so."

"I know where it is," she said, staring down the trail.

William's nerves felt like piano wires vibrating with the low tones a man could feel but not quite hear. He and Kath had once been a perfect song. She'd brought the high notes into his life with her cheerfulness and a natural optimism. She had more goodwill than any person he'd ever known, which explained why she'd put up with him when he'd been at his worst.

Aching to fill the silence, he prayed again for wisdom. There had to be something he could do to prove he'd changed, but for every step he took in her direction, she took two back. He had to make *her* come to *him*. But how?

They rode in silence with his nerves thrumming, each lost in thought until they reached a stand of pines. The arid climate was surprisingly hard on evergreens, but they had discovered a stand of blue spruce the first time they'd hunted for a Christmas tree.

"This is the spot," he said, trying to sound jovial. "The best tree has to be here somewhere."

Kath almost smiled, but the light didn't reach her eyes. Turning, she lifted the blankets off her lap and climbed out of the sleigh. She'd always been a graceful woman and that hadn't changed. But watching her now, he recalled the way she had looked a year ago. She had been three months along and he'd rushed to help her out of the sleigh, teasing her because it took them back to how they had spent the morning. While climbing out of bed, she had complained that she'd lost her waistline. He'd pulled her back under the covers, showing her with his hands that a waistline wasn't all it was cracked up to be.

Dear God, he wanted to make love to his wife. Never again would he take that privilege for granted. After swallowing his loneliness, William looped the reins and walked to her side of the sleigh.

Wishing he could give her a forest of perfect trees, he motioned to the evergreens with an outstretched hand. "Lead on," he said, sounding gallant.

Kath raised her face to the sun, closed her eyes and inhaled through her nose. When the gesture pulled her lips into a smile, his heart pounded. For the first time in months, his wife looked happy.

"It's a beautiful day," she said wistfully.

"Perfect for finding a tree."

He held out his hand, but Kath stepped ahead of him, kicking the snow and making clouds of crystal dust. It was noon and the sun couldn't have been higher. She barely made a shadow as she headed toward a cluster of blue spruce. In the past she had inspected every tree within a quarter mile, but this year was different. She glanced at a few that were as tall as he was, but she didn't seem impressed.

Huddled inside her cloak, she trudged past the stand of pines to a field of untouched snow where she stopped in her tracks. Curious, William approached from an angle that gave him a view of her face. What he saw stole his breath. Kath's eyes were alive with love and her cheeks had a pink glow. Full of purpose, she strode across the empty snow to a tiny blue spruce growing all by itself on a slight rise. The tree was only three feet tall, but it was perfectly formed with branches raised to the sky.

William couldn't move. The tree reminded him of their son—small and perfect. He didn't want to chop it down and bring it home. He'd see it every day and be reminded of the life he'd cut short with his foolishness. Besides, he reasoned, the point of today was to help Kath get past her grief.

Squinting against the brightness, he ambled up the hill and stood at her side. The tree looked even tinier than it had from the bottom of the hill and he frowned. "It's kind of small, don't you think?"

His wife touched the tip of a bluish needle. "It's perfect."

William grunted. "We'll come back for it in a few years. It'll be even better."

"No," she said evenly. "It'll be gone."

She was right. The spruce would grow to maturity and be unrecognizable, or else it would die in a fire or a drought. Change was part of life. Nonetheless, William didn't want to take it home.

"What about Alex?" he said. "She wants a big tree."

"No," Kath said, dragging out the word. "She wants the *best* tree."

"This isn't it." William crossed his arms over his chest. "Let's look some more."

He was about to add to his case by mentioning Sunday's Christmas party when Kath spun to face him. He'd seen dozens of reactions in her eyes in the past months, but the most dominant by far had been a frozen grief. Today he saw a firestorm of emotion and it confused him.

"I want this one," she insisted.

Anything you want, Kath. I'll do anything…

But he felt sick at the thought of looking at the little tree for the next ten days. He didn't want reminders of that night. He'd made his amends and stayed sober. That had to be enough. It was time to start over. He tried to sound reasonable. "It won't hurt to look around."

"Yes, William. It *will* hurt. It hurts all the time."

"I know that, Kath."

"No, you don't!" Her cheeks burned red. "You hide in your study and preach your sermons! You talk to people every day as if *he'd* never been born. You want to forget. I don't."

"That's not true, Kath. I think about it every day."

"That's my point. You think about *it!* I think about *him.*"

She ran down the rise, stumbling in the snow. William followed her to the back of the sleigh where he'd stowed the ax. She grabbed it with both hands and whirled to face him.

"Kath—"

"Don't say a word! I'll cut it down myself."

Count to ten. Hold your temper.

But he was lost in a storm of his own. The fall had been an accident, but he'd still hurt his wife and killed his son. He'd denied Alex a little brother. He hated the man he'd been…and sometimes still was. But the anger was rising like a tide, pushing up his chest to his throat. His vision blurred to a red haze, and his jaw throbbed with the effort of keeping it closed.

One…two…three…

He never got to four. He snatched the ax from her hand, strode up the hill and felled the baby tree with three swings. It landed on its side with a plop, sending a puff of crystal flakes into the air. Furious with himself, William lifted the tree by the trunk and marched down the hill to the sleigh. After setting it in the back seat, he strode to the stand of taller pines where he chopped down the first one he reached, dragged it to the sleigh and stowed the ax on the floorboard.

The two-seater wasn't big enough for both trees, so he maneuvered the smaller one into an upright position and put the tall pine next to it. When a branch prickled against his cheek, he became aware of Kath's rasping breath. She was standing on the far side of the sleigh, clutching the flaps of her cloak and breathing in shallow pants. Her eyes, usually serene, were blurred by tears.

Dear God, what had he done? The Bible told a man to love his wife with honor and sacrifice, to put her needs before his own. William had just bullied Kath in the worst way. He should have been *glad* to cut down the tree. He should have moved the whole mountain for her. Instead he'd been the same selfish fool who'd once drowned his cares in a bottle of whiskey.

The air went out of his lungs. "Kath, I'm sorry. I—"

"I want to go home."

She meant Philadelphia, but he pretended not to understand. "Of course. Alex is waiting."

After giving him a look of blatant pity, she glanced at the rise where she'd found the baby tree. The snow, once pristine, bore the swish of her skirt and the mark of his angry stride. Someday the tracks would melt, but William would never forget the tears coursing down his wife's cheeks.

With the sun blazing, he prayed to the God who'd made the mountains, the snow and the perfect little tree. He was the Lord of second chances. There *had* to be a way to make things right. William just needed to find it.

Chapter Three

"**Y**ou did it, Mama. You found the best tree."

"I think so, too."

As Alex leaned against her, Kath put her hand on her daughter's shoulder. They were gazing at the little tree she had set up this morning. William had offered to help, but she wanted nothing to do with him after yesterday's episode. When they had returned to the house, she'd asked him to leave her tree in a bucket of water at the back door.

Kath had planned to tote the little thing up to her bedroom, but what was the point? She spent most of her day downstairs. After William had left this morning, she had moved a coatrack, filled a Dutch oven with rocks and water and put the tree in a corner of the entry hall. The tree fit perfectly, but Kath felt bad about placing it in such a prominent spot. In spite of yesterday's anger, she had no desire to rub William's nose in the argument. Deep down, he had a good heart. With Christmas just nine days away, he was collecting donations for the poor. Last year Kath had made the calls with him and felt nothing but pride. She'd never known a man more committed to helping people in need.

As for yesterday's upset, he'd apologized with bone-jarring sincerity.

Kath, forgive me. I'm a weak man right now....

She had almost reached for his hand. How many times had they argued in the past ten years? Dozens...but they had always settled their differences and sealed their forgiveness by making love. Kath had adored those nights. She'd married a hot-blooded man and rather liked the passion...but not anymore.

Alex's voice broke into her thoughts. "When can we decorate the tree?"

"How about now?"

Her daughter's eyes lit up. "That'll be fun. Let's get the box."

Kath thought of the decorations she kept in the Christmas trunk. Over the years, she'd collected piles of ribbon, strings of beads, paper cutouts and a handful of glass ornaments her mother had given to her when she and William had left Philadelphia. Opening the trunk always made her smile, but she wanted the little tree to be special.

She ran her fingers through Alex's hair. "We'll need everything for the big tree and the party on Sunday. I have something special in mind for this one. How would you like to help me make angels?"

"Out of what?"

Kath thought of the fabrics in her cedar chest. Most of them were too colorful for what she wanted to do, but one of the scraps was perfect in spite of the memories it evoked. She had used it to make a nightgown she'd never wear again. "I have some white satin," she said to Alex.

"And lace?"

"Lots of it." She'd bought five yards for the trim on their bedroom curtains and had used only three. "Let's get started."

Together they went upstairs to Kath's sewing room, where she had two rocking chairs, good light from a window, a worktable, dress forms and all the tools they'd need for today's project. She knew exactly what the angels looked like. After she had lost the baby, she'd made a sketch of the statue she wanted on her son's grave. Her angel was a little boy with his face lifted to heaven and his wings poised for flight. She had considered adding a halo to the drawing and had decided against it. Any child that carried William's blood—and hers, too—was sure to get into mischief.

Instead of feeling sad, Kath felt a bittersweet warmth as she spread the satin on the table. Next she retrieved a sheet of brown paper and a pencil, drew an angel and cut the pattern while Alex watched. "You can pin this on the satin while I cut some more."

Together they pinned and snipped until they had dozens of little boys with wings. As Kath put down the scissors, Alex smoothed the stack of satin angels. "I wish he'd lived," she said.

Stunned by her daughter's perception, Kath covered her small hand and squeezed. "So do I, honey."

"I wonder what he would have been like."

"Probably like most little boys."

Kath blinked and saw toy trains, pennywhistles and muddy shoes. She and William had been elated when she'd missed her monthly. Never would she forget the evening she'd told him…. They'd almost made love in the kitchen! But then they had thought of their daughter, reading in her room. With her buttons gaping, Kath had grabbed her husband's hand and led him upstairs.

She didn't know why, but babies hadn't come easily to them. They'd been married for three years before Alex was conceived, and they had been disappointed every month for the next several years. Eventually she'd given up hope. Then they'd had the miracle…and the loss.

Alex looked up from the angels. "What do we do next?"

"We sew on the wings."

The little girl scrunched her brows together. "They need faces."

Kath glanced at her original drawing. She'd given the angel wide eyes and wavy hair. "I think you're right."

"Could we embroider them?"

Kath loved needlework and had been teaching her daughter simple stitches. She stepped to the shelf where she kept her embroidery basket and lifted it with both hands. "That's a good idea. Can you make the eyes?"

"With knots like you showed me?"

"Exactly."

Kath sat in the rocking chair with the basket in her lap. She'd been a bit older than Alex when her grandmother had given it to her with sage words of advice.

You can always mend a tear, Kathy dear. If you can't make it the same, make it better with pretty stitches.

Kath had used that advice on everything from made-over dresses to recipes, but she doubted it applied to the shreds of her marriage.

As she opened the wicker lid, Alex leaned closer for a look at the rainbow of threads. Over the years, Kath had collected dozens of colors for the scenes she had embroidered. She had ten shades of blue, a true brick-red, a garden of pinks and several shades of brown, green and yellow for nature scenes. As always, the rainbow lifted her spirits. "What color should we use for the eyes?"

"Blue," Alex answered. "Like Papa's."

William Junior had been born with blue eyes, but so had Alex. Would his eyes have turned brown like hers, or would they have stayed the color of a summer sky? Kath wouldn't know until she saw her little boy in heaven, but something in her heart knew—just knew—that his eyes would have been as true blue as his father's.

"Blue's my choice, too," she said as she handed Alex a length of thread she'd once used to embroider a blue jay.

"What about hair?"

"Let's see…" She fingered through the skeins. Her own hair was sparrow-brown. William's hair bordered on red. Alex's was a mix of them both, but what would their son have inherited? After rejecting three shades of brown, she selected a color that matched William's hair perfectly and set it on the table. "I like this one."

Alex lifted the blue thread first, snipped a piece and threaded the needle with a seriousness that made Kath worry. The child had seen too much in her short life. Even before the accident, she'd heard her parents shouting at each other when William had come home smelling of whiskey and slurring his words. Kath couldn't erase those memories, but she could make new ones—even better ones, as her grandmother had suggested.

She made a point of admiring Alex's handiwork. "Those stitches are perfect."

"I'm trying, but yours are better."

"That's because I've been doing it so long." She threaded her own needle, lifted an angel and rocked in the chair as she gave the boy wavy red hair. "Do you know who taught me to sew?"

"Your grandma."

"That's right. She was from Ireland."

For the next two hours, Kath chatted with her daughter about everything from Alex's favorite books to where the birds went in the winter to the holidays Kath recalled as a girl in Philadelphia. "We put a candle in every window," she said. "And your grandmother made snowflakes out of lace she stiffened with sugar water. That's what we'll do with the angels when they're stitched."

"Didn't you do that to your petticoats?" Alex asked.

A smile curled on Kath's lips. "I sure did, at least until I got caught in the rain after church one Sunday. My legs were sticky for days."

Alex giggled and Kath chuckled at the memory of dissolving into a puddle of sweetness. Before she knew it, her sides were hurting from laughing so hard and she had to wipe her eyes. Dear God, it felt good to laugh again. Just as wonderful was the happiness in her daughter's eyes.

As their giggling faded to a peaceful silence, Alex held up an angel with blue eyes and red hair. "Now he needs lace on the wings."

Kath took the ornament and pinned two layers of the delicate fabric over the satin. With a few quick stitches, the angel was ready to fly. "If I show you how to do the hair, we can finish today."

Alex was already giving another angel blue eyes. "Papa will be surprised."

"I'm sure he will." Kath tried to keep her voice light, but her tongue felt heavy as she worked on the second angel. To fill the silence, she started to hum "Greensleeves." Shortly before they had come west, the melody had been turned into a Christmas carol. The words whispered in Kath's thoughts.

What child is this, who lays at rest,
In Mary's lap is sleeping?

"Mama?"

Alex's voice pulled Kath out of a bittersweet memory of rocking her son. He'd been so tiny and he hadn't been able to suck at all. She'd tickled his chin, but he'd only moved his lips. Praying for a miracle, she had dripped what little milk she'd had into his mouth, only to worry that he'd choke on it. Kath bit her lip until the pain replaced the pictures of her son. Some recollections were truly so painful they had to be locked away.

Reminding herself that Alex needed a mother, she forced a smile. "What is it, honey?"

"I want to hear a story."

That suited Kath just fine. It was a chance to hint to her daughter about the trip to Philadelphia. "How about the one about Aunt Becky and the beehive?"

Alex shook her head. "Tell me the story about your first Christmas with Papa. The one where the donkey came to church."

Kath drifted back to a simpler time. "It was the coldest night ever. The church wasn't built, so Papa told everyone to come to the saloon where it was warm. He was telling the story about the baby Jesus and the manger when an old miner came in."

"The man with the beard," Alex added.

"That's right. He was wrapped up in a blanket and wearing a floppy hat all covered with snow."

"And everyone just kept listening to Papa."

"He was getting to the best part of the Christmas story, where Mary and Joseph are in the stable with the animals, when all of a sudden—"

"The man's donkey kicked at the door."

"And Papa said to let him inside because God cares about jackasses no matter how many legs they have."

Warmth welled in Kath's middle. But then she recalled how the night had ended. After learning they were almost newlyweds, the barkeep had given them his room above the saloon. Kath had left first and undressed for bed. With the covers pulled to her chin, she had lain in the dark, waiting for her husband's touch on their first Christmas Eve. Two hours later she had still been waiting. She'd already discovered that William wouldn't leave a lost soul to suffer alone. She understood that calling and accepted it. But when he'd come to bed smelling of whiskey, she'd felt sick to her stomach and had faked being asleep.

Kath reached for her scissors and snipped the thread holding the lace. How naive she had been that night. The next morning she had made a comment about his drinking, but he had shrugged.

"If I don't take a drink now and then, these men won't trust me." Then he'd quoted the Bible verse about being all things to all people.

She had accepted his reasoning at the time, but she'd come to see those words for what they were—an excuse to drink. Kath sealed her lips as she reached for another strip of lace. The years had taken a terrible toll on her patience. How many times had she begged him to break the habit? Too many to count. When he refused, she had closed her eyes to it. What more could she have done? She'd married a stubborn man who thought he was right about everything. But he wasn't.

The Harlequin Reader Service® — Here's how it works:

Accepting your 2 free books and 2 free mystery gifts places you under no obligation to buy anything. You may keep the books and gifts and return the shipping statement marked "cancel." If you do not cancel, about a month later we'll send you 6 additional books and bill you just $4.69 each in the U.S., or $5.24 each in Canada, plus 25¢ shipping & handling per book and applicable taxes if any.* That's the complete price and — compared to cover prices of $5.50 each in the U.S. and $6.50 each in Canada — it's quite a bargain! You may cancel at any time, but if you choose to continue, every month we'll send you 6 more books, which you may either purchase at the discount price or return to us and cancel your subscription.

*Terms and prices subject to change without notice. Sales tax applicable in N.Y. Canadian residents will be charged applicable provincial taxes and GST. All orders subject to approval. Credit or debit balances in a customer's account(s) may be offset by any other outstanding balance owed by or to the customer. Please allow 4 to 6 weeks for delivery.

If offer card is missing write to: Harlequin Reader Service, 3010 Walden Ave., P.O. Box 1867, Buffalo NY 14240-1867

NO POSTAGE
NECESSARY
IF MAILED
IN THE
UNITED STATES

BUSINESS REPLY MAIL

FIRST-CLASS MAIL   PERMIT NO. 717-003   BUFFALO, NY

POSTAGE WILL BE PAID BY ADDRESSEE

HARLEQUIN READER SERVICE
3010 WALDEN AVE
PO BOX 1867
BUFFALO NY 14240-9952

GET FREE BOOKS and FREE GIFTS WHEN YOU PLAY THE...

Lucky 7

SLOT MACHINE GAME!

Just scratch off the silver box with a coin. Then check below to see the gifts you get!

YES! I have scratched off the silver box. Please send me the 2 free Harlequin® Historical books and 2 free gifts for which I qualify. I understand I am under no obligation to purchase any books, as explained on the back of this card.

349 HDL EF4L   **246 HDL EF4E**

FIRST NAME	LAST NAME

ADDRESS

APT.#	CITY

STATE/PROV.	ZIP/POSTAL CODE

7	7	7	**Worth TWO FREE BOOKS plus 2 BONUS Mystery Gifts!**
🍒	🍒	🍒	**Worth TWO FREE BOOKS!**
♣	♣	♣	**Worth ONE FREE BOOK!**
🔔	🔔	🍒	**TRY AGAIN!**

www.eHarlequin.com

(H-H-10/06)

Offer limited to one per household and not valid to current Harlequin® Historical subscribers.

Your Privacy - Harlequin Books is committed to protecting your privacy. Our Privacy Policy is available online at www.eHarlequin.com or upon request from the Harlequin Reader Service. From time to time we make our lists of customers available to reputable firms who may have a product or service of interest to you. If you would prefer us not to share your name and address, please check here ☐.

She jammed the needle through the lace. "Ouch!"

"Mama? Are you all right?"

"I pricked myself, honey. That's all."

She popped her finger into her mouth and tasted blood. She was tired of the pain, tired of everything. In nine days she'd be on an eastbound stage and nothing would change her mind.

William lifted his coat off the hook in the church office and shrugged into the heavy wool. He'd spent the day collecting donations of food and clothing for families in need this holiday season. There were three altogether, but Jed Rush's situation was the one that kicked William in the gut. The man had a wife and a new baby. Two months ago he'd been putting a roof on the new hotel, when he'd fallen and injured his back. He was in terrible pain and couldn't work, but his wife's eyes had shone with pride when she'd spoken to William at church.

"We're going to be fine, Reverend," she had insisted. "We have each other and that's everything."

William grimaced at the memory of Cynthia Rush and her confidence. There was a time when Kath would have stood by *him* with that conviction. Now he didn't feel welcome in his own home. He'd never been so lonely in his life. In the past, he'd have gone to the saloon and found friends among the miners and mountain men traveling through town.

Why not? Just one drink…

He snuffed out the lamp and stood in the dark.

What's the harm? You've already lost her.

"Shut up," he said to himself.

He strode out the back door, pausing on the top step for a look at the church cemetery. A split-rail fence outlined the place where thirteen people were buried. William had preached all the funerals, except the one for his son. He'd tried, but he hadn't managed a single word. Dr. Hayden had stepped forward and delivered a eulogy that had left William begging God for help.

Guilt tightened his throat as he glanced at a single set of footprints in the snow. He wondered if they belonged to Kath. She visited more often than he did, though not a day passed that he didn't stand on this step and remember. The pause usually gave him strength, but today he felt chilled to the bone as he walked down the steps and headed home.

The parsonage and the church were a block apart, separated by the schoolhouse and a handful of shops. As ice crunched beneath his boots, he looked at the second-floor windows where he saw lamps burning through the dusk. He imagined warm stoves and families talking at the supper table. His belly rumbled in anticipation of Kath's good cooking, but he wanted her company even more.

He walked faster, lengthening his stride until he saw the parsonage. Gold light was spilling from the kitchen window where he saw Kath move from the stove to the table with a bowl in her hand. She would have already laid out the place mats she had embroidered, maybe the set with wildflowers. Alex would have arranged the silverware. More than anything, William wanted to walk in the back door and kiss his wife hello. Such a simple thing…such a joy. And he was about to lose it forever.

His long stride slowed to a halt. He couldn't stand the thought of sitting at the table across from his wife, talking about nothing when their marriage was falling apart. But neither could he look away from the golden light. This, he realized, was hell—standing alone in the dark with the light just a few feet away, feeling love and not being able to give it.

Dear God, he wanted a drink.

Count to ten, he told himself. But when he reached six, he glimpsed Kath in the window again. She motioned to Alex and together they sat at the table and bowed their heads. Alone in the dark, William mouthed the words of the grace she always said.

For this food for our bodies and the love in our hearts, we thank Thee, Lord. Amen.

A year ago she would have held supper until he came home, but those days were gone forever. It was all his fault, he knew that. Clenching his jaw, he fought the snake of longing twisting in his gut. The saloon was three blocks away. He'd find friends there. He'd listen to jokes and tell some of his own. For an hour or so, he'd be free from the burden of being a man. He could almost smell the tobacco in the dimly lit room. When he swallowed hard, he tasted the amber cure.

"Don't be a fool," he said with a growl.

But he couldn't stand the thought of going home. Instead he walked past the parsonage and headed for the edge of town. By the time he reached the last street, the sky had turned black and the air felt even colder. Stars glimmered from one end of the heavens to the other, reminding him of summer walks he'd taken with Kath.

Please, God....

William prayed until his fingers were numb, but he found no peace. He had a bottle of whiskey on a high shelf in his study. He kept it there to remind himself of what he'd done. It had dust on it now.

Just one drink.

He closed his eyes and counted to ten. He made it all the way, but the craving grew stronger with each breath. When he looked at the stars and saw only the fog of his thoughts, William knew he was a doomed man. He wasn't strong enough to lose Kath *and* stay sober. He just couldn't do it. To tired to fight, he walked back to the parsonage and let himself in the front door.

Except for a lamp turned low in the entry hall, the house was dark and still. William shrugged out of his coat and stepped to the corner, where he expected to find the coat tree. Instead he saw Kath's blue spruce. It was covered with angels, each made of a fabric that was vaguely familiar. He touched an angel wing and realized where he'd seen it. She had bought the white satin for the wedding dress she had never made because they had eloped. Later she had made it into a nightgown she'd worn on their first anniversary. She'd knocked his socks off that night.

The lace was familiar, too. She'd used scraps from their bedroom curtains. Caressing the fabric, he recalled the morning light casting shadows on their bed as they woke up in each other's arms. His gaze shifted from the wings to the angel's face. Judging by the awkward stitches, he figured Alex had worked on this one. He looked at another, and then a third, before he realized the angels were little boys with red hair and blue eyes.

I'd like something special, William. I drew a picture.

His stomach churned at the memory of Kath handing him a piece of paper. She'd sketched a baby angel with its face lifted upward and wings spread wide. He'd shaken his head and insisted on a simple cross.

How selfish he'd been...but no more. William grabbed an angel off the tree and charged out the front door.

Chapter Four

"**K**ath! You look wonderful!"

Hilda Dixon had been the twelfth person to arrive at the parsonage for the annual Christmas party and the tenth to compliment Kath's appearance. Instead of the gray gown she had planned to wear to the decorating party, she had chosen a red crinoline with a velvet bodice and matching trim.

The choice had been inspired by a wakeful dream. With the sun streaming into the bedroom, she'd thought about the red tulips she'd planted in front of the parsonage the year Alex was born. If she left, she wouldn't see them bloom.

If...

Where had that come from? Baffled, she hugged Hilda. "Thank you. I'm feeling better."

"Must be the holidays," her friend said. "It's either that, or William's charmed his way into your good graces."

Hilda meant well, but the mention of William made Kath yearn for the somber gray. Two nights ago he hadn't come home for supper. Alone in her bed, she had heard the front door open and had listened for his steps in the kitchen. As much as she resented him these days, she didn't want him to go to bed hungry. She'd been on the verge of offering him a late supper when he'd left again.

She'd shivered in the dark and told herself that she didn't care where he went. If he wanted a drink, it was none of her business. But she'd still felt the panic.

Kath forced herself to smile at Hilda. "Actually, William and I have a bit of news."

Hilda clasped her hand. "Are you—"

Expecting. Kath interrupted before her friend could finish. "No. Nothing like that." She tried to sound cheerful. "It's about time Alex met her grandparents. I'm taking her to Philadelphia for a visit."

"Oh, Kath." Hilda had seen right through her.

A knock on the door gave Kath an excuse to walk away. As she passed the little tree, she told herself again she was doing the right thing. William had joined them for supper last night, but he'd gone out after midnight. This morning his eyes had been red with exhaustion, but she hadn't smelled anything but shaving soap. In fact, he'd been so charming that she'd smiled at him.

After smoothing her skirt, she opened the door and saw the Bodine sisters. Betty was Kath's age and a dedicated spinster. Her younger sister, Deidre, was dressed in a blue gown that matched her eyes and showed too much cleavage for an afternoon gathering. The women were new arrivals from Atlanta, a city torn apart by war. Kath liked Betty a lot, but Deidre tried her patience.

"Hello, Katherine," the blonde said in a Southern drawl. "I hope you don't mind. Betty and I brought something for the party."

Smiling her thanks, Kath took the cloth bag, peeked inside and saw a sprig of mistletoe. In the past, Kath had put it up in every room and enjoyed the playful teasing it inspired, not to mention being caught under it by her husband. This year she had ignored the tradition.

Forcing a smile, she thanked the sisters and escorted them to the front room, where a crowd had gathered and was waiting to decorate the tree. Earlier, Kath had laid out the ribbons and paper globes. Everyone who visited today would put a few ornaments in place. By dusk, the tree would be drooping with paper, ribbons and lace.

As the Bodine sisters mingled, Kath wondered what to do with the mistletoe. She felt obligated to hang it, but where? The threshold to the dining room where the refreshments were laid out was a possibility, so she walked to the side room, stood on her toes and hung it on a nail from last year.

"Do you need some help?"

Startled by William's voice, she wobbled until he clasped her waist in both hands and lowered her to the soles of her feet. He was behind her and almost whispering into her ear. She didn't dare turn around. Instead she broke away from his grip and stepped into the dining room, leaving him in the doorway where she had just hung the mistletoe.

"You should be with our guests," she said.

"I'll go back in a minute. I just wanted to warn you— word's out about your trip."

"I know. I told Hilda."

William's eyes were on the empty bag in her hand.

"What's that?"

"A hostess gift from Deidre Bodine."

"If I know Miss Bodine—"

"It's nothing," Kath said.

But her eyes darted to the mistletoe hanging over William's head. He followed her glance, noticed the leaves and looked straight into her eyes.

That look… She'd forgotten how it felt to be pinned in place like a butterfly. Her heart was fluttering and she could barely breathe.

William lowered his chin. "I remember the first time I kissed you. It was in your mother's garden."

They'd been standing next to a red azalea in full bloom and he'd just asked her to marry him. As soon as she had breathed a yes, he'd brought his mouth to hers with a possessiveness she'd come to cherish. Warmth quivered in her belly, but she didn't trust it. "I'm not that girl anymore."

"And I'm not the same man."

"How can I believe you?" she said.

His eyes turned into blue lakes. "I want to fix things between us. We had a good life."

"We used to have a lot of things," she retorted.

She watched his face as he searched for words. "Kath, I'm—"

"Reverend! There you are!" Deidre came around the corner. "I have news about the food baskets."

Kath lifted a platter of cookies off the table. "I was just getting a tray to pass around. If you'll excuse me—"

"Of course," said Deidre with a gleam in her eyes. "I just heard about your trip. You must be *so* excited."

Kath forced a smile. "I am."

As she approached the doorway, William stepped back to give her space. For some foolish reason, his consideration made her mad. She'd had enough of his remorse and the pity of her friends. She was just plain sick and tired of it all. But instead of telling him what she thought, she gripped the tray and walked out the door.

She was halfway across the entry hall when she heard Deidre's voice dripping with Southern honey.

"If you get lonely, Reverend, my sister and I would be *delighted* to have you for supper."

Kath had a good mind to tell Deidre to take her mistletoe straight back to Dixie, but the urge faded as quickly as it had risen. Once she left Denver, what William did with his time was no longer her concern. Balancing the tray of cookies, she pasted on a smile and went to serve her guests.

William tried to focus on the letter he was writing to a friend in Brooklyn, but his thoughts kept drifting back to this afternoon's party. He usually enjoyed the festivities, but this year's gathering had been a trial. Between the whispers and questioning looks about Kath's trip, he'd wanted to shout the truth.

I love my wife!

The only good that had come from today had been Deidre Bodine and her prattle. She'd driven him batty, but he'd enjoyed the hard looks she'd inspired from Kath. It wasn't often that his wife acted with anything but kindness, but she'd been shooting daggers at Deidre all afternoon.

William set down his pen and glanced at the pocket watch on his desk. Lukas Schmidt wasn't expecting him tonight, but neither would the stonecutter be surprised by a midnight knock on his door. Three nights ago, when William had forgone the whiskey and taken Kath's angel, he'd walked to the man's cottage and found him singing to a slab of stone in his workroom. He had shown the artisan Kath's drawing and asked if he could make a statue of the angel by Christmas.

"I don't know," Lukas had replied. "Tell me why you need such a thing."

"It's for my wife."

"She has gone to heaven?"

"No, Lukas. She's as far from heaven as a woman can get."

William had stayed until after midnight, telling the stonecutter more than he'd shared with anyone about his trouble with Kath. His heart had started to bleed that night, and the steady drip hadn't let up. If the statue didn't convince Kath to forgive him, nothing would.

Time was *not* on William's side. That night he had tried to exact a promise from Lukas that the angel would be finished by Christmas, but the old man had been circumspect.

"I sing to the stones and they come alive," he had said in his heavy accent. "I will do my best, but the angel must emerge on its own."

Lukas had an odd way about him, but William liked the man. He'd arrived last August with a freight wagon full of Indiana limestone, found William at the church and introduced himself as if he were a king.

"I'm a stonecutter, Reverend. I'm in the business of honoring life."

Later William learned that Lukas had emigrated from Munich and studied his craft in Paris. He'd come to America because he wanted to be free and had settled in Gettysburg until a hatred of war had driven him farther west. Eventually he'd arrived in Denver and had generally kept to himself.

After capping the inkwell, William pushed to his feet. Late or not, he wanted to see Kath's angel. He stepped into the hallway and fetched his coat, being careful not to make a sound as he left the house. He didn't want his wife to know about these late-night visits because he couldn't explain himself, at least not yet.

As he stepped into the yard, snow crunched beneath his

boots. Being careful of ice, he trekked across town, passing shops, gambling halls and the saloon that didn't tempt him in the least. With his breath turning to steam, he hurried to Lukas's cottage on the outskirts of town.

Made of stone with a shingled roof, the little house resembled the pictures in Alex's book of fairy tales. William half expected an elf to pop out of the chimney as he neared the cottage. Or maybe a family of mice would appear in the beam of light pouring from the window and dance a Christmas jig. William grimaced at his own whimsy. Apparently he didn't need liquor to see things, nor did he need it to hear beautiful music. Lukas's tenor voice was raised in song.

Stille Nacht, heilige Nacht
Alles schläft, einsam wacht.

William couldn't understand the words, but he recognized the melody to "Silent Night." Hoping he'd feel calm and bright when he saw Kath's angel, he rapped on the door.

"Do *not* come in!"

That wasn't the greeting William had been expecting. "Lukas? It's me."

"Stay out!"

"But—"

An exasperated sigh poured from under the door as a shadow flapped in the window. The gold light flickered and then steadied as Lukas yanked open the door. "*Now* you can come in."

William scanned the crowded workshop for Kath's angel but saw only slabs of stone and a sheet of canvas covering something in the middle of the room. Judging by the tools on a nearby table, Lukas had been working on the statue when William interrupted him.

"Is that the angel?" he asked.

"Not yet."

"Can I see it?"

Lukas huffed. "Of course not."

"But that's why I came."

"No," Lukas countered. "You came because you are afraid."

William glared at the stonecutter, who had stepped to a potbellied stove and lifted a red enamel coffeepot. The liquid came out in a trickle, causing William to wonder if the old man did anything fast. "When will it be done?" he asked.

Holding a cup in each hand, Lukas turned to William with an expression that was old and young all at once. His eyes, rheumy and blue, held the wisdom of suffering, but he had the muscles of a much younger man. How many tons of stone had he moved in his life? William couldn't guess, but he saw the weight of those stones in the man's patient expression. Time had marked him in other ways, too. His hair, white and gossamer thin, hung past his shoulders, while a scraggly beard made his face appear even thinner than it was.

Lukas handed William a cup. "Am I right? Are you afraid?"

"You're damn right I'm afraid," William countered. "I've been thinking. Maybe I should tell Kath about the statue."

"That would be a mistake."

"Why?"

The old man shook his head. "For a smart man, you don't know much about women."

William thought he knew a lot. "I know my wife."

"You know the girl you married. But what about the woman she's become?"

He couldn't answer.

"That's my point," Lukas said. "Her heart is hard like the stone. You must sing to the stone until you can see its true form."

Half the town wondered if Lukas was tetched in the head. William was sure of it. "If I start serenading Kath, she'll throw a bucket of water on me."

"I'm talking about the music in your heart. Let her hear it."

William turned and stepped to the window. The moon had passed from view, giving the night an even darker hue. He thought of their home, filled with resentment and cold rooms. Loneliness stabbed through him. "I've tried to talk to her, but she won't listen."

"Then show her in other ways that you love her. Find out what she wants the most and give it to her."

William latched on to that rope of hope. "She wants the statue," he said. "You've *got* to finish it by Christmas."

Lukas chuffed. "That's not the answer, William. No matter what I make of *this* stone, it's your wife's heart that matters."

William turned back to Lukas and indicated the room with a sweep of his hand. "You have more chisels and hammers than I can count. You've learned from masters. You know what you're doing."

"So?"

William's throat tightened with frustration. "I have no idea how to reach my wife. I've apologized. I've quit drinking. What more can I do?"

"Show her your heart. Charm her like it was the first time you met."

"But how?"

"*Ach,* you're impossible." Lukas threw up his arms in disgust. "Come with me, Reverend."

The old man rummaged in a drawer for a burlap sack, put on his coat and marched out the door with William in his wake. The stars glimmered in the blue velvet sky, giving shape to the broad canopy of an oak tree several feet from the cottage. Lukas made a beeline for the sturdy trunk. Then he faced William, jammed the sack in his hands and pointed into the branches.

"There's mistletoe in that tree," he said. "*Now* do you know what to do?"

Kath pushed aside the quilt, rolled out of bed and paced to the window overlooking the front yard. The stars still had a grip on the sky, but she had given up any hope of sleeping. Earlier she'd heard the front door open and had peeked outside just as William strode into the yard. When he turned toward Main Street and its three saloons, she had felt sick to her stomach.

Until that moment, she had been enjoying the glow of the party. In spite of Deidre Bodine and her mistletoe, Kath had enjoyed herself. When the last guest had departed, she and William had cleaned up like old times, comparing notes about the day. He'd tickled Alex until she was giddy, then the three of them had sat in front of the tree while William read a story about a family of mice celebrating Christmas with nothing but a crumb of cheese and each other.

Kath had felt a lump in her throat. She had a special gift for Alex this year—a sewing basket full of embroidery thread—but she hadn't expected to be spending Christmas with William. For the past ten years, she had made him a new shirt, each one different and special in some way. It was too late to start one now, but for Alex's sake, she had to give him something. She had been thinking about shopping at the Emporium when she'd heard him leave the house.

Unable to sleep, she had paced between the window and the bed. As the moon sank in the sky, her anger simmered until the pot ran dry, leaving behind a crust of worry as she peered into the night. Denver was a rough town. Gambling halls attracted drifters who'd think nothing of ambushing a clergyman and robbing him blind. Not that William needed to be ambushed. If he saw a stranger in need, he'd give him the coat off his back.

Kath stayed at the window, thinking about broken promises and broken bones, until she saw William pace around the corner. Out of habit, she gauged his mannerisms. His stride, fast and even, told her that he hadn't been drinking. So did his straight spine and the defiant jut of his chin. As he turned into their yard, she noticed a burlap sack slung over his shoulder. It was bulging at the seams but didn't appear to be heavy.

Annoyed and curious, Kath slipped into her wrapper and tiptoed down the stairs. She reached the bottom step just as William closed the door with a soft click.

"Where were you?" she demanded from the dark.

"Good grief, Kath!" He spun to face her, tightening his grip on the sack. "You scared the daylights out of me. What are you doing up so late?"

"That's the wrong question." She stepped into the entry hall, where a draft pebbled her skin. Aware of the thin wrapper and the curves it revealed, she crossed her arms over her chest and waited for his answer.

"It sounded like a good question to me," he replied. "You've got to be tired after the party."

"Don't change the subject."

"All right," he said, drawing out the word. "In that case, I'll tell you the truth. I went to see a friend."

"At this hour?"

"Why not?"

"Who were you with?"

With the sack still draped over his shoulder, William spread his boots in defiance. "It's Christmas. A man's entitled to a few secrets."

"I don't care what time of year it is. I want to know where you were."

Kath matched his stare, but it came at a cost. His eyes…they were as blue as the sky and full of certainty. He wasn't going to tell her a thing, and he had the nerve to be self-righteous about it. Anger seared them together in a battle of wills she didn't want to lose.

She saw the same fire in William's expression. "Does it matter to you, Kath?"

He'd deepened his voice to a husky drawl, the one she'd heard when he'd clasped her hand for the first time.

I believe we met yesterday, Miss Adams.

Yes, Reverend, we did. You were in quite a hurry as I recall.

I still am.

A month later he had asked for her hand in marriage. She'd been eighteen and crazy enough to say yes. Looking at him now, she felt just as muddled but for different reasons. She'd loved him for ten years, but he'd hurt her so profoundly. Tonight's absence opened those scars. "Of course it matters where you've been. You're Alex's father."

"And?"

"There's nothing else to say. If you want to be stubborn, you can. I'm going to bed."

Alone.

She stared at William to make her point, but the remorseful man she expected was nowhere to be seen. Instead she saw the rake who had informed her father that a wedding was inevitable.

I love your daughter, sir. I intend to be a good husband to her.

They had given Reginald Adams a week to change his mind, but he had refused to honor his daughter's wishes. His reasons, Kath knew, were less than noble. He had expected her to marry the son of his business partner. Until William had ridden into her life, she hadn't known a thing about love and had been content with the arrangement. But everything had changed the moment William had whipped past her on that lonely road.

It had changed again when she'd lost the baby. Refusing to think about that night, Kath walked up the stairs like a queen—a lonely one, but she still had her pride. No way would she ask him what was in that burlap sack.

Chapter Five

"I don't see why you want my company," Kath said to William as she cleared the breakfast dishes. Her husband had just asked her to go with him on his morning calls. There had been a time when she had enjoyed making visits with him, but she hadn't made the effort in months.

"Do you remember Jed Rush?" William asked as he slathered jelly on a bite of toast.

"Of course." After Jed's fall from the roof, Kath had organized a week's worth of meals for the young family.

"I want to talk to him alone before the committee shows up with the Christmas basket. I was hoping you'd spend the morning with his wife."

In spite of her sympathy for Jed and Cynthia, Kath doubted William's good intentions. He'd been trying to get her out of the house all morning. First he'd suggested they go shopping for a new cloak for Alex. Then he'd mentioned visiting old Mrs. Griggs and her six cats. Everyone in Denver knew that Ardith Griggs preferred felines to people, especially around the holidays.

Besides, Kath had plans of her own. She wanted to

know what was in the burlap sack and planned to search his study for it. More than curiosity had driven her to that decision. Last night, after she'd left William at the bottom of the stairs, she'd slid into bed and pulled the covers to her chin. For the first time in months, she had missed his company. If only she could believe that he wouldn't stumble back into a bottle of whiskey…. If only she could trust him.

Kath had forced herself to stare at the ceiling, where she'd seen the moonlit shadow of the tree in the yard. The barren branches had stretched across the room and down the wall, reminding her of the birds she fed. If she left, who would put out crumbs? Wide-eyed, she had dared to hope that William would knock on her door and tell her where he'd been. Instead she'd heard nothing. Tears had spilled from her eyes and she had realized how futile it was to ache for things she couldn't have. If he had a surprise planned for Christmas, she needed to be prepared.

She poured a kettle of steaming water over the dishes in the sink. William would have to find another way to speak to Jed alone. "I can't go this morning," she said. "I have plans."

"What about this afternoon?"

"I have things to do for Christmas."

"I can't argue with that," he said. "So do I."

Refusing to be curious, Kath sealed her lips as William carried his plate to the sink. Even with the steam dampening her cheeks, she felt the size of him as he stood next to her. A year ago she would have tipped her head and they would have kissed. He'd have rubbed her back until she relaxed. A year ago the baby would have been on the way.

She stared at the grease spiraling in the dirty water, then lifted a plate and scrubbed with a vengeance.

William didn't move. "It's a beautiful day. Maybe you'd enjoy getting out."

"No!"

Why couldn't he understand? She didn't want to feel the sun on her skin or admire the winter sky. Close to losing her temper, she hunched over the sink and scrubbed even harder. He didn't budge an inch.

"Do you want something?" she said irritably.

"I want to make you happy."

He stroked her back with his palm, sending whispers of forgotten pleasure from her scalp to her toes. How long had it been since he'd touched her with such sweetness? He'd tried, but she'd always stepped away. Somehow knowing that she'd be gone in a week made the moment bittersweet. Instead of pulling away, she said, "Tell me where you went last night."

"I can't. It's a surprise for Christmas."

It wasn't the answer she wanted, but the one she had expected. She stared at the dishwater, gray with the remnants of breakfast. It would never be new again and neither would their marriage.

William stepped back without a word, leaving an uncrossable chasm in place of the closeness of his body. Silently, he left the kitchen and walked out the front door.

Kath peered through the window as he passed by the house. As soon as he rounded the corner, she dried her hands and hurried into his study to look for the burlap sack. She hadn't been in the room for months, but she imagined William sitting at his desk. Over the years, they had fallen into a habit. On Friday nights he'd read his sermons to her, asking for her opinion and changing words when she shook her head. She missed those exchanges. William had respected her ideas in a way no one else ever had.

I couldn't preach without you, Kath. You're ten times smarter than I am.

It wasn't true, but she enjoyed the praise.

Pushing away the memory, she looked at the books gathering dust on the shelves. William owned everything from novels to Shakespeare to collections of theological essays. Wanting to understand her new husband, she had read all of them during the first years of their marriage. When babies hadn't come right away, sharing William's books had been a comfort.

Swallowing back a lump, Kath stepped to the trunk positioned under the window. William had owned it since he'd left Brooklyn, and it had carried their things from Philadelphia to Denver. Now he used it to store letters and sermon notes. As she touched the latch, she relived the first time she had opened the trunk. It had been their wedding night. After taking vows at a tiny church north of Philadelphia, they had stopped at a roadside inn.

Closing her eyes, she recalled every detail—the feather bed, the scent of bay rum on her husband's neck, her nakedness beneath a night rail. She had been a trembling bride, knowing only a hint of the passion they'd share that night. William had slipped the cotton from her shoulders, telling her with his eyes and touch how beautiful she was to him. With her insides melting, she had listened and waited until she couldn't stand the wonder. Then she'd kissed him on the mouth.

The highwayman had taken his bride and made her his

own that night. She'd been full of awe, joy and a well-being she hadn't imagined. Her mother had warned her about the first time and she had been expecting pain, but she had felt only pleasure and the sensation of being stretched. Little did she know that the stretching of her body was just the beginning of the ways she'd accommodate her husband, and that the pain would come later.

Kath lifted the lid of the trunk and saw three pairs of William's long johns. Tucked below them were two shirts, his clerical collars and a pair of black trousers. He'd been sending his things to the laundry since she lost the baby, but seeing his clothes in the trunk startled her. It was as if he'd embarked on a journey of his own. Kath felt a wave of compassion for him, but then she recalled his stubbornness about the little Christmas tree.

After closing the lid, she searched the office for the burlap sack, found it behind his desk and dragged it to the window, where she had more light.

"Kath? What are you doing?"

She whirled and saw William in the doorway. Heat raced to her cheeks. "I—I was looking for, uh…"

He leaned against the door frame, then pointed his chin at the sack. "Go ahead and open it."

"Maybe I will," she replied.

"Just be ready when you do."

As she pinched the string closing the sack, she caught a whiff of greenery. She knew that smell and didn't like it. Judging by the size of the bag, William had gathered enough mistletoe to decorate the entire house, maybe even the city of Denver.

Kath bit her lip. The gesture was just like her husband—full of good intentions but not quite right. She didn't want a kiss. She wanted her baby back. But how could she be angry with him? He was trying to please her, telling her he loved her the only way he knew how. She wanted it to be enough, but she felt empty and cold in spite of the heat in his eyes. He needed her, but how could she trust him? Stubborn men quit drinking all the time. Weak ones lifted the bottle at the first sign of trouble.

She let go of the string but didn't walk away. "I'm not interested after all."

"Then why are you here?"

Kath couldn't answer, but neither could she leave.

William had come back to the house because he'd forgotten a letter he needed to post. The last thing he'd expected was to find Kath in his study. She hadn't set foot over the threshold in months. It had gotten so dusty that he'd cleaned it himself, everything except the whiskey bottle.

She still hadn't answered his question, and he wasn't about to make it easy for her. He'd given a lot of thought to Lukas's advice about singing to his wife's heart, and he wanted to start right now. He felt no guilt about blocking the door. She was trapped by her own design and he was enjoying the sight of her. Her hair, up in a careless knot, gave her a womanly air. But the blush on her cheeks belonged to a child who'd been caught with her hands in the cookie jar.

William risked a smile. "You remind me of Alex right now. Remember last year?"

"Of course. She went looking for the doll you'd bought, the one with the porcelain face."

Their daughter had been admiring the doll for weeks. When it disappeared from the store, she had hunted through the entire house. William smiled at the memory. "As I recall, she found it under *our* bed."

The slight emphasis on *our* made Kath's cheeks flush, but it also put anger in her eyes. "This is different, William. I wanted to look in the bag because I don't trust you."

"You used to have cause to feel that way."

"I still do."

He didn't agree. The dusty bottle was on a high shelf, a testament to his love for her. The baby angel was emerging from stone even as he and Kath stood glaring at each other. He wanted to tell her those things, but they were his best cards. If he played them now and lost, he'd have nothing left. Instead he motioned toward the bag with his chin. "Open it. It tells the whole story."

Kath glared at the bag, then turned to the window where dust motes were swirling in the light. With her hands clasped at her waist and her chin tilted to the sky, she reminded him of the young bride who had defied her family to marry a man with nothing more than a vision.

He'd failed her badly. He'd failed himself and God, too. But the price had been paid with the gift of God's own son. The guilt had to stop right now.

William ambled across the room, stood behind his wife and clasped her upper arms. She trembled at his touch, just as she had the night he'd asked her to become his wife. They had been in her mother's garden, sitting on a bench beneath a sycamore tree.

I'm a restless man. I want to go west.

I do, too.

Would you like to do it together?

Her mouth had made an *O* and her eyes had brightened with the twilight sun.

I love you, Kath. I want you for my wife.

She had cupped his cheek with one hand. Turning slightly, he had kissed her palm as she'd murmured, "Yes, William. *Yes!*"

He wanted her to say "yes" again, but how could he persuade her? If he kissed her now, he risked blowing out the small flame. But if he did nothing, it could die on its own. He needed to fan the spark as gently as he could, so he settled for matching his breath to hers. With their chests moving in perfect time, William inhaled the scent of her hair, exhaling gently so that his breath grazed the shell of her ear.

She must have felt it, because her head snapped back. A year ago he would have pulled her to his chest and kissed the spot behind her ear. He'd have held her in place, nuzzling until she turned in his arms to kiss him back. But today that instinct was all wrong. The air was crackling like the seconds before a lightning strike. William took it as a warning. He wanted to rekindle their love, not start a firestorm. He let go of her and stepped back, watching as she stared out the window.

Sunlight turned her into a silhouette with soft edges. William saw softness as a good sign. He had plans for tonight and intended to carry them through. But first he had to get Kath out of the house. Knowing that she wouldn't leave without some prodding, he picked up the bag of mistletoe, headed for the door without a goodbye and went straight to Hilda Dixon's house. He needed an ally and Kath's closest friend was his best hope.

Chapter Six

"**P**romise to think about what I said."

The words had come from Hilda, a friend Kath trusted to always tell the truth. They were walking up the steps to the parsonage after an afternoon that had included a fancy tea at the new hotel. Hilda had been blunt.

It's time to snap out of it.

That's what I'm trying to do. It's why I have to leave.

If you go now, you'll be taking the bitterness with you. Why not wait until spring?

Hilda had also informed Kath that punishing William wouldn't bring back her baby. Then she mentioned something Kath hadn't realized. Her husband had been preaching on forgiveness for months, not as a minister teaching his flock but as a man who needed it.

Determined to make her point, Hilda also pointed out something Kath *had* noticed. Women liked her husband, and Deidre Bodine had already staked her claim. Yesterday she'd come by the parsonage with a bag of Christmas cookies, supposedly for Alex. Kath hadn't been fooled. The woman barely knew her daughter and had made a point of asking where William had gone.

"Kath?" Hilda's voice pulled her back to the porch. "This is the biggest decision of your life. Don't rush into it."

"I won't."

"And think of Alex. She loves her father."

"I know."

But Kath was also aware that Alex had witnessed things a child should never see. If she stayed and William went back to drinking, Alex would see those things again. By taking her daughter to Philadelphia, Kath believed she was protecting her. But the cost… Alex was too young to understand.

Kath rested her hands on the railing and looked up at the cottonwood. The day had turned warm and the ice encasing the tree was melting in teardrops. The branches had lost their exquisite beauty, but she could imagine spring. It was a good feeling…almost.

As she lowered her chin, Hilda pulled her into a hug. "If you want to talk, come and see me. I don't care if it's the middle of the night."

"Thanks."

Kath swallowed a lump. If she left, she'd never see Hilda again. They were as close as sisters, maybe even closer. They had arrived in Denver City within days of each other, each one far from home and newly married. And madly in love with men who had promised them heaven on earth.

As Hilda left with a wave, Kath stepped through the door to the parsonage. What she saw made her gasp. William had hung mistletoe everywhere—over all the doors, from the wall sconces and even from the beam above the stairs.

Her heart melted like the ice on the branches but instantly froze into daggers. A kiss wouldn't heal the rift between them. Her gaze shifted to the door to William's study. It was the one opening without mistletoe and she wondered why. As she slipped out of her coat, she glanced at the baby tree. An empty branch caught her eye. Curious, she counted the angels and found nineteen. She counted again and knew for certain that someone had taken the twentieth angel.

"You better move if you don't want to be kissed."

Whirling around, she saw William coming down the stairs with a hammer dangling from his hand, a sign that he'd hung mistletoe in the upstairs rooms, as well.

"You can wipe that cocky grin off your face," she snapped at him. "This isn't amusing."

"Maybe not," he said easily. "But I'm not going to let you leave without a few reminders of what we've shared."

"I don't need any reminding," she said, struggling to hold her temper. The bitterness in her voice tasted vile, but that's how she felt.

"I think you do." William motioned toward the study. "I want to show you something."

Her heart felt like bread dough expanding in a sealed tin. With each beat it got bigger, threatening to squeeze right through the casing. Was pain causing the sensation? Or hope? But with hope came danger. What if she trusted her husband and he failed her again? Kath sucked in a deep breath. She simply couldn't risk it.

With the mistletoe dangling from every door frame, she couldn't imagine what awaited her in the study. Her husband was determined to break her will, and she knew from experience he could do it.

Don't cry, love. If it's meant to be, children will come. But what if they don't?

We have each other. It's enough, Kath. More than enough.

Each month she'd cried and somehow he'd lifted her up. When trying to conceive had turned into a worry, even a chore, he'd turned it back into making love. Heat rushed from her womb to her chest, causing her heart to burst with the memory of William's hand gliding across her belly. Recollection taunted her, but Kath frowned. "You can say your piece right here."

"No," he said evenly. "I have to show you something."

"Then go get it."

He squinted in disgust, as if she'd asked him to touch a dead body. And not just any body, one that had been decaying in the grave and stank to high heaven. Kath didn't understand, but neither did she care. She was *not* going into the study. With the angels dangling from the little tree, she crossed her arms and raised her chin. Unless he was willing to tell her where he'd been going at night, she had nothing to say to him.

She watched as he stood straighter, matching her gaze with a defiance she hadn't expected. An old shiver ran up her spine as she realized the study held something more threatening than the mistletoe. He'd made her curious, even hopeful. She wanted to look over her shoulder into the softly lit room, but refused to give in.

Ignoring the clumps of greenery over her husband's head, Kath brushed by him and went up the stairs.

William snatched his coat and stormed out the front door. How the devil was he supposed to sing to Kath's heart when she wouldn't listen to him? He had spent hours thinking of ways to woo his wife and decided it was time to remind her of their fiery courtship.

It had nearly killed him to give up an evening with Alex knowing that Kath might still leave with her, but he had asked Emma's mother to keep her for the night. Then he had set up a table for two in the study, ordered a meal from the hotel and set up candles on the little table. He'd had it all figured out. He was going to show Kath the dusty whiskey bottle, tell her how much he loved her and pray that she'd invite him back to their bed.

But how did a man romance his wife when she wouldn't even look at him? Hoping Lukas had an answer, William strode to the old man's cottage. The windows were dark, but he pounded on the back door anyway.

"Lukas! Are you there?"

No answer.

William jiggled the knob and felt it turn in his hand. He opened the door a crack. "Lukas?"

Chilly air filled the room, telling William that the old man was gone. Good manners told him to close the door and come back later, but he was hurting inside. More than anything, he wanted reassurance that Kath would stay. His hopes landed square on the slab of stone. Had Lukas covered it with the tarp? A peek…that's all William wanted.

"You're tempted, I see."

William turned and saw Lukas striding toward the cottage from the stable behind the house. "You bet I am."

"In that case, come in. I will show you the angel."

"It's finished?"

"That's for you to decide."

What did *that* mean? William wasn't sure as he followed Lukas into the chilly room where dusky light was pouring through the southern window. He looked to the pedestal holding Kath's angel and saw perfection emerging from the stone. The gown was finished, but the wings were just taking shape. But it was the angel's face that captured William's attention. The little boy was looking up to the sky, but was weighted down by the rock still holding his spirit.

"It's not done," William said, suddenly fearful that Lukas wouldn't finish in time.

"We have five days, Reverend. I'll finish my work before Christmas morning. But what about yours?"

William dropped down on a stool. "How do I get through to her? She won't listen to me."

"I'd tell you to have faith, Reverend. But it's entirely possible that she'll leave."

William hung his head. "I can't stand the thought."

Lukas studied William with rheumy eyes, poured lukewarm coffee from the pot on the stove and handed him the cup. "Did it occur to you that what you want and what your wife needs are not the same thing?"

"But it is," William insisted. "We're a family."

"It comes down to this, my friend. Does her happiness matter more than your own?"

"Of course."

"Then are you willing to let her go?"

"No!"

"Think again," Lukas said. "Would she be happy as a prisoner? A creature like the angel is right now? I think not."

William felt the coffee warming his palm. Without the heat of the stove, the dark liquid would turn cold. Eventually it would freeze. He didn't want that for Kath. "You're saying I have to let her go."

Lukas pushed to his feet and paced to the window. "You need to think of her first. That's what I'm saying."

William looked at the half-finished statue. When he'd brought the angel to Lukas, he'd wanted to give something to Kath that would honor their son and prove that he loved her. What good would the statue do if she left? Not much. An idea took root in William's mind. "I know time's running out," he said to the stonecutter. "But I need another favor."

"What is that?"

After William told Lukas what he had in mind, the old stonecutter pushed to his feet. "That, my friend, is a wise plan, but I doubt I'll have time. Have you ever carved stone?"

"Me?"

Lukas made a point of looking around the room. "I don't see anyone else in here."

"I don't know a thing about it."

"Then you'll have to learn."

Chapter Seven

"**M**ommy, when will Papa be home?"

"I don't know, sweetie," Kath replied. "He's at the food basket meeting."

The two of them were making Christmas cookies from a recipe Kath had learned when she was Alex's age. Her mother had named them "Moon Cookies" because they could be shaped into either circles or crescents before they were baked and dipped in sugar. The first year she and William had been married, she'd made them alone in a tiny kitchen, missing her mother and sisters terribly. They'd sat together and eaten the entire batch, remembering their families and dreaming of children of their own. They had wanted at least four, two boys and two girls.

Thank God for Alex. She was a smart and caring child. Kath didn't mind giving William a large part of the credit. In spite of his drinking, he'd been a wonderful father. He'd taken Alex fishing and had taught her to ride. The two of them talked all the time. Leaving would be hard on them both.

Holding in a sigh, Kath glanced out the window and into the night. It was after nine and her daughter should have been in bed, but Kath wanted the company. With William staying out every night, the house had become unbearably still. She heard every tick of the clock, the flop of snow when the breeze stirred and the thudding of her own heart as she stared down the tunnel of her future.

Hilda's comments, particularly the reminder that women found William attractive, had added ghosts to the long journey back to Philadelphia. Those pictures shouldn't have mattered to Kath, but they did. The thought of William rubbing elbows with Deidre at the food basket meetings made her irritable.

As Alex set a circle of dough on the tray, she gave a loud yawn. "I wish Papa would get home."

"He might be late, sweetie."

"He's late a lot," Alex said. "I guess because it's Christmas. Maybe he's planning a surprise."

"There's lots to do with the church," Kath said, sounding mild. She wanted to put Alex at ease, but her own belly was churning. As long as they were sharing a roof, she had a right to know where her husband was going at night. What was he hiding? Alex had the innocence to believe in a Christmas surprise, but Kath didn't. She didn't like the secrecy at all.

To get her mind off William, she watched as Alex scraped the sides of the bowl to form another ball of dough. She loved the sight of her daughter's little hands and the way she concentrated, as if making a cookie were the most important thing on earth.

After flattening it between her palms, she placed it on the tin. "Papa likes cookies a lot, especially these."

And especially lately. He had taken to munching on penny candy from morning until bedtime. Butterscotch was his favorite. Peppermints were second. Kath thought about the Christmas gift she had purchased for him at the Emporium. On a high shelf she had spotted a crystal candy jar shaped like a train. It reminded her of the day they had left Philadelphia, heading west by railcar to St. Louis, where they had stayed for a few years. Getting to Denver had been much harder. They had joined a wagon train and experienced both the harshness and grandeur of nature. By some miracle, Alex had been conceived at the end of that journey. The candy jar seemed like a fitting gift. William could keep it on his desk instead of filling his pockets with sticky butterscotch.

As she rolled a ball of dough, Kath glanced at her daughter who was yawning again. Guilt washed through her. Was she wrong to take Alex away from her father? The answer wasn't clear. Leaving would put tears in her daughter's eyes, but Kath's deepest fear was that William would start drinking again. She simply couldn't live with that threat, nor could she stand the thought of Alex living with the arguments, the smell of alcohol on her father's breath.

Where was he going at night? Two days ago he'd stayed out until dawn. Wondering if he had slept in the church, she had bundled up, gone to the empty building and ended up with more questions. Annoyed, she had stood in her bedroom window until he'd walked through the door. She had been ready to confront him if he'd been drinking, but his steps had been straight and sure. The next morning she'd sniffed the air for a hint of whiskey but had smelled only soap.

As she set a cookie on the tin, Kath had a frightful thought. If he wasn't filling his nights with liquor, had he found something else to fight the loneliness? Or more precisely, had he found *someone* else? Kath knew her husband. William was loyal to the core. He'd never even looked at another woman. But that was before she had thrown him out of their bedroom. Before Deidre Bodine started bringing him cookies and batting her eyelashes.

With her fingers aching, Kath molded the dough into a crescent. The food basket meeting would be over any minute. If it hadn't been for Alex, she would have marched over to the church to see for herself what was happening. But she couldn't leave her little girl alone. Nor did she want to start gossip by asking Mrs. Howell to sit with Alex.

Kath couldn't search for William, but she'd be ready for him when he walked through the door. She wanted an explanation and intended to get it.

Alex yawned again.

Kath rubbed her daughter's back. "Why don't you go upstairs, sweetie. When Papa gets home, I'll give him the cookies."

"And milk?"

"Sure," Kath answered. Cookies, milk…and a plateful of questions.

William had never been so exhausted in his life, but time was running out. Christmas was just three days away. Lukas was doing well with his part of Kath's gift, but William had proven to be all thumbs. Still, he'd done his best. To his surprise, the stonecutter even praised his work.

"It's not perfect, Reverend. But it sings. If you'll allow me to put on the finishing touches, I believe your wife will be pleased."

Please, God…

Aware of the grit under his nails and his aching arms, William turned the knob and stepped into the parsonage.

"I want to know where you've been, and I want to know right now."

Kath's voice came from the front room. She was wearing the same dress she'd had on this morning, a gray gown that matched the color of the stone, and she was holding a candle at her waist. The gold light illuminated her straight nose, the stubborn chin he loved, the brown eyes that were full of fury.

William stalled by taking off his coat. If he told her the truth, he'd take away from the impact of the statue. The angel had to speak for itself, but neither did he want to give up this opportunity to win back a piece of her heart.

After hanging his coat on the hook, he motioned to the study with his chin. "I want to show you something."

When her eyes narrowed, he knew she was thinking about the mistletoe. "You can't charm me, William. I asked a simple question."

"And I want to answer it," he said evenly. "But not with words."

Curiosity filled her eyes, but she had her pride. She'd drawn a line for herself and wasn't about to step over it. She stood straighter in the doorway. "Just tell me this…were you with Deidre Bodine?"

"Was I what?"

"You heard me."

William seethed with anger. Not once had he looked at a woman with impure thoughts, at least not since he'd taken Kath as his wife. Some men had a problem with their eyes, but not him. He'd married the loveliest girl on earth, a woman made just for him. They fit together with utter perfection. He had no interest whatsoever in other women and was offended by the accusation.

He was on the verge of telling her so, but Lukas's advice played through his head like a waltz. *Entice her, Reverend. Make her want to know you.*

A little jealousy wasn't a bad thing, not if the fire would burn away the frost. William crossed his arms over his chest and leaned against the door frame in a display of self-assurance. "Suppose I *was* with Deidre. I'm not saying I was, but let's suppose…would it bother you?"

"Of course!"

"Why?"

"Because you're Alex's father and I'm still your wife. We're still living under the same roof. Because I—I—" *I love you.*

"Say it, Kath."

She bit her lip.

"Then I'll say it. We love each other and always will."

Her eyes, wide and questioning, locked on his face, but her hands were trembling. The brass candleholder wobbled, causing the light of the flame to flicker dangerously across her face. William reached her in two strides, took the candle and set it on the half table. As the flame steadied, he gripped her arms and looked into her eyes. Their faces were a breath apart. He could smell the rosewater scent of her hair and see each one of her lashes. Her cheeks had a healthy glow—from anger, no doubt—but he didn't care. His wife looked alive.

He longed to kiss her but settled for brushing her cheek with his index finger. "Katherine Merritt," he said in his sternest voice, "you are now—and always will be—my wife. Not once have I looked at another woman and I never will. You are the loveliest creature God ever put on this earth. Those brown eyes of yours…they're beautiful. They do more to wake me up than strong coffee and you *know* what I'm talking about. I can't look at you without feeling a love so deep I can't even describe it."

He was looking into her eyes, waiting for her to say something in reply. Her lips parted, but she sealed them again. He couldn't bear the thought of letting her go, so he cupped her face in his palms. "You're my heart, Kath. You make me whole."

"Oh, William."

He tried to read the inflection in her voice, but he couldn't tell if she'd meant "Oh, William. I forgive you," or "Oh, William. I pity you." As much as he wanted to kiss her, he couldn't do it until he knew where he stood. The thought of tasting her sweet lips again and then losing her was too much to endure. Instead he stared into her eyes, daring her to look away.

He watched as she swallowed, causing her throat to twitch as she broke silence. "How can I trust you?" she said in a whisper.

"Come with me into the study."

She stayed still for a good five seconds, and William prayed for every one of them until she led the way into the study. He followed with the candle, guiding her to the bookshelves where he raised the single flame. Light danced on the spines of the books, then higher still until the trinkets on the top of the case were illuminated.

"What do you see?" he asked.

He watched her face as she took in the vase that belonged to his mother, the brick to honor his father, a picture frame

holding the family photograph they'd had made two years
ago. He saw the precise moment she noticed the dusty jug
of whiskey. Her eyes narrowed and she pulled back. Her
gaze snapped to his face. "What's that?"

"It's what you think it is," he said evenly. "But look at
it, Kath. Look close."

She turned back to the bottle, studied it, and then
stepped closer for a better look. Her breath caught. "I see
dust."

"That's right. I haven't touched it since that night and
I never will again. I can live with it *and* without it. I had
to prove it to myself and I have. I won't tell you it's easy.
Sometimes I want a drink in the worst way. But I want you
and Alex even more."

Please, God. Let it be enough.

When she turned and looked into his eyes, he prayed
even harder. She wanted to trust in him, he could feel it.
But something was holding her back. As a man of God,
William knew all about forgiveness—both the needing
and the giving of it. He didn't like being on either side of
that fence, but he'd made his peace with needing it from
Kath. He could only pray that she'd find it in her heart to
give it.

Still looking into his eyes, she bit her lower lip as if the
words were fighting to come out of her. William knew that
feeling. *Lord, I'm a drunk. Forgive me for my ugly ways.*
That confession hadn't come easily.

He couldn't pressure Kath. It would only make her
more confused and possibly angry. So instead of kissing
her like he wanted, he took a step back and indicated the
bottle with his chin. "That's what I wanted to show you."

Before he could change his mind about pulling her

close, he turned on his heels and strode out the door of the study and into the entry hall. As he passed the little tree, the angels fluttered in his wake.

As soon as William stepped out of the study, Kath grabbed her coat and charged out the front door. Clutching the wool across her body, she hurried the two blocks to Hilda's house and pounded on the door. When a dim glow filled an upstairs window, she stepped back to reveal herself. As she expected, Hilda's husband appeared in the window and glared into the yard.

Hoping he'd recognize her and send Hilda downstairs alone, Kath waved. When the curtain fell back in place, she stepped back on the porch, letting her coat flop open. The temperature had dropped to below zero, but she was burning up. She'd never felt so confused in her life. One minute her heart was on fire; the next she felt numb.

She watched as lamplight loomed in a downstairs window. A moment later, Hilda opened the door and pulled her inside. "It's freezing out there! Come in and tell me what happened."

Hilda slipped her arm around Kath's shoulders and walked her into the kitchen where the stove had a trace of warmth. Slipping out of her coat, Kath dropped onto a ladder-backed chair. It was so much like her own kitchen—the house she might never see again if she left. Instead of feeling calmer, she felt her chest heaving with a mix of hope and panic.

"Oh, Hilda," she gasped. "I'm so scared."

Her friend patted her shoulder. "Take slow breaths while I make tea. You'll warm up in a minute."

Kath tried to focus on the air entering her lungs, but

every breath put her back in the study. When she'd first seen the bottle—or more correctly, the dust—she had wanted to tell William how proud she was of him. If her husband could resist the temptation to drink, they had a chance at a fresh start. Hope had softened her heart. But just as quickly, the old anger had wiped away every ounce of her goodwill. She didn't want to feel that bitterness. William loved their son as much as she did. His guilt had been monumental and she didn't doubt his regrets. So why had the words stuck in her throat?

"Drink this," Hilda said as she set a cup of tea on the table.

Kath took two small sips. The heat melted the tension in her throat and she let out a deep breath. "I don't know what to do."

She told her friend about the dusty bottle and everything it signified. "I never thought I'd say this, Hilda. But I might be able to trust him again. I still don't know where he's going at night, but I know he's not drinking."

"That's good," Hilda said. "But if I were you, I'd still be worried."

"You mean Deidre."

"Yes, I do."

Kath shook her head. "I thought about it, but after tonight…" The memory of William's declaration stole her voice. For those few moments, she'd felt the longing she'd known as a bride. He'd made her feel young and beautiful again. Considering how she'd let herself go, he was either half-blind or in love. Kath knew that his eyesight was just fine. He'd made her feel hopeful again. Even happy.

Hilda raised an eyebrow. "Any man can be tempted, Kath."

"Not William." The warmth in Kath's belly turned to

anger—not at William but at Hilda, who didn't understand. She made her voice firm. "For all his faults, my husband's a good man. He's kind and he loves Alex with his whole heart. He's true blue, Hilda. He loves me and I love him."

Her friend's eyes twinkled. "So why are you sitting in my kitchen and not in your own?"

"Because…" Kath's voice dropped to a hush. "I can't forgive him."

"Ah, Kath."

"I can't do it, Hilda." Tears pushed into her eyes, burning her skin as they ran down her cheeks. She knew that forgiving William was the right thing to do. She worshipped the God who'd forgiven the sins of the world and sacrificed his own son to do it. But somehow, the thought of forgiving William filled her with rage. In some strange way, she'd be losing the baby all over again.

Hilda reached across the table and took her hand. "Kath, I'm going to be harsh, but you need to face the facts. William Jr. is gone from this earth. Holding on to the anger won't bring him back. Not only that, it's a betrayal to him. That dear boy wouldn't want his mama hating his father for something that was essentially an accident."

"One that could have been prevented," Kath insisted.

"But it happened, didn't it?" Hilda's voice was both kind and firm. "And nothing can change that fact."

A sob pushed into Kath's throat. "I want to forgive him, but I can't."

"You can't make yourself feel it, but you can say the words. You can march home right now and tell William that you're at least willing to try. Once you plant that seed, let God do the rest."

A Son Is Given

Kath's heart raced again. "Do you really think it's possible?"

"I'm sure of it. The hardest part is the first step."

A faint smile curled Kath's lips. She'd always admired Hilda for her honesty. "You're not going to let me off the hook, are you?"

"Absolutely not," Hilda replied. "There's too much at stake."

Chapter Eight

"It is finished." Lukas's tenor voice rang with awe.

If William hadn't known about singing to the stone, he might have thought the stonecutter was boasting. But that wasn't the case. Lukas had cut the stone with his hands, but the old man counted that talent as a gift from God.

With the afternoon sun pouring through the window, William took in every detail of the statue. The boy's face was pointed upward and his wings were wide, as if he were eager to take flight. With his hands pressed together in prayer, the child was the picture of soaring dreams and tender need. Lukas had matched Kath's angel to perfection.

It had taken hours of hard work, but the stonecutter had finished the statue just in time. Tonight was Christmas Eve. As the children put on their pageant, William would tell the Christmas story in a booming voice. He hadn't been home much, but he knew that Alex had the job of holding up the Christmas star. A smile lifted his lips. At breakfast this morning, she'd told him she was mad. She'd wanted to be the camel, but the Sunday school teacher said she wasn't tall enough and had given the part to a *boy*.

Papa, aren't there girl camels?

There sure are. Maybe next year you can be a camel.

William's heart squeezed at the memory. He couldn't bear the thought of a Christmas without his little girl. The best part of the day was sitting with Kath on the divan, holding hands while they enjoyed their daughter.

William ran his hand along the statue and swallowed hard. "It's perfect, Lukas."

"But not as perfect as your gift, Reverend."

William shook his head. "Your work is magnificent. Mine doesn't compare."

"You're judging the outside," said the stonecutter. "Your wife will see the love you've put into her gift."

"I hope so." William's voice dropped an octave. "Last night, we talked a bit. Just for a minute, I thought…" His voice cracked. When he'd shown Kath the dusty bottle, he'd seen a flash of pride in her eyes. He'd felt like the young preacher who had been full of dreams and wild hopes. But then her face had turned rigid. That's when he'd left the study.

By choice, he hadn't seen her since. The statue and the gift he'd made with his own hands were his last hope.

"When shall we take it to the cemetery?" Lukas asked.

William glanced out the window. It was just past noon and the sky was clear, but he didn't want Kath to see the statue before tonight's church service. There were things he still needed to say to her. Afraid that she'd run if they spoke in private, William had written this year's Christmas message with his wife in mind. He'd done all he could to save their marriage. The rest was up to her.

"Would you mind doing it late tonight?" he said to Lukas.

"Whatever time you say."

"Right after the service," William said. "I'll leave the minute it's over."

"Then tonight it is." Lukas smiled. "I wish you well, Reverend. You've done your best. That's all a man can do."

Instead of looking forward to an evening of carols and holiday cheer, Kath was walking to church with her stomach in a knot. She wanted to think she was nervous for Alex, whose white dress was a little too long, but her daughter wasn't the cause of her upset. Ever since she had left Hilda's house, Kath had been churning inside. That night, alone in her bedroom, she had dropped to her knees and whispered the only honest prayer she could say.

I want to forgive him, Lord. But I can't. Help me to do what's right.

She'd climbed into bed and fallen into a deep sleep. When she woke up, the sun had already climbed high in the sky. It was the first time in months that she'd slept so well. Blinking, she had discovered a note from William on the nightstand. He had fixed breakfast for Alex and taken the girl to Emma's house. The note had said nothing about his own whereabouts, leaving Kath alone in a storm of emotion. One minute she had wanted to feign a headache and skip the church service. The next she felt compelled to look her very best. After going through her wardrobe, she had selected the red paisley, put up her hair and pinched her cheeks to give them color.

After getting Alex dressed in her costume, Kath had taken her daughter's hand and headed out the door. They were turning the corner to the church when Alex tugged on her hand and pointed west.

"Mama, look at the sky!"

Swirls of silver and royal blue were rolling down the mountainside as if the clouds were the breath of a living creature. Kath inhaled and held the air in her lungs, savoring the smell of an approaching flurry. "It's going to snow," she said to Alex.

"I hope so."

So did Kath. She loved the purity of new flakes, especially when the morning sun made them sparkle. She was imagining that picture when they reached the fence surrounding the cemetery. At the sight of the wooden cross marking her son's grave, her throat constricted with resentment toward William. She still wanted an angel for her baby, even if she weren't in Denver to appreciate it.

But what good would that do anyone? The disturbing thought lingered in Kath's mind as she guided Alex up the steps and left her with the other children. In the corner she spotted a group of women standing around Cynthia Rush, admiring her infant daughter. She was about to turn away, when Hilda called out to her. "Kath, come over here. Cynthia needs advice on colic."

Memories of Alex screaming for hours welled into a river of compassion. Kath marched over to Cynthia, looked at her adorable little girl and felt nothing but sympathy for the tired mother. She touched the baby's cheek, saw the rosebud mouth and felt all the joy and pain of loving a child.

"I know all about *that*," she said, referring to colic.

She was sharing stories when a handbell summoned them. After taking her seat, she scanned the sanctuary for William. Alex had looked adorable in her white dress, and she hoped to share a smile. It wasn't much, but it was a start. Before she could spot him, the first chords of "O Come All Ye Faithful" echoed from the old piano. Expecting to see the children, she turned to the back of the church, where she saw William leading the processional.

Dressed in the long black coat he saved for special occasions, he was holding his Bible and looking straight at her. Just as it had ten years ago, the sight of him took her breath away. With his reddish hair and wide shoulders, he filled the doorway with a confidence that made King David seem timid. When the pianist started the final chorus, he broke away from her gaze, focused straight ahead and strode down the aisle. When he reached the pulpit, he set down his Bible and faced the congregation.

"Glory to God in the highest," he declared. "Peace on earth and good will toward men."

And so began the Christmas pageant. The children, costumed as animals, the wise men and Mary and Joseph, walked down the aisle and took their places at the front of the church. A boy named Todd recited his verse and stepped back, making way for another child to be in the limelight. Some repeated the words perfectly; others mumbled and stumbled with an innocence Kath felt to her toes. When "Joseph" forgot his lines, William charmed the congregation by whispering them in the boy's ear.

To Kath's pride, Alex raised the star right on time and got a round of applause. It was all so sweet, so full of love and mercy. Her heart was beating with hope. She wanted to be happy again. She wanted to love her husband. Could she do it? Could she find a way to forgive him? She was praying with her whole heart when Cynthia's baby started to whimper. The child was just a row away, behind Kath and to her left. Twisting her handkerchief, she waited for tears to fill her eyes, but they didn't come. Instead she felt a warmth in her chest as if she were holding her own child. As Mrs. Hawkins played "Hark the Herald Angels Sing," Kath dared to hope that she had crossed a line.

William stood in front of his flock. "Ladies and gentlemen, it's true that the Christmas message is one of joy. We give gifts to honor the gift that God gave us—the life of his very own son. With that gift comes the promise of forgiveness."

Kath wanted to stare into her lap with shame. It was true that William had wronged her. She had good cause for her resentment, but what did that prove? Only that she had a reason to become bitter, a hard-hearted wife who'd forgotten her vow to love her husband for better or for worse. Her throat swelled shut as she held William's gaze with her own.

"None of us is perfect," he said to her. "I've made tragic mistakes in my life, one so bad it cost me my son."

Kath felt his pain in her marrow. She wanted to tell him that she finally understood and that she loved him, but he'd turned his attention to the crowd.

"By the grace of God a man can still breathe after a mistake like mine. But it's only by the grace of the people who love him that he can start fresh. If there's a harder gift to offer—forgiving someone who's hurt you so badly you can't face the day—I don't know what it is."

As he paused to let the words sink in, the baby wailed once and stopped in mid-cry, plunging the room into silence, as if the cry had never happened. In that moment, Kath understood her own bitterness. Being angry with William was a way of keeping her son alive. As long as she felt the pain of the loss, he wasn't gone. But Hilda was right. Nothing could bring him back. Not her bitterness. Not a statue to mark his grave.

In the silent church, Kath accepted a simple truth. Never again would she hold her son in her arms. Never would she kiss the top of his head. But that didn't mean she couldn't love him. The way to keep William Jr. alive was by loving his father and sister. How foolish she'd been.... How close she'd come to losing the family she held most dear.

Blinking back tears, she watched as her husband paced across the front of the church, finishing his sermon with words of love and hard-earned wisdom. Wanting to show him her heart, she willed him to turn in her direction.

Look at me, William. I love you.

He wanted to face her. She could feel it. But his eyes stayed focused on the congregation. After the last prayer and a heartfelt amen, he nodded to the pianist, who played the first notes of "What Child is This?"

Instead of feeling the ache of loss, Kath felt unbridled joy. As her heart soared with the music, she closed her eyes and breathed a prayer of thanks. All around her the voices rose in a tribute to the birth of another son. As the last note rang, Kath opened her eyes and looked for William.

When she didn't see him, she turned to Alex. "Where'd Papa go?"

"Out the back door."

Ignoring the people crowding around her, Kath hurried to the door and stepped outside. She looked down the path, then farther up the street. William was nowhere in sight and she had no idea where he'd gone. It wasn't like him to race away from a service. Kath's heart pounded with the knowledge that her husband was suffering. Praying silently for his peace and safety, she walked home alone with Alex.

* * *

In spite of the subzero temperatures and flurries of snow, William's back was damp with sweat. He was a strong man and so was Lukas, but getting the statue into the freight wagon had required a system of pulleys and a mule. Unloading it hadn't been any easier, but together they'd positioned the statue at the head of William Junior's grave.

The hard work had been a blessing. Without it, William would have gone crazy thinking about Kath. When he'd talked about the grace of forgiveness, he'd been begging her to stay in Denver. He could only pray that the marker would touch her heart, and that the gift in his pocket would prove his sincerity.

Lukas interrupted his thoughts. "Reverend, it's been a joy to sing to this stone in honor of your wife. I wish you all the best."

"Thank you, Lukas. I hope it works."

The old man motioned to the eastern sky. "You better hurry. The sun is rising."

As the stonecutter climbed into his freight wagon, William glanced at the pink-and-gold sky where the sun was pushing away the black night. With fresh snow coating the ground, the light split into a thousand diamonds of hope. He couldn't have asked for a lovelier day. Hoping it was a good sign, he hurried home.

Being careful not to wake Alex, he climbed the stairs and tiptoed into the bedroom where Kath was hugging a pillow in her sleep. Leaning down, he touched her shoulder. The heat of her skin pushed through the nightgown and warmed his hand.

"Kath? Wake up, love."

She rolled to her side. "William! I—"

"Me first," he said. "I want to show you what I've been doing at night."

When her eyes locked on to his, William battled an onslaught of doubt. What if the statue deepened old wounds instead of healing them? He almost let her talk, but there was no point in risking his plan. The statue was the most eloquent statement he could make. "I'll wait outside while you get dressed."

"All right," she said. "I just need a minute."

As he stepped into the hall, he thought about how good it would feel to sleep next to his wife. To hold her in his dreams…to love her in all the ways God intended for a husband and wife to care for each other.

Please, Lord…

As soon as Kath emerged from the bedroom, he guided her to the stairs. Without a word, he took his place in front of her, protecting her lest she trip on the hem of her dress. Silently he helped her into her coat as if they were courting, then they went out the front door and emerged on the street where the snow was twinkling in the golden light.

"Where are we going?" she asked.

"You'll see."

"Is it far?"

William steered her around the corner to the cemetery. "We're already there."

As they walked down the path, she lifted her eyes to their son's grave. When she saw the angel, she picked up her pace, hurrying until she stood at the foot of the grave.

"Oh, William!"

He saw rivulets cascading down her cheeks and worried

that he'd hurt her again. He came up behind her and clasped her arms. She deserved to hear the whole truth.

"The day after we cut down the little Christmas tree, I nearly went crazy," he said. "I almost drank, Kath. I was going to open the bottle and climb inside. But then I saw the tree and the angels you made and I remembered."

"I wanted a marker."

"And I said no because I was so ashamed." He took a deep breath. "I'll never forget our son, Kath. I wish I could say more about that night, but I have to be honest with you. I don't remember it. I don't know if I stumbled and knocked you down, or if you were running away and tripped. I just know that I was drunk and you got hurt."

Kath looked up with tears in her eyes. He wanted her to say something that would end his purgatory. Instead she turned back to the statue and caressed the angel's upturned face. With William looking on, she kissed the top of the little boy's head.

"I can't make it right," William said to her back. "But I want you to know that your happiness means more to me than my own. That's why I have something else for you."

As she faced him, he lifted the smaller gift out of his pocket and held it out to her. It was wrapped in a white cloth, almost like swaddling. She took it in both hands, felt the weight and held it in the crook of her arm as she peeled back the cloth.

"William, it's lovely."

"It's a replica of the statue on the baby's grave. I hired Lukas Schmidt to carve the big angel, but I made this one with his help. That's where I've been at night—working with Lukas."

He watched as Kath stroked the statue's hands, the

wings and finally the baby's face. She looked up with love shining in her eyes. It gave him hope, but he needed words. When they didn't come, he clasped her shoulders.

"I want you to stay, Kath. But if you decide to leave, I'll understand. I made the little statue so you can take it with you."

He'd done his best. The rest was up to Kath, who was looking at the angel as if it were the most precious thing she had ever seen. Gently she covered it with the cloth and slipped it into her coat pocket. With her eyes shining, she stood on her toes and kissed his lips.

Shocked to his bones, William couldn't move. "Kath, does this mean—"

"It means I love you with my whole heart. I'm not leaving, William. Not now. Not ever. I've been punishing you and I'm sorry for that. You suffered as much as I did. I hope you can forgive me for being so bitter."

All he could do was shake his head. "There's nothing to forgive. I love you, Kath. I'd do anything for you."

"Anything?" she said, grinning.

"Just name it."

Standing as close as she could through their heavy coats, she pushed up on her toes and whispered the sweetest words he had ever heard. "Take me to bed, husband. Now, before Alex wakes up."

William didn't need to be asked twice, but he wasn't about to let the moment end without sealing the deal on the spot. With the sun sparkling on the snow, he brought his mouth to hers with a tenderness that turned into the promise of passion. The kiss was a sign of things to come, a melting that would bind them again as man and wife.

With the sun glistening through his tears of joy, William

lifted Kath off her feet and spun her in a circle. As her laughter rang in the air, he whispered a prayer.

Thank You, God.

It was Christmas, and he'd just been given the greatest gift of all.

* * * * *

ANGELS IN THE SNOW

Elizabeth Lane

Dear Reader,

If there's one thing I've always believed in, it's the eternal power of love. I've felt that power many times, most recently when my father passed away at ninety-one, and the hospital room was filled with a sweetness that could have come only from his lingering spirit.

Christmas is a time when the power of love is very strong. If we let it into our hearts, it can work small miracles—miracles of healing, redemption and forgiveness. But before we can reach out to others, we must first forgive and accept ourselves. This is the lesson Della must learn in our story. I hope you'll read it as it was written—with love.

My best wishes for a heartwarming holiday season.

Elizabeth Lane

For Olivia Tanya
November 1, 2005
Welcome to our world!

Prologue

South Pass, Wyoming
December 22, 1866

Della struggled up the rocky slope, her lungs screaming in the thin mountain air. Thickets of bare aspen, their trunks as white as bone, loomed through the gathering darkness. The ground was slippery with their fallen leaves.

A hungry wind, its moist breath heralding the winter's first blizzard, whipped tendrils of light brown hair around her face. It lashed the ends of her woolen shawl, threatening to rip it from her shoulders. Her work-worn hands clutched it desperately as she staggered into the gloom.

Where was the cabin? Della had seen the curl of chimney smoke from the wagon trail and judged it to be less than a mile away. But now she could find no trace of human habitation—no gleam of firelight through the darkness, no scent of wood smoke or simmering food on the cold night air. She stumbled on, realizing that she had lost all sense of direction. She no longer knew where she was. But there was one thing she *did* know. She would rather freeze to death than go back to the wagon train.

Them soldiers at the fort, they told us what kind of work you done back in Saint Jo! They said you'd spread your legs for any man what had money to pay! So why not me, you little slut? The wagon master's words had stung like lye in a wound. Earlier tonight he'd caught her alone, gathering firewood in a clearing. When he'd backed her against a tree and started fumbling with his trousers, Della had jabbed a knee into his groin and fled.

She'd hoped to find the cabin she'd seen and throw herself on the mercy of whoever lived there. But now she was lost in the darkness with a storm blowing in. Every step she took brought her closer to dying out here alone in the wilderness.

For the past year, Della had struggled to make a clean break from her old life, taking any menial job she could find, washing dishes, scrubbing floors, doing laundry, anything to keep from going back to those upstairs rooms at the Crimson Belle. But she'd known she couldn't survive another winter in Saint Joseph. Her sister's letter from Oregon, with enough money in it for Della's passage West, had come as a godsend. But it had arrived late.

By the time Della had the money in her hand, it was mid-October. She'd found only one band of travelers reckless enough to set out on the Oregon Trail so late in the year. Desperate to get away, she had paid her passage and joined their wagon train.

So far, the trip had been one long chain of disasters. The wagon train passengers, members of a close-knit religious sect, were resentful and suspicious of outsiders. The wagon master they'd hired was a brute and a bully. Worse, he was incompetent. Many of the delays that had put the wagon train weeks behind schedule had been his fault. Della, wiser than most of the travelers, suspected that he'd taken the cash they'd paid him, bought broken-down wagons, ailing horses and wormy flour with part of it and pocketed the rest.

Things had gone from bad to hellish after the wagon train had stopped at Fort Kearny. At the fort, Della had tried to stay out of sight, fearful that some of the soldiers might have patronized the Crimson Belle in the past. But she couldn't stay in the wagon all the time. Inevitably, she'd been recognized. Now everyone in the wagon train knew about her former profession. The women shunned her. The men cast her sidelong looks that made Della's flesh crawl. Even the children had been ordered to leave her alone.

She glanced back the way she'd come, wondering if anyone from the wagon train would come looking for her. Not likely, she surmised. To most of the passengers she was a nonperson, of no more consequence than a stray dog. Some of them, especially the women, might even be grateful she was gone.

In any case, they'd have more pressing concerns than finding a friendless runaway. With the storm blowing in, everyone was anxious to reach South Pass City, which lay about ten miles ahead. There'd been talk of pushing on into night without stopping to make camp. No one wanted to be stranded on the trail in a Wyoming blizzard.

Della gave a little cry as her ankle caught a tree root. Her foot twisted in its worn boot, and she pitched forward, catching her weight with her hands as she went down. Only the carpet of leaves that covered the rocks saved her from a painful injury.

For a moment she lay still, her breath coming in gasps.

She had to keep moving. If she didn't get up she would die right here.

Gathering the last of her strength she clambered to her feet and forced herself to go on. Somewhere there had to be a place of shelter and safety. Somehow she would find it.

Around her, the snow had begun to fall. Lacy white flakes drifted down through the bare trees to settle on her hair, on her shawl, on her skirt. Years ago, when she was a little girl, her grandmother had told her that when snow fell, angels were shaking the dust from their wings. For a long time, Della had believed the story. What a pity she didn't believe it now. She could use an angel or two on this dangerous night.

Only as Della thought about angels did she remember that it was almost Christmas. Once upon a time, she had loved the holiday. That was before the years above the Crimson Belle, where every day was the same and Christmas only meant that the men who climbed the stairs were drunker than usual. It had been a year ago, on Christmas Day, that she'd walked out of the place for the last time. Life had been hard since then but not hard enough to make her want to go back.

This year she'd looked forward to spending a real Christmas with her sister's family in Oregon. But as the wagon train met with delay after delay, she'd realized it wasn't going to happen. The best she could have hoped for was to spend the holiday in South Pass City. Now, even that wretched prospect was out of reach. But celebrating Christmas no longer mattered. Nothing mattered now except staying alive.

The snowfall had thickened. Snowflakes rippled around

her in silvery curtains, coating her hair, her eyelashes, her clothes. She could feel the icy wetness through the thin soles of her boots. If she didn't find that cabin soon she'd be in danger of freezing her feet.

She peered frantically in all directions, searching for the faintest glimmer of light, but between the darkness and the swirling snowflakes she might as well have been blind. The layer of snow that covered the leaves on the ground was treacherously slick. Time and time again her feet slipped and she pitched forward, skinning her hands on rocks and low-growing scrub.

She was getting tired…so very tired. How sweet it would be to lie down and rest, pillowed by downy feathers of snow. By the dust from angels' wings…

Della felt a curious warmth as the darkness folded around her like a quilt. She sank into it, closed her eyes and drifted into sleep.

Chapter One

Hunter McCall finished his coffee, laced up his high-topped boots and reached for the sheepskin coat he'd hung on a chair near the stove. It was still dark outside, but the animals in the barn would be awake and hungry. With last night's snowfall heavy on the ground, the morning chores were bound to take longer than usual. As long as he was awake it made sense to get an early start.

He took a moment to add another stick of firewood to the stove so the cabin would be warm when Joey got out of bed. Some would say that he took too much care with the boy, but Joey was barely five and he was all that Hunter had.

Climbing the ladder to the shadowed loft, he crouched beside the low bed, gazing down at his son, who lay curled like a puppy beneath the patchwork quilt. Joey was fair, as his mother had been. His flaxen hair was tousled, and his golden eyelashes lay soft and sweet against his rosy cheeks. Hunter tucked the quilt over one exposed shoulder. Then he descended the ladder, walked back across the cabin to the door and went outside.

The brunt of the storm had passed, but snowflakes still

drifted like fine white mist from the pewter sky. The wind had sculpted the snow into knee-high drifts. Hunter pushed through them, breaking a path to the barn. By now it was almost seven, but the dawn was just beginning to pale in the east. The December sun wouldn't be up for nearly an hour.

Hunter didn't need a calendar to tell him what the date was. It was December 23, the day before the first anniversary of Rachel's death. She had wanted to live through Christmas, but consumption had ravaged her frail body until there was no life left. She had died in his arms on Christmas Eve, December 24, 1865.

Hunter had spent Christmas Day carving her grave out of the frozen earth and lining it with soft pine boughs. At sunset, he and Joey had laid her to rest on a wooded hillside above their homestead. The Christmas holiday had been ignored last year. It would be ignored this year, as well. Hunter had no heart for it, and Joey would never know the difference. As far as they were concerned, December 25 would be just another day.

The dog, a shaggy collie-shepherd mix, came bounding out of the barn as soon as Hunter opened the door. Seeing the snow, it sprang into a drift with a joyous yelp, scattering white in all directions. For all his gloomy frame of mind, Hunter couldn't help chuckling. "Go to it, Sam," he said. "Somebody might as well have a good time in this blasted snow."

Inside, the small barn was dark and peaceful, warmed by the breath of stirring animals and the rank aroma of fresh manure. Hunter lit the lantern and hung it on a metal hook. By its flickering golden light he fed the cow, the chickens and his two horses. Buck, the rangy tan gelding, nuzzled Hunter's shoulder as he filled a pail with oats.

Sadie, the cat-footed blue mare, had been bred last season and was due to foal in the spring. Hunter patted her rounding belly, thinking of the money the colt would fetch and the new wagon he would buy with it. If the pelts from this winter's trapping brought a fair price, he might expand the barn as well. He had saved, scrimped and worked his fingers to the bone to build this homestead into a place he could be proud of. At first he'd done it for Rachel and the family they'd hoped to raise. Now he did it for Joey.

He'd just finished milking the cow when he heard the dog barking—not its usual, playful bark, but an urgent, come-quick sort of yapping that Hunter had learned to recognize and heed.

Grabbing the spare rifle he kept loaded on a rack above the barn door, he raced toward the sound. If Sam had cornered a bear or a treed cougar, which had happened before, he wanted to be ready.

The knee-deep snow made for rough going, but at least Sam's trail was easy to follow. A hundred yards from the cabin, Hunter spotted the dog pawing furiously at a place where the snow had drifted against a fallen tree trunk. Maybe he'd found a woodchuck den or a badger hole, with the owner at home. Whatever it was, it didn't appear to be dangerous—yet.

"What is it, boy?" Hunter plowed along the last few feet of trail and reached the drift. The dog glanced up at him, then resumed its frantic digging.

"Here, now, get out of the way and let me see." Hunter pushed the quivering animal aside and knelt in the snow. The only tracks he could see were Sam's big paw prints. Whatever the dog had found, it had been here through the storm.

Sam sat back on his haunches, whining anxiously as

Hunter used his boot to scrape away more of the snow. There was no sound, no sign of movement. Any creature buried by the drift would either be holed up deep or—

"Lord Almighty!" Hunter gasped, staring down at what he'd just uncovered.

It was a fold of faded blue calico cloth.

Dropping the gun, he fell to his knees and began scooping frantically at the snow with his bare hands. He uncovered two narrow feet, clad in thick woolen stockings and worn-out boots, then part of a skirt. Judging from the curled position of the knees, he calculated where the head would be and plunged his arms into the snow. The woman would be dead, of course. Even if she'd been warmly dressed, which she wasn't, it would take a miracle to survive a night in a Wyoming snowstorm.

Poor creature, where had she come from? It was late in the season for travelers. Maybe she was the wife, daughter or sister of a neighbor family, who'd fled a quarrel or become lost on some small errand and wandered aimlessly into the storm. Such things sometimes happened in blizzards, where the swirling snow could cause a person to lose all sense of direction.

He would wrap her body in his coat and carry it to the barn, where the sight of it wouldn't upset Joey. Then he would make the rounds of his neighbors and try to discover who her people were. If no one claimed her, he would spend another Christmas digging a grave.

Hunter's chilled fingers touched the edge of a knitted shawl, then moved into an open space beneath the fallen tree. The trunk's curved shape had formed a pocket of air above the woman's face, protecting her from suffocation. Not that it made much difference now. Dead was dead.

Working his hands beneath her body, he lifted her out of the snow. She was slender, as Rachel had been, but taller by several inches. The wet tangle of her light brown hair hung over his arm as he stared down at her pale, fine-featured face. She'd been a pretty thing. Still was. Damned shame, Hunter thought as he laid her on the snow, stripped off his warm sheepskin coat and bundled it around her chilled body. The woman was far beyond knowing the difference, but somehow it didn't seem decent to carry her without a wrap.

The wind bit through his woolen shirt as he lifted her in his arms again and set off with the dog trailing behind him. It was rough going with her added weight, especially since he couldn't see where he was placing his feet. Halfway to the barn, he stepped in a hole and stumbled forward. Reeling, he caught his balance, but in the process he nearly dropped the woman's body. Catching her just in time, he jerked her upward, hard against his chest.

She gasped, then groaned.

Hunter's heart lurched as he stared down at her. Her eyes were closed, but he could see the barest flutter of a pulse in the hollow of her throat. Tiny, vaporous puffs of breath emerged from between her blue lips.

Heaven help him, she was alive!

Plunging through the drifts, he raced toward the cabin. She was so cold, so tenuously connected to life, that even if he got her warm, Hunter knew she could still slip away. Even if she survived, she could lose fingers and toes, even hands and feet, to frostbite. As for the state of her mind…

But he wouldn't let himself think of that now. He could only concern himself with one thing at a time, and his first task would be to get her warm.

* * *

Joey stood in the open doorway, dressed in one of Hunter's old flannel shirts cut off at the sleeves. His blue eyes widened at the sight of his father, staggering up the snowy path.

"What's that, Pa?" he piped. "What'd you find?"

"One very cold lady." Hunter stomped the snow off his boots on the porch and carried the woman inside. "Close the door and get out of the way. She needs warmth."

Joey swung the door shut and hooked the latch. Bouncing with curiosity, he stared up at the pale, still face. "She looks dead," he announced.

"She's not far from it. I'm going to need your help, all right?"

The boy nodded solemnly.

"Good. Run upstairs and get dressed while I put her to bed. Wear your warm shirt and those new wool stockings we bought you in town. It's a bitter day, and I don't need two frozen people on my hands. Oh—and toss down the quilt from your bed. We're going to need it."

Joey raced up the ladder to the loft. While his son got dressed, Hunter carried the woman into his own bedroom, laid her on top of the patchwork coverlet and opened the coat he'd wrapped around her.

Lord, where should he start? She was still breathing, but her pulse was thready, her work-worn fingers stiff with cold. He inspected them for signs of frostbite. There were none, thank heaven. But the surface of her skin was icy. If the dog hadn't found her, Hunter surmised, she wouldn't have lasted the morning.

Working fast now, he unlaced her boots and peeled off her snow-encrusted stockings. Her long, pale feet were chilled but, likewise, free of frostbite. He held them between his hands, gently massaging and flexing them to improve the circulation. The temperature outside was well below freezing, but the snow must have acted as a blanket, trapping her body heat for the few precious hours she needed. She could count herself as one lucky woman—if she survived.

The snow that encrusted her woolen shawl and thin calico dress was already melting in the warmth of the cabin. If he didn't get her clothes off, she would soon be soaking wet. Tossing the shawl over the back of a chair, Hunter bent close and began undoing the tiny buttons down the front of her dress.

It had been a long time since he'd undressed a woman. Rachel had been so ill during those last months that making love had been out of the question. Since her death, he had slept alone. There were girls to be had in the saloons and brothels of South Pass City. But the very thought of that mindless butting and thrusting, with no more love or respect than a dog had for a bitch, left him cold. That aside, what would he do with Joey while he went off to spend time with a whore? What would he tell the boy when he came back?

Someday soon, he supposed, it would behoove him to find the boy a new mother—a good woman, honest, hardworking and tender. But he didn't feel ready to go out courting. Truth be told, he didn't feel much of anything except a dull, empty ache where his love for Rachel had been.

Hunter's fingers had opened up the woman's dress to the point below the waist where the buttons ended. Underneath she wore a threadbare chemise, a loosely fastened corset and a ragged petticoat. For all her shabby clothing, her slender body was beautiful—strong and well-shaped, with small but perfect breasts that strained against the thin muslin. Her cold-shrunken nipples were as hard as spring raspberries.

Hunter tried not to notice those things as he worked the sodden dress down over her shoulders and off her arms. She made little animal sounds, but her eyes remained closed, the lashes like the dark edges of a feather against her ivory cheeks. He couldn't help wondering what color those eyes would be when she finally opened them. Was she aware of him at all? Did she feel the warmth of the room, the touch of his hands? Or was she lost in some dark dream where no one could reach her?

He stripped the damp petticoat down off her hips, along with the dress, and tossed them over the chair with the shawl. Now she was wearing nothing but the corset, the chemise and some mud-stained drawers underneath. These were dry enough to leave alone, Hunter decided, struggling to avert his gaze. But she needed warming, and, in any case, it wouldn't do for Joey to see her so scantily clad.

Taking his own gray flannel nightshirt from its hook on the back of the door, he maneuvered it down over her body. Hunter was a big man and, apart from her height, she was no more than a slip of a woman. The nightshirt fit her like a tent, but at least she'd be warm and modestly covered when she woke up—*if* she woke up.

Lifting her limp body in his arms, he slipped the unconscious woman into the warm hollow of the bed and tucked the covers up around her chin. Her hair lay in damp tendrils on the pillow. Tiny gold freckles dotted her pale ivory skin.

Joey had come into the room. He pressed close to Hunter's side as he stared down at the woman in the bed. "Is she going to die, like Ma did?" he asked.

Hunter tried to ignore the familiar gut clench that hit him every time Joey mentioned his mother. "Not if we can help it," he said.

"If she dies, we can bury her on the hillside. Then Ma won't be all alone up there."

"Your mother isn't alone, Joey," Hunter said. "She's with the angels in heaven, watching over you."

A wistful look passed across the small face that was so like Rachel's. "Ma said she'd come back to visit if she could. Sometimes I feel like she might be here. But I can't tell for sure. I wish I could see her."

"You can't see angels." Hunter squeezed his son's shoulder. "But if you can feel your mother's spirit, she's here."

"Do you ever feel her spirit, Pa?"

"Sometimes." It was a lie. Hunter had never felt Rachel's spirit. He wasn't at all sure he believed in spirits or angels, or anything else, for that matter. But he would not deny a small boy a scrap of faith to ease his loss.

"Stay here and watch the lady for me," he said. "I'll hang her clothes up by the stove and make us some breakfast. Call me if she moves."

Hunter turned his attention to putting more wood in the stove. The stones he kept on the floor underneath were warm to the touch. He wrapped one in a towel, carried it back into the bedroom and slid it under the covers against the woman's icy feet. He felt her stir in response to the pleasant heat. She didn't speak or open her eyes, but her breathing, he noticed, had deepened to the rhythm of normal sleep.

Encouraged by these signs, he returned to the kitchen and put the oatmeal porridge on to cook, adding a few of the precious raisins that Joey liked. Then he draped the wet clothes over a chair near the stove, where they soon began to give off little rising threads of steam.

The next time he glanced toward the bedroom, Joey was seated on a nail keg, his cornflower eyes fixed on the woman's sleeping face.

The first thing to penetrate Della's benumbed senses was warmth—a slow, delicious warmth that crept over her like sunlight through a dark winter fog. Little by little it seeped into her body. She felt it penetrate her chilled toes, her feet and legs, her hands and arms. She could feel the steady beat of her own heart as her blood lost its sluggishness. Her limbs stirred, responding to her will. Miraculously, she realized, she was alive.

Other things stole slowly into her awareness—the sound of water dripping off an eave, the faint creak of a floorboard; the simmering aromas of meat, onions, carrots and potatoes and the sharper smell of hot coffee.

With effort, she opened her eyes. The first thing she saw was a towheaded cherub of a boy staring down at her, his freckled face inches from her own.

"Pa!" He spun away from her and raced out of sight. "Pa, come quick! She's awake!"

Raising her head, Della looked around her. She was lying on a double bed, covered with a pile of quilts so thick and warm that she was beginning to sweat. The room was spacious, with man-sized clothes hanging from a row of pegs near the door. Thin gray light streamed in through a high window set in a sturdy log wall. She was in a cabin, Della surmised, maybe the very one she'd been searching for last night when the storm struck.

"Hurry, Pa! See, she's got her eyes open!" The boy bounded back into the room, tugging at the hand of a tall man.

He stood scowling down at her, his presence filling the room. Della calculated his height to be well over six feet, with shoulders that spanned the width of the door frame.

He was dressed in work clothes—canvas trousers, a homespun shirt of dark brown wool and heavy boots, still wet with snow. The dark chestnut hair that fell in crisp waves below his ears matched the heavy mustache and beard that concealed the lower part of his face. His deep-set brown eyes were as fierce as a golden eagle's.

As a child, Della had loved reading her grandmother's book of Norse tales. Her favorite stories had been the ones about Thor, the god of thunder and lightning, with his brawny physique, flowing beard and turbulent nature. Now it was as if Thor himself, clad in the trappings of a homesteader, was looming above her from the clouds.

"How are you feeling?" His speech was a Yankee's, the consonants crisp and the vowels well honed. Whoever he was, he impressed her as a man who'd had some schooling.

Della glanced past him, through the doorway, expecting to see a woman bustling around the kitchen, but there appeared to be no one else in the cabin.

"I feel as if I just fell out of the sky," she said. "Where am I? How did I get here?"

"Our dog found you in a snowdrift," the boy piped up. "Pa dug you out and carried you into our cabin. I thought you were dead. You looked like my ma when she—"

"Never mind, Joey," the man said gruffly. "We haven't had company in so long that we've forgotten our manners. I'm Hunter McCall. This is my son, Joseph. And you're lucky to be alive, Miss—"

"Brown," she said. "Della Brown. And I have you to thank for my life, Mr. McCall."

"You can thank the dog. He's the one who found you. And there's no need to stand on formality. Hunter will do fine." He glanced around the room, edgy now, as if he didn't quite know what to do with her. "Stew's hot on the stove. I'll bring you a bowl to eat in here."

Della struggled to sit up. "Don't trouble yourself. I can certainly get up and—"

"No." His big hands pushed her shoulders back onto the pillow. "You were almost dead when I brought you inside this morning. I don't want you getting up and passing out on me."

He turned back toward the kitchen, then paused in the doorway. "Your people must be worried about you. If you'll tell me where to find them, I'll ride over and let them know you're here."

"No! Please—" Della's pulse slammed as she remembered the wagon train. Again she struggled to sit up, then fell back onto the pillow, unable to summon the strength.

"No?" He frowned at her, his eyebrows almost meeting above the bridge of his nose. "What are you, a fugitive from justice?"

"After a fashion." Della's attempt to laugh emerged as a nervous gasp. "I ran away from a wagon train."

"A wagon train?" He stared at her, then shook his head. "What are you talking about, woman? It's winter! There haven't been any wagon trains on the road since the end of October!"

"I can understand why. But this wagon train was late, and the people were anxious to get to Oregon. I was going there to join my sister—she's all the family I have left."

Della battled the deep weariness that threatened to drag her under again. "Things happened. Broken wagons, sick horses, supplies that didn't show up. We never thought the trip would take this long."

Hunter shook his head again and muttered something that sounded like "Damn-fool idiots!" "You say you ran off. What happened?" he demanded.

"There was a man, the wagon master. He tried to—" Della glanced at the boy, who was all ears. "He tried to hurt me. But I got away and ran into the woods. Earlier I'd seen the smoke from a cabin, maybe yours, but I couldn't find it. Then it started to snow…"

Unable to look into the earnest eyes of her listeners, Della turned her face toward the wall. She hadn't lied, but she hadn't revealed the whole story, either. How could she? What would this man do if he knew who—and what—she really was?

"The snow's deep out there, and it's still coming down," Hunter said. "The folks in your wagon train could be in trouble. If you don't mind looking after Joey, I'd rest easier if I could ride down the trail and make sure they're all right."

Dread clenched like a fist in the pit of Della's stomach. What would happen if Hunter found the wagon train? What would he do if they told him about her?

"Is something wrong?" He stared down at her, a puzzled frown on his face.

She shook her head. "It's just…that awful man. I don't want him coming after me again. If you find the wagon train, please don't tell anyone I'm here."

"What if they're looking for you?"

Della glanced at Joey. As a good father, which he appeared to be, Hunter had surely taught the boy the importance of being truthful. How could she ask the man to lie in front of his son?

She forced herself to meet Hunter's piercing eyes. "I doubt they'll care enough to look for me," she said. "But if they ask, you'll know what to tell them."

He nodded brusquely and went back to the kitchen, returning a few minutes later with a tray that held a bowl of stew with a spoon, a mug of hot black coffee and a slice of brown bread. Still frowning, he placed the tray on the bedside table. "I'll be back before dark," he said. "Joey's a good boy. He won't give you any trouble."

Della watched from the bed as he shrugged into his heavy coat and strode out the front door into the falling snow. She'd done her best to protect her secret, but if Hunter found the wagons and somebody mentioned a runaway whore, the truth would be impossible to hide.

Hunter McCall was a good man, exactly the sort of man who would ride out in a storm to look for a band of lost travelers. But no good man would want a fallen woman sharing a roof with his innocent young son.

Not that she planned to impose on his hospitality for long. She had run away from the wagon train with nothing but the clothes on her back, but it wouldn't be the first time she'd been stranded and down on her luck. In South Pass City she could always get work as a cook, dishwasher or cleaning woman until she had enough money to go on to Oregon. If there was no other choice, she could even rejoin the wagon train and endure more weeks of misery.

But whatever happened, Della vowed, she would never return to the life she'd left behind. She was a different woman now. She would rather die than go back.

Chapter Two

Della pushed her pillow against the top of the bed and eased herself to a sitting position. Joey watched her shyly as she lifted the tray and placed it across her knees. His eyes were the color of the morning glories that had spilled over her grandmother's porch every September of her childhood.

Feeling a bit self-conscious, she dipped a spoonful of stew and brought it to her lips. The broth was gluey and wanted seasoning, but Della was too hungry to care. She wolfed down the meat and vegetables, savoring their nourishing warmth. She was already feeling stronger.

"Did your father make this stew, Joey?" she asked, sopping up the last of the broth with a chunk of the bread.

The boy nodded solemnly. "Pa's a pretty good cook. Ma was better, but she's in heaven now." His eyebrows knitted in a pensive scowl that reminded her of Hunter's. "What do you think angels eat? Is there any food up there?"

Della took a sip of coffee. The tarry brew seared a path down her throat. "I don't know," she said. "I've never been an angel."

"Maybe I ought to ask Ma the next time she comes to visit me."

"Your mother comes to visit you?"

"I don't know for sure." He looked down at his small, chapped hands. "She promised me her spirit would come back, and Ma always kept her promises. Sometimes, like at night, I think she might be here. But I can't see her, and she doesn't say anything, so it's hard to tell."

Della battled the impulse to reach out and gather the little boy into her arms. Hunter wouldn't want her touching his son, she reminded herself. Not if he knew about her old life in that gaudy upstairs room with the red brocade wallpaper, the gilded brass bed and the men trudging up and down the stairs.

She imagined Hunter walking through the door after having found the wagon train. She pictured his eyes glaring down at her as if she were something that had stuck to the sole of his boot. She could almost hear the contempt in his gruff voice as he ordered her out of his home.

Setting the tray aside, Della sank back into the bed. She had long since learned to seize small moments of pleasure, hoarding them like precious souvenirs to remember when times were bad. Her childhood memories had sustained her through those black days at the Crimson Belle. They had even lent her the strength to walk away.

Hunter could be gone until nightfall. For the few hours that remained she would savor her time in this cozy cabin with a child who needed a few good memories of his own. That way, when the ugly truth surfaced, she would have some trace of sweetness to carry away with her.

And maybe she could leave some sweetness behind.

"So how do you and your father celebrate Christmas,

Joey?" she asked the boy. "Do you decorate a tree and hang up your stockings? Sing songs? Read the Bible?"

He stared at her as if she'd just spoken to him in a foreign language. "I don't know," he muttered, shaking his golden head. "What's Christmas?"

Snowflakes whitened Hunter's beard as he rode down the long hill toward the wagon road. The going was slow and treacherous. Deep drifts covered the trail, hiding rocks, holes and tree roots that could cause his mount to stumble. He gave the big tan gelding its head, allowing time for the horse to find its own secure footing.

Nothing could have stopped him from going out to look for the wagon train. If the wagons were marooned in the snow he would need to get the women and children to shelter, and maybe the men, as well. Otherwise they might perish from cold and sickness.

This wouldn't be the first time he'd rescued stranded travelers, and it wouldn't be the last. In fact, Hunter had come to think of it as his duty. If anyone died on this stretch of the Oregon Trail, when he could have saved them, part of the blame would be his.

Once again his thoughts flew back to the woman in his cabin. Della. He liked her name. He liked the deep moss agate color of her eyes, the husky timbre of her voice and the way her mouth dimpled at the corners when she spoke. He had always been a fair judge of people and, even though he knew almost nothing about her, his instincts told him she was honest, gentle and kind.

Della. His lips and tongue played with her name, liking the feel of it, the taste of it.

She had run away from the wagon train—or more precisely, from the wagon master, Hunter reminded himself. His gloved fists clenched around the reins as he thought of that pretty, delicate woman, chased down and cornered by a panting brute intent on having her. Seeing the man again would be the last thing she'd want. But if the travelers needed shelter in his cabin or barn, there'd be no way around it.

He would protect her, Hunter vowed. If he had to beat the bastard to a bloody pulp, he would do it. He had never been a violent man, but in this case he would take satisfaction in every crunching blow.

Now, through the thinning trees, he could see the open strip of ground that marked the Oregon Trail. Under different conditions, the road would be deeply rutted, worn down by the wheels of countless passing wagons. Today it was flat and white where drifting snow had filled in the ruts.

There was no sign of the wagon train.

Dismounting at the edge of the trees, Hunter stepped into the middle of the road, dropped to a crouch and began scraping away the snow. He had uncovered several feet of ground before he found what he was looking for—fresh horse droppings, trampled against the muddy earth. It was a sign, at least, that the wagons had passed this point and moved on. More than likely they'd been trying to reach South Pass City before the storm stranded them on the trail. But that didn't mean they'd made it.

Mounting up again, he rode west along the road for a few more miles. Now and then he dismounted to look for signs of the wagon train. At last he stopped and turned around. Between this point and South Pass City there were several homesteads, some within shouting distance of the road. If the travelers had made it this far before the heavy storm struck, they should be all right.

Behind him, sunset blazed crimson and purple above the snowy peaks. Hunter nudged his horse to a trot back along the trail they'd already broken. He'd promised to be home before dark. Joey would worry if he was late. Maybe Della would worry, too. It had been a long time since he'd come home to a house with a woman in it. Even though she was a stranger, Hunter found himself looking forward to sharing supper in the cozy warmth of the little cabin.

How long would she stay? he wondered. For the next few days she would need to rest and recover. But what would happen when she was strong enough to leave?

The people on the wagon train would likely wait out the storm in South Pass City. Since Della had paid her passage all the way to Oregon, she might want to rejoin them. If that was her choice, Hunter resolved, he would confront the wagon master himself and make sure the man understood his attentions weren't welcome. After that, he could only hope she'd have the sense to stay with other women and avoid being alone.

But what if she didn't want to go back to the wagon train? Or what if they'd already left her behind?

He could hardly ask a lady to share the intimate space of the cabin for more than a few days. He could take her into town, maybe find her a place with a family or some elderly widow who needed a pair of helping hands. Then in spring, when the wagon trains were coming through again, she could take up her journey to Oregon.

Still, why was he grinding out plans as if he were the one in charge of Della's life? She was a grown woman with a mind of her own. The decision would be hers to make.

By the time Hunter spotted the cabin through the trees,

it was nearly dark. The snow had stopped falling and the sky was beginning to clear. A sprinkle of stars glimmered through the thinning clouds, promising a cold, bright day tomorrow.

The dog came bounding out of the barn to welcome him as he rode into the yard. Dismounting, Hunter scratched the shaggy ears. Then he led the horse to its stall, removed the bridle and saddle and rubbed down the gelding's wet coat with a towel. After making sure that all the animals were fed and comfortable, he closed the barn and trudged across the snowy yard to the front porch. He was tired and hungry. Even a bowl of the same tasteless stew he'd eaten for lunch would satisfy him as long as it was warm.

Standing under the eave that covered the porch, he stomped the snow off his boots. He was reaching for the latchstring when the door swung inward, flooding his senses with light, warmth and savory aromas that made his mouth water.

Joey stood in the doorway, grinning. "Come on in, Pa," he said. "Miss Della and me, we're making Christmas!"

Della's heart dropped as Hunter walked into the cabin. The pan of hot oatmeal cookies she was lifting from the oven tipped in her hands. She grabbed the edge of it, searing her fingers as she saved the sliding treats from crashing to the floor.

She risked a glance at Hunter's face. The only emotion she could read there was surprise. If he'd found the wagon train and learned about her past, he showed no sign of it. But even if he knew, Della reasoned, he wouldn't raise such a tawdry issue in front of Joey. He would wait to confront her after the boy was asleep.

"What's going on here?" he demanded, his eyes taking in the cutout snowflakes and strings of paper-doll angels hung around the cabin.

"It's Christmas, Pa!" Joey's eyes danced. "Miss Della told me all about it. After supper she's going to read me the Christmas story out of Ma's Bible!"

Hunter's scowl deepened, and Della's heart sank. True, she should have asked him before flinging herself into Christmas preparations. But Joey had been so taken with the whole idea, it had simply happened.

What if she'd done something wrong? What if he had something against Christmas? Hunter could be furious with her for reasons that had nothing to do with her past.

"I hope you won't mind," she said. "It started innocently enough. When I found out Joey didn't know anything about Christmas, I started to tell him, and one thing led to another."

Hunter unbuttoned his sheepskin coat and hung it on the back of a chair. The lantern over the table etched tired shadows beneath his eyes. "I've never been much for celebrating," he said. "As long as it pleases the boy, it's fine. Just don't try to drag me into it."

He washed and dried his hands at the basin, pulled out a chair and sat down at the table, which was covered with a gingham cloth and set with plates, bowls and mugs. "Smells good," he muttered.

"Miss Della made biscuits!" Joey said. "And Christmas cookies!"

"I also added a few things to your stew. I hope you like it." Della filled the bowls from the simmering kettle. She had found the cellar well stocked with vegetables, and a back corner of the cupboard had yielded a store of little-used spices. Starting with Hunter's bland venison stew, she'd expanded the ingredients—more onions and carrots, dried peas, some cabbage, salt and pepper, a pinch of sage and, finally, a batch of fluffy egg dumplings. Hot biscuits, ice-cold milk and spicy oatmeal raisin cookies completed the offering.

Hunter bowed his head and mumbled a few words of grace. The gusto with which father and son fell to eating spoke volumes about how long it had been since they'd had a well-prepared meal.

"This is right tasty," Hunter said, buttering his third biscuit. "But I haven't forgotten that I told you to stay in bed and rest. The last thing I need is a sick woman on my hands."

"I'm fine," Della said. "Getting up and doing a few things was just the medicine I needed." She took a deep breath, summoning her courage. "Did you find the wagon train?"

He shook his head. "The trail was snowed over. My guess is, your friends headed on to South Pass City before the worst of the storm hit."

Della's knees had gone liquid with relief. Hunter hadn't spoken with anyone from the wagon train. For now, at least, her secret was safe.

But not forever. If the wagon train waited out the weather in South Pass City, the travelers would talk. Sooner or later, when Hunter went to town, he was bound to hear the story.

But she would likely be gone by then, Della reminded herself. Whatever the circumstances, she could hardly expect to spend more than a few days under his roof.

"Can we put up a Christmas tree tomorrow, Pa?" Joey bounced on his chair. "Miss Della told me how her folks used to cut a little pine tree down and bring it right in the house. Then they'd hang popcorn strings and paper angels and things on it. At night, they'd hang their stockings up by the fire, and when they woke up on Christmas morning, there'd be presents in them! Can we do that? Please, Pa?"

Hunter shot Della a rueful glance, as if to say, *Now look what you've done!* "I don't know about that, Joey," he said. "There's not much room in here for a tree, and presents don't pop out of thin air. Somebody has to buy them or make them." His gaze lingered on his crestfallen son. "We'll talk about it in the morning, all right? Now finish your supper, and maybe Miss Della will let us have some of those warm cookies for dessert."

Joey sighed. "But you'll still read me the Christmas story, won't you, Miss Della? You promised."

"Certainly." Della gave him a smile. "The Christmas story is the most important part of Christmas—much more important than trees and presents. We'll read it after the kitchen's cleaned up and you're ready for bed." Her eyes narrowed in Hunter's direction. "Maybe your father would like to listen, too."

Joey brightened. "I can wipe the dishes," he said. "Pa lets me. I've only broken one."

"That's fine, Joey." Della's eyes remained fixed on Hunter. What was going on behind that stern, bearded mask of a face? The man seemed to care deeply for his son, and the presence of a Bible on the corner bookshelf gave mute evidence of his religious beliefs. But how could a loving, believing father deny his child the magic of Christmas, the most joyful day of the year?

Something was wrong here—and if it took her all night, Della vowed, she was going to find out what it was.

* * *

Hunter sat in the wooden rocker that had been Rachel's, watching as Della settled herself in the armchair, pulled Joey up beside her and opened the Bible that lay on her lap. He noticed how she paused, her eyes lingering on the first page where the family record was kept—the dates of his marriage to Rachel, Joey's birth and Rachel's death. For the briefest moment her lips parted. Then, avoiding his eyes, she thumbed swiftly through the pages to the place where the Book of Luke would be.

"There it is, Joey," she said, pointing to the page. "Soon you'll be learning to read. Then you can read the story for yourself."

Joey snuggled close to her, his eager eyes following the movement as her fingertip traced each line. Her voice, unlike Rachel's clear soprano, was rich and throaty, with a little catch that Hunter found strangely fascinating. Hearing her read was like listening to the contented purr of a cat.

With her attention focused on the Bible and Joey, Hunter had ample time to study her. She had donned her dry clothes while he was out searching for the wagon train. Despite its shabby condition, the blue calico dress, with its modest, round neckline, was becoming. But Hunter couldn't help remembering how her slender, feminine body had looked without it or the way she'd felt in his arms when he'd slipped the nightshirt over her underclothes and tucked her into his bed.

When he wore the nightshirt again it would carry the scent of her body. That scent would surround him, stealing into his senses as he slept, arousing forbidden dreams and hungers.

But what was he thinking? Rachel had been gone for a year—a proper time as some might measure it. But he still felt her loss like a shaft of winter ice in his soul. Although his body might be tempted, Hunter knew that his heart was far from ready to love anyone else.

Even so, he could take pleasure in the glow of firelight on two bent heads. Joey's tousled thatch of hair was as pale as milkweed. Della's neat braids were the color of coffee laced with cream. She was not the most beautiful woman he'd ever seen—her fair skin was dotted with tiny freckles, and she had a sliver of a gap between her front teeth. But those tiny imperfections lent interest to her pretty face. She was also warm, giving and unafraid of hard work—Hunter had recognized that last fact when he'd touched the calluses on her hands.

Maybe there was a man waiting for her in Oregon, one who would love her, give her children and make her happy. If so, Hunter could only hope that man would realize how lucky he was.

By the time Della had finished the story, Joey's head was nodding against her shoulder. Stirring, he gazed up at her. "Would you tuck me in, Miss Della?" he murmured drowsily.

"Do you mind?" She glanced at Hunter.

"It's fine, if you don't mind climbing up to the loft," Hunter said, then added, "I'll take a quilt and sleep up there with Joey while you're here. You can have my bed—is that all right with you, Joey?"

"Sure. I don't mind sleeping with you, Pa, not even when you snore. But your bed is big enough for two. You could sleep with Miss Della, just like you slept with Ma."

The heat that flamed in Hunter's face matched the becoming rose that flooded Della's. For an instant both of them stared at the floor. Then she had the grace to laugh.

"Men and women don't usually sleep together unless they're married, Joey," she said. "Besides, I can't abide snoring."

Before Hunter could come up with a witty rejoinder, she rose and offered Joey her hand. "Lead the way to your loft," she said.

Hunter's eyes lingered on the pair as they moved toward the ladder. Joey clung to Della's fingers, his bare legs showing below his nightshirt as he pattered sleepily across the floor. Maybe it was best if the boy didn't get too attached to her. Joey was hungry for a mother's affection. He could be hurt when the time came for Della to leave.

"Can you sing me to sleep?" Joey's voice drifted down from the loft. "Ma used to do that. It was nice."

Hunter sensed Della's hesitation. "Would you like to hear a Christmas song?"

"Uh-huh," he sighed, already drifting.

Della cleared her throat and began to sing. "Away in a manger, no crib for a bed…"

Rachel, once a soloist in her church choir, had been gifted with a voice like a silver bell. Della's untrained alto was not even fit for comparison. All the same, her whispery, off-key notes drifted like smoke through Hunter's senses, stirring little tendrils of heat that crept pleasantly through his body. He sat listening with his feet on the hearth as the fire burned down to embers. For the moment, he felt warm, well-fed and filled with the peaceful contentment of things as they should be. The fact that the magic couldn't last made it, somehow, all the more precious.

Della's song faded into silence. A few seconds later he heard the creak of a floorboard as she moved toward the ladder. Hunter settled back in his chair to wait for her return. The thought of spending time alone with her, talking quietly in front of the fire, filled him with pleasure. He found himself wanting to know everything about her, where she'd come from, what she'd done with her life and why she was on her way to Oregon.

Then she walked around the chair and sat down, facing him, with her hands clasped tightly in her lap. Her expression put him instantly on guard. She looked like a woman who'd just stepped into a pen with a wild buffalo bull, determined to grab its horns and wrestle it to the ground.

"I've been trying to figure you out all evening, Hunter McCall," she said. "It perplexes me that a man would refuse to celebrate Christmas with a child he loved. Now that I've seen the front page in your Bible, I can guess part of the reason. But there has to be more. If I'm going to help Joey celebrate his first Christmas, I need to know where you stand."

"Where I stand on Christmas, you mean?" Hunter scowled at her. "Why should that be any concern of yours, Miss Della Brown?"

Her jewel-like eyes probed into his. "The memory of this Christmas will stay with Joey for a long time. Next year, when I'm gone, he might want to celebrate again. If you tell him Christmas is nothing but a lot of balderdash, the boy will be crushed."

"I see," Hunter muttered guardedly.

"I don't want him hurt," she said. "And I don't want to stir up trouble. But I need to understand my limits—and for that, I need to understand *you*."

Chapter Three

The stillness was broken only by the hiss of burning pine pitch and the light scrape of a twig against the side of the cabin. Della willed herself to wait, forcing Hunter to speak first. It might take some time, she sensed. Over the years, she'd learned a few things about reading men. This one was in pain.

She was taking a gamble, confronting him like this. But Joey's bedtime prayer had touched her deeply, igniting a spark of fierce, protective courage.

Bless Pa that he won't be sad anymore, Hunter's son had murmured into his clasped hands. And as she'd listened, Della had glimpsed a vision of a young boy growing to manhood in the company of a bitter, remote father who'd allowed grief to take permanent root in his soul and suck all the joy from living. Joey deserved better, Della had resolved. Maybe it was beyond her power to change things, but she would never forgive herself if she didn't try.

Hunter stirred uneasily, looking trapped. "If you saw the front page of that Bible, you already know that my wife died a year ago, on Christmas Eve."

"Yes, I know."

"Isn't that enough?"

"Enough?" Della would not let him dismiss her so easily. "Enough for what? Enough to make you forget about celebrating Christmas last year? Yes, that's perfectly understandable. But what about the year before, or even the year before that? When I asked Joey about Christmas, he didn't even know what it was!"

Hunter glowered at her above his beard. "Last year, when Joey was four, his mother died. The year before that, when he was three, he had whooping cough. He was so sick that the idea of celebrating Christmas never entered our minds. Before that, I was off fighting in the Union Army. His mother may have done a few things for the holiday, but Joey would have been too young to remember. Now, are you satisfied?"

Della let her silence hang in the air before she spoke. "What about this year? Were you planning to do anything at all for the boy?"

Hunter picked up the iron poker and jabbed it into the smoldering log, sending up a shower of fresh sparks. "It didn't seem right, celebrating on a sad anniversary. I reasoned that Joey would be in school next year. He'd have friends his own age. He could wait that long to learn about Christmas."

"Shame on you, Hunter."

His eyebrows shot upward.

"Joey's just a little boy, and he's had a lot of sadness in his life. He needs a day of hope and joy, not a father who can't dwell on anything but his own grief."

"I said you could go ahead and celebrate with him. What more do you want?"

"You, celebrating with us."

He shook his head. "Leave it be, Della. You can keep Christmas with the boy. That's fine. But if you want to know the truth, I've hated the day for as long as I can remember. Losing my wife on Christmas Eve only made it worse."

"I wish you'd tell me more. I don't mean to pry, but I need to understand for Joey's sake."

He leaned toward the fire. For a long moment he stared into the glowing coals. At last he turned back to face her. "Give me your shoes," he said.

"My shoes?" She blinked at him.

He rose, picked up a long wooden box that was stowed against the wall and placed it on the hearth. "Your soles are worn through. You'll freeze your feet in this weather. Here—"

Kneeling on the rug in front of her, he lifted Della's left foot, cradled her ankle-high walking boot between his knees and began loosening the worn leather laces. Pulling up the tongue, he eased the boot off her foot and held it up for inspection. Lamplight glimmered through the worn place in the leather sole.

"That boot walked most of the way from Missouri," she said, thinking of the long days she'd trudged behind her assigned wagon rather than face the animosity of the couple who shared it.

"So I see." Hunter set the boot aside and reached for her other foot. "When I'm through fixing them, your boots will last you all the way to Oregon."

His hidden message was not lost on Della. Hunter would not allow any excuse, even something as trivial as worn-out boots, to keep her from leaving as soon as the weather cleared. Well, that was fine with her. She had a new life waiting in Oregon. Why would she want to stay here with this gruff, stubborn, infuriating hulk of a man?

She extended her foot and allowed him to slip off the other boot. His fingers were deft and gentle. She could imagine those fingers unbuttoning the front of her dress, chastely avoiding any contact with her skin.

"Your feet are still cold," he murmured. "Your toes are like ice."

Without asking permission, he tugged off her thread-bare wool stockings and pressed her toes between his big, warm palms. Della felt the tension leaving her body as his strong hands massaged the tender balls of her feet, the weary arches, the battered heels. A little moan of pleasure escaped her lips. Of all the men she'd known, not one of them had ever rubbed her feet. The sensation was pure heaven.

His head was at the level of her lap. She found herself wanting to reach out and rake her hand through his glossy chestnut hair and feel its crispness curling around her fingers. But if she did that, Della reminded herself, he might stop rubbing her feet—or he might take it as an invitation to do more.

His fingers brushed her bare ankles, the gesture as intimate, somehow, as if he'd stroked her breast. Hunter McCall struck her as a man of strict morals. He was touching her in innocence, seemingly unaware of the shimmering heat that spiraled up her legs to pool between her thighs.

In those dark years at the Crimson Belle, Della had frozen her natural responses to physical contact. However deeply her body might be violated, there was a part of her that no man could reach, let alone possess. Now she felt those responses beginning to thaw. And Hunter was only touching her feet!

His fingers seemed to be growing warmer, their pressure more intense. The low cadence of his breathing began to quicken as his fingers inched higher. Della's hammering pulse sent hot shivers through her body. Heaven help her, she didn't want him to stop.

Something clenched in the pit of her stomach, and suddenly she felt afraid. She'd been vulnerable once, and the pain of what had happened was something she never wanted to feel again. In a protective move, she yanked her feet away from him and tucked them beneath her skirt.

"My feet are much warmer, thank you," she said with an awkward little laugh. "Now, if you don't mind, I'd like to take you up on your offer to fix my shoes."

With a long exhalation, he rose from his knees and opened the wooden box he'd placed on the hearth. Inside was a set of fine cobbler's tools—hammers, nails, trimming knives, glue, a cast-iron shoe holder and several rolled pieces of leather.

Avoiding her eyes, he unrolled the thickest piece. "My father was a cobbler back in Albany," he said, picking up one of Della's boots. "I learned the trade and could have taken over his shop, but I wasn't ready to settle down. For a while I took a job with the railroad. Then the war came along. My father died while I was in the army, and I never went back home. My sisters sold the shop to pay his debts. They sent me his tools as a legacy."

"Why not move into town, then, and set yourself up in business?" Della ventured. "The money would be good, and Joey would have more chances to meet other children."

Hunter used a carpenter's pencil to trace the outline of her boot sole on the leather. "I've thought about it. But growing up in a town, with no animals to tend or chores to do, isn't the best thing for a boy. And while I don't mind mending shoes for my neighbors, I've no wish to spend my days hunkered over a workbench the way my father did."

"But what about courting?" Della asked boldly. "Surely you'll be wanting to find Joey a new stepmother and give him some little brothers and sisters. How are you going to find a suitable woman clear out here?"

He glanced up, shooting her a narrow-eyed scowl. "I'll cross that bridge when I come to it," he snapped, and sank into silence.

Della watched as he used a short, curved knife to cut along the outline he'd drawn. She was learning more about the man, but she had yet to unravel the mystery of why he disliked Christmas so much.

"You mentioned your sisters. How many do you have?"

"Two. Both married and living in the East. No brothers." He put the boot over the iron shoe holder, then coated one side of the newly cut sole with thick glue.

"What about your mother?" Della persisted. "Is she still living?"

He fitted the new sole onto the boot, pressing it into place. "Can't say as I know. Or care." His brown eyes flashed at her. "Since I know you'll worry me till I tell you, I'll save you the trouble. My mother was a beauty, but she wasn't exactly what you'd call a pillar of society. Every few months she'd disappear for a week or two. Then she'd come back, laughing and hugging, with her pockets full of candy and presents for all of us. My little sisters were always glad to see her. But once I was old enough to know how she paid for those treats, I didn't want anything to do with them, or with her. She'd usually make a foray right before Christmas. Afterward she'd walk in the door laughing, with her arms full of presents and the money in her pocket for a fine Christmas dinner. I came to despise the day!"

Della sat frozen in her chair, willing the expression on her face to remain unchanged. "What about your father?" she asked softly.

"He tolerated her ways because he loved her and didn't want to break up his family. His one great fear was that she'd leave and never come back." Hunter pressed a small nail into the rim of the sole. The blows of his hammer punctuated his words. "Finally his fear came true. She ran off with an actor who promised to put her on the stage. My father was a kind man, and she broke his heart."

Yours, too, Della thought. Her throat had gone dry. Her hands lay cold and clammy on the arms of the chair as she watched Hunter hammer in the rest of the nails.

"We never celebrated Christmas after she left us. For me it was a relief." He lifted the shoe off the holder and began trimming the edge of the sole.

Della watched him, feeling as if she were walking a tightrope where every word she spoke would be another dangerous step.

"So you're punishing your innocent little boy for your mother's sins."

He gave her a withering look. "Enough," he growled. "I said you could celebrate with the boy. Now leave it alone, Della. You've been here for less than a day. If you think you can just step in and rearrange our lives, you don't know me, and you don't know Joey."

Della lifted her chin, refusing to be cowed. "I'm not even pretending to know you. But you were kind enough to take me in, and I'd like to do something nice for you in return. You saw Joey's face when he talked about Christmas. You saw how happy he was."

"Yes, I did, and we're talking in circles now. You know where I stand, and that's that."

Hunter turned away from her and picked up the other worn boot. The blasted woman was as persistent as a horsefly. As if it wasn't enough to fill Joey's head with star shine and angel dust. What would he do when she went away, leaving a disappointed little boy to learn all over again that the real world was grim and tough and cruel, and happiness was something that dissolved in a flash if you tried to hold it, like spun sugar in your mouth.

He glanced back at Della. She was watching him like a cat, her bare feet tucked primly beneath her skirt. He remembered the feel of those feet in his hands, the skin cool and soft, the bones delicate beneath. He remembered the little pleasure moans she'd made as he manipulated each arch and hollow. It had been impossible not to imagine the sounds she might make if he touched her in more intimate places. Even now, as he thought about sliding his hand along the silky inside surface of her leg, Hunter felt his body harden and strain against his trousers. He battled the forbidden feeling, first by trying to focus on his work, then by making trivial conversation.

"I take it your own childhood was less dismal than mine," he said.

She curled deeper into the armchair. "Yes, I suppose my sister and I were lucky. We didn't have a lot of money, but our parents did the best they could for us. And our grandmother lived just down the block. Anytime we wanted a cookie or a story or a hug, all we had to do was knock on her door. Our family always celebrated Christmas at her house. First we'd go cut the tree and bring it back on a sled. Then we'd help Grandma make gingerbread men and popcorn strings to hang on the tree, along with paper stars and paper angels. On Christmas Eve we'd hang up our stockings and sing carols. It was wonderful."

Her face shone like a child's as she described the glorious holiday. Hunter couldn't help thinking how beautiful she looked, leaning toward him, with the firelight glowing on her skin. For two cents he would have abandoned his shoe mending, gathered her up in his arms and swept her into the bedroom.

But what was he thinking? Della wasn't the kind of woman a man could fling onto the bed and ravish till his lust was slaked. She was a lady, just as Rachel had been. And a lady was entitled to a proper courtship, a gold ring and a tender wedding night.

As for himself, Hunter was nowhere near ready to court another woman. Maybe in six months, maybe in a year, but not yet. Rachel's death had left him so empty that he wasn't a fit companion for any woman—and maybe not for a small boy, either. Joey deserved someone who would make him smile, sing him songs, mend his overalls and teach him manners.

Sadly, the boy deserved a mother.

"So what happened to you, Della?" he asked, testing the fit of the sole he'd cut on the bottom of her boot. "Why were you on your way to Oregon alone, in a wagon train full of fools, with winter coming on?" He glanced up, meeting her eyes. "What were you running from?"

She hesitated, but only for a heartbeat. "Not running *from*. Running *to*. My sister wrote me about her life in Oregon and sent me the money to join her. I'd had…a spell of bad luck and was ready for a new start. My one mistake was not having the patience to wait until spring."

"A spell of bad luck, you say?"

Again, Hunter sensed that tick of hesitation. "Let's just say I had no money, no family and no future. My sister gave me the chance to make a new start, and I jumped at it."

Hunter would have asked more questions, but she yawned wearily, stretching her arms and flexing her wrists. "Forgive me, I know it's early but tomorrow's going to be a busy day, and I'm awfully tired. Would you mind if I excused myself and went to sleep?"

"Not at all." Hunter might have suspected her of evading his questions, but Della really did look exhausted. Her face was pallid and there were violet shadows under her eyes. She had nearly died out there in the snow, he reminded himself. After her ordeal, she should have spent the whole day resting in bed and drinking hot liquids. Instead she'd gotten up to bake cookies and fix that wonderful supper. No wonder she was worn-out.

"I'd be happy to share the loft with Joey," she said. "Or, for that matter, I can sleep right here in this big chair of yours. It doesn't seem right that I should take your bed."

Joey's practical solution flashed through Hunter's mind, but bringing that up now would likely get his face slapped. "You need your rest," he said. "I'll sleep fine in the loft. Just let me get a pillow and the spare quilt, and the bedroom's yours. I can finish this boot sole and add the new heels after you're asleep. The hammering shouldn't bother you much if you close the door."

She eased her feet to the floor, her bare toes resting on the braided rug. "You're a good man, Hunter McCall," she said. "I'll be grateful to you for the rest of my life."

"Anyone else would have done the same." Hunter laid his tools on the hearth and rose to his feet.

"No, that's where you're wrong." Her soft hazel eyes held his for an instant. "Believe me, I know."

"Then maybe you've been spending too much time with the wrong kind of people."

Uncomfortable with praise, Hunter turned away and strode into the dark bedroom. There were two pillows at the head of the carefully made bed. He took one of them, along with the quilt that was folded over the back of a chair. The loft was the warmest part of the cabin. He wouldn't need much in the way of covers.

He was just turning back toward the door when he heard the sound of something falling. Rushing back into the lighted room, he saw Della lying on the rug, her eyes closed, her face chalk-white.

Hunter fell to his knees beside her, feeling for the pulse at her throat. Several fear-filled seconds passed before he found it, beating strongly against his fingertips. Her breathing was shallow but regular. She had simply stood up too fast and fainted, he concluded. The best thing he could do would be to put her to bed and let her rest.

Scooping her up in his arms, he carried her into the bedroom. Could she be pregnant? he wondered as he balanced her against his shoulder and turned down the covers with the hand he'd freed. Was that why she'd been so anxious to get to Oregon?

But no, that wasn't likely, Hunter told himself. He'd seen her in her underclothes. Her flat, taut belly was almost hollow, her small, perfect breasts unswollen. She was simply exhausted, done in by her ordeal and an afternoon of work. He should have insisted that she go back to bed right after supper. His desire to spend time alone with her had been plain selfish.

But she was clearly fleeing from something. The bad luck she'd been so evasive about could have been an unhappy marriage or love affair, heavy debts or even a brush with the law. But that was none of his business, Hunter reminded himself. If she wanted to tell him more, fine, he would give her a sympathetic ear. Otherwise, he would not press her for secrets she wanted to keep.

As he prepared to lower her to the bed, Hunter felt a strange reluctance to let her go. The warm weight of her was sweet in his arms, the fit of her head against his shoulder so natural that it seemed meant for that very spot. He knew next to nothing about the woman, but he loved touching her, loved holding her.

Briefly Hunter weighed the idea of taking off her dress and replacing it with his nightshirt. Surely she would rest more comfortably that way. But no, if Della woke up and found him undressing her, she might get the wrong idea and be deeply upset. He would not take that chance.

Still holding her, he leaned over the bed and placed her on the soft flannel sheet. She stirred and moaned but her eyes remained closed as Hunter pulled up the covers and tucked them under her chin. Her breathing had deepened into the slow cadence of sleep. She would be all right, he told himself. And if she needed anything, the loft was right above the bedroom. He would have no trouble hearing her.

For a moment he gazed down at her, remembering how her eyes had sparkled like a child's when she'd talked about Christmas. She looked like a child now, slumbering in peaceful innocence, as if she were dreaming of Christmas in happier times.

Impulsively, he leaned down and brushed her cool forehead with his lips. She flinched as his beard tickled her nose, and he drew back, but Della was sound asleep. She did not awaken as Hunter stole out of the bedroom and quietly closed the door.

The logs in the fireplace had burned down to crumbling coals, but the stove was still warm. He would bring in more wood after he checked on the animals, Hunter decided, reaching for his coat. Then he could take his time resoling Della's boots.

After that, if he could find a looking glass, he had something else to do.

Della woke to the mouthwatering aromas of bacon and fresh coffee. The brightness of sun on snow was spilling through the small, high east window of the cabin.

Still groggy, she sat up and rubbed her eyes. She had a vague memory of waking up in the middle of the night, taking off her dress, corset and petticoat and flinging them over a chair. Aside from that, the last thing she remembered was Hunter fixing her boots and asking her questions that she didn't want to answer.

Had she gone to sleep in the chair? Had he carried her to bed? Was that why she'd awakened in the night with her clothes on?

Stretching, she sat up and pulled her chemise down over her body. Tonight would be Christmas Eve, she reminded herself. She was facing a busy day.

At least she'd slept well—better than she had since the start of that miserable wagon trip. She felt strong and rested, ready to face any opposition Hunter McCall might fling in her way. Whatever it took, she would give Joey one good Christmas to remember.

As she swung her legs to the floor, she saw her boots sitting on the rug. Hunter had done a splendid job with them. They were freshly oiled, with sturdy new soles and heels to protect her feet from the snow. Her stockings, washed and dried, lay folded beside them.

A hard lump tightened in Della's throat as she pulled the stockings and boots on her feet. The men in her adult life had used, abused and exploited her, treating her as if she were of no more worth than the dirt under their feet. This simple kindness from a gruff, bearded giant of a man almost undid her.

Hunter bore her no love, she knew. Mending her boots had been nothing more than an act of compassion, something he would have done for any stranger in need. Still, she would miss him after she moved on. And she would never forget what he'd done for her.

But enough woolgathering! It was December twenty-fourth, and she had a Christmas celebration to prepare. Moving swiftly now, Della fastened her corset and pulled on her dress and petticoat. Her fingers flew as she did up the buttons, then splashed water on her face, finger-brushed her mouth and twisted her braids on top of her head.

Back in her time at the Crimson Belle she would have slept until early afternoon, then spent a leisurely hour applying cosmetics to her face and curling her thick brown hair with a heated iron. But those days, thank heaven, were gone forever. Now Della did only what was fast and practical. No one, not even Hunter, would notice or care how she looked.

With her mind on the tasks ahead of her, Della flung open the bedroom door, stepped into the bacon-scented warmth of the kitchen—and halted dead in her tracks.

Standing next to the stove, pouring a mug of coffee from the blue-enameled pot, was a tall, handsome, clean-shaven stranger.

Chapter Four

"Good morning," Hunter said, sipping his coffee. "How do the boots feel?"

Della stared at his clean, rugged features—the strong cheekbones, the square, slightly cleft chin. She'd seen her share of good-looking men. Most of them she'd found to be vapid, conceited, even cruel. If Hunter stopped her breath now, it was only because she'd come to know the man behind the face—a man who would save a half-frozen woman, take her in, warm her, feed her and even mend her shoes. A man who hurt as deeply as he had loved.

He was handsome enough to play a Greek god on the stage, she thought. But Hunter didn't belong on a stage. He was perfect right here, in this cozy mountain cabin, wearing a dark plaid woolen shirt and tending breakfast on a big iron stove.

Joey was sitting at the table. He grinned as he sopped up the last of his fried egg with a hunk of biscuit. "Pa shaved," he said, stating the obvious.

"He looks…right fine," Della said, noticing the way

Hunter's russet-brown curls had been awkwardly self-trimmed in back, making them fall in soft tangles down his neck. Her fingers itched to comb them out and even off the ends with scissors. Maybe later she would offer, although the thought of it made her feel strangely weak in the knees.

"Thank you for mending my boots," she said. "They'll carry me a long way now."

A long way from here, she thought; and as her eyes met his, an ocean of unspoken words seemed to flow between them. Here in this small, warm space was everything she had ever wanted—four strong walls, a man she could come to love and a lonely child who needed her. But remaining here was out of the question. When Hunter learned about her past—a secret she had no power to hide—he would never want to look at her again.

Hunter cleared his throat. "Now that the snow's stopped, I've got work to do in the barn," he said. "Some loose boards need nailing down, and I've been meaning to widen the mare's stall, so there'll be more room when she foals. The work should take me most of the day." He thrust a plate of bacon and eggs into Della's hands and motioned her toward the table. "After breakfast, I'll clear out of here and leave the cabin to you two, so I won't be underfoot. And don't worry about making lunch for me," he added. "I'll come in and find something when I get hungry."

The stubborn set of his jaw made his message clear, as his words had made it last night. He wanted no part of their Christmas preparations. And now that he'd shared the reason why, Della was to respect his wishes.

But what about Joey? How could the boy have a real Christmas with his mother dead and his father refusing to be involved?

True to his word, as soon as he'd finished eating, Hunter put on his coat and strode outside, the dog frisking at his heels. Minutes later, Della heard the echoing ring of hammer blows against the side of the barn.

Forcing his image to the back of her mind, she set about cleaning up the kitchen. Then she popped a kettle of corn, threaded a needle and showed Joey how to string the popped kernels onto a thread. The task was a challenge for his eager little hands. Joey broke and ate more popcorn than he strung. But he had fun long enough for Della to get two apple pies into the oven. Later, when the sun was high, she promised him, they would go out and cut a Christmas tree.

By the time Joey had wearied of popcorn stringing, Della had mixed up a batch of thick, spicy gingerbread dough. "This was always my favorite thing to do at Christmastime," she said as she washed his hands and sat him down at the table, where she'd placed a floured breadboard. "I still love making gingerbread men."

With gentle patience, she helped Joey roll and pat out a figure with dried black currants for eyes and a sliver of apple peel for its mouth. Joey was entranced.

"Can I make a dog?" he asked. "Can I make a horse?"

"You can make anything you want to," Della replied, resisting the urge to hug him. "But remember to make them skinny, because they'll puff up and get fat in the oven!"

Joey giggled. "That's Pa," he said, pointing to the finished gingerbread man. "Now I'm going to make Sam."

The little fingers went to work, rolling and patting out the shape of a dog. For a young child with no art experience, he was amazingly adept. The finished form actually looked like the big collie-shepherd mix Della had glimpsed outside.

Next he fashioned two horses. "The tall one is Pa's horse, Buck," he said. "This fat one is Sadie. She's going to have a baby in the spring. Pa says we'll need to sell it when it gets old enough, so we can buy a new wagon. I'd rather have a colt than a dumb old wagon, but Pa's the boss."

He said it so matter-of-factly that Della had to smile. She watched as he modeled a smaller version of the first gingerbread man. "This is me," he said. "And now I'm going to make a lady."

He used the last of the gingerbread dough to shape a female figure with a nipped-in waist and a long skirt. "There," he declared, giving his creation two currant eyes and a smile. "All done!"

"Is that your mother?" Della asked gently.

"Ma's an angel. I'd need to put wings on her, and the dough's all gone." He glanced up at Della, his eyes sparkling. "This is you!"

Even inside the barn, Hunter could not escape the aromas that wafted from the cabin. Cinnamon, ginger, apple pie and fresh, hot bread floated into his nostrils, making his mouth water. He had left the house because he wanted nothing to do with Christmas. But Christmas, it seemed, was doing its level best to find him.

Steeling his senses against the fragrant seduction, Hunter hammered another board onto the newly reframed side of the mare's stall. This job could have waited months. But he'd needed an excuse to get out of the cabin. Now he couldn't leave the stall unfinished.

From outside, the playful yapping of the dog caught his attention. Through the partly opened door of the barn he caught sight of Della and Joey trooping up the hill through the untracked snow. Della, wrapped in her shawl, was carrying the hatchet from the woodpile. Joey was prancing along beside her, looking as if the circus had come to town. Sam raced around them in circles, barking happily.

It was easy enough to guess where they were going. A hundred yards up the hill, beyond the wide ribbon of aspens, was a stand of young pines. It would be as good a place as any to look for a Christmas tree.

Would they be all right? Hunter hesitated, the hammer sagging in his hand. Della didn't strike him as an accomplished woodcutter. She could easily swing the hatchet and cut her leg or even injure Joey if he got in the way. And with the snow driving deer down from the high meadows, there might even be a cougar or a bear in those pines. If anything were to happen to Della or his son, Hunter knew he would never forgive himself.

With a sigh, he laid the hammer on the floor of the barn and lifted the rifle from the rack. He didn't want Della to think she was dragging him into their celebration, but he had to make sure she and Joey were safe. He would keep well behind them and out of sight, Hunter resolved. Unless something went wrong, they wouldn't even need to know he was there.

He could hear the two of them singing as he followed their trail through the deep snow. Della was teaching the boy "Deck the Halls." Her merry, untrained voice coaxed Joey to sing along. Hunter had never heard his son sing— or if he had, he'd never really listened. Only now did he realize that the boy had inherited his mother's exquisite soprano. In another time, another place, Joey might have sung in a grand church with candles and stained glass windows. Here his pure young voice floated on the crystalline air, blending with the piping song of chickadees and the rustle of a breeze through the bare aspens. The sound of it took Hunter's breath away. It was almost like hearing Rachel again.

The singing stopped as they reached the pines. Hunter hung back, out of sight, listening as Joey raced giddily from tree to tree. "This one!" he shouted. Then, "No, this one! No, wait—"

There was a moment of silence, followed by a whoop of boyish delight. "This one! It's the best tree of all! Come on, Miss Della, let's chop it down!"

Again, there was silence. Then Hunter heard Della's voice. "But, Joey, that one is so...so big. I don't know if we can even get it into the cabin. Let's keep looking. Maybe you'll find one you like even better."

"No." Hunter's son had a stubborn streak, and it came out now. "We want to have the best Christmas ever, and this is the best Christmas tree ever."

Della's sigh was audible, even from a distance. "All right. Stand way back over there, Joey, and keep Sam with you. That's it. Hold on to his collar."

Hunter waited, then heard exactly what he'd expected— the dull *thunk* of metal bouncing off wood. There was a brief pause. Then he heard the same sound again, followed by a breathy mutter and yet another impotent *thunk*. There was no getting around it. Christmas or not, Della was going to need his help.

He strode up the hill, through the aspens and into the pines, following the winding trail of trampled snow. At its end, he found Della, sprawled on her rear at the foot of a tree that was seven feet tall and a good six inches through the base of the trunk. A wide-eyed Joey stood a dozen feet away, clutching the dog.

Frustrated, she glared up at him. "Don't even start with me," she muttered.

"How about if I just start on the tree?" Hunter pried her cold fingers from around the handle of the hatchet. A full-sized ax would have been better suited for the job, but he would make do with what he had.

Della moved over to crouch next to Joey as the chips began to fly. Hunter cut the tree high, leaving a good eighteen inches of stump and trimming off the branches above the cut. What was left would just fit beneath the roof of the cabin, in the gravel-filled bucket he planned to use as a tree stand.

Joey cheered as the tree toppled, and Della's pretty face wore a smile once more. But they both looked cold and tired. It was time he got them back to the cabin.

With Hunter dragging the tree through the snow, they trudged down the hill. "Sing with us, Papa," Joey piped, breaking into "Fa-la-la-la-la." Hunter, no singer, was mumbling along with the words when a movement through the aspens caught his eye.

"Shh!" he hissed, motioning them to stop. "Get down behind the tree. Hang on to the dog and keep quiet!"

Della circled Joey with one arm and pulled him down behind the Christmas tree. With her free hand she grabbed the dog's collar. Hunter had cocked his rifle and was creeping down through the aspens. Her throat tightened as he rounded a snowy hillock and vanished from sight.

The dog strained against her hand, whining low in its throat. What was down there? A bear or cougar? A man? Della drew Joey close against her. Her eye caught the gleam of sunlight on the hatchet Hunter had left behind. Could she reach it if she had to? Could she use it?

A single shot from the rifle shattered the winter stillness. Startled by the sound, a flock of magpies exploded out of the trees, sending down showers of snow. Then there was nothing but silence.

Della's ribs ached from holding her breath. Her snow-dazzled eyes probed the whiteness, straining to see against the bright sun.

"There!" Joey said, pointing. "There's Pa!"

Hunter had just come back around the hillock. In one hand he carried the rifle. In the other he was holding a long, dark shape.

"It's a turkey!" Joey shouted, twisting free of Della and bounding down the slope to meet him. "Pa's shot a wild turkey!"

Hunter was grinning broadly. "Look at this!" he exclaimed, hefting his prize. "Here's Christmas dinner!"

The fire had burned down to crackling embers, casting its glow on a Christmas tree decorated with paper chains, paper stars, paper angels, six gingerbread figures and one rather short string of popcorn. It was the most beautiful tree Hunter had ever seen.

From the armchair, he watched Della in the kitchen. She was mixing a batch of sourdough rolls for tomorrow's dinner, and the motion of her arms made her firm breasts quiver beneath the fabric of her dress. The stirring of desire he felt now was warm and pleasant, something to enjoy. But he knew it wouldn't take much to make him want more. If he let himself dwell on the fantasy of her in his bed, the ripe weight of her breasts in his cupped palms, the curve of her small, taut rump, the satin slickness of her thighs as they opened to him like the gates of heaven...

Hunter felt the heat flood his loins. He willed the tempting thoughts away, knowing this wasn't the time or the place. For now he would content himself with the aromas of fresh pine and good food and the presence of this luminous woman in his home.

All in all, it had been a long, satisfying day. The wild turkey hung in the springhouse, plucked, singed and ready for the oven. Even with all the excitement, he'd managed to finish the work on the mare's stall. Best of all, it was Christmas—the first real, honest Christmas he'd ever experienced. And he owed it all to this strong, passionate stranger he'd found half-frozen in the snow.

He knew nothing about her, Hunter reminded himself. Aside from the fact that she'd had a happy childhood, the woman who called herself Della Brown was a mystery. But tonight, that didn't seem important. The only thing that mattered was that she was here.

Hunter smiled at the sight of his son's bare legs coming down the ladder from the loft. Joey was dressed for bed in the old flannel shirt that served as his nightgown. Clutched in one small hand was one of his new woolen stockings.

"I need to hang this up by the fireplace," he said. "Will you help me, Pa?"

"Let's see." Hunter studied the rough stone fireplace. The mantle was fashioned from a split log with the top surface smoothed. It would be an easy matter to hammer in a small nail from his cobbler's box. A more pressing question was what to put inside the stocking. He had thought of nothing to give his son.

A few taps of the hammer and the stocking was in place. Joey stepped back to admire it. "Miss Della's grandma used to tell her that if she was naughty she'd get a lump of coal in her stocking," he said. "But she never did."

"I suspect Miss Della was a very good little girl." Hunter settled back in his chair, his eyes on Della's slender back.

"Can we read the Christmas story again?" Joey darted to the bookshelf and tugged down the Bible. "Will you read it this time, Pa? You come listen, too, Miss Della."

Hunter pulled the boy onto his lap as Della dried her hands on a towel and settled onto the seat of the rocker. This had been his mother's chair, Joey had told her earlier that day. Now Della sat uneasily, feeling the presence of the woman whose death had left her son and husband alone—the woman she felt unworthy to replace, even for this brief holiday.

As soon as Christmas was over, she would find an excuse to leave, she vowed. Every day she remained here increased the chance that Hunter would find out about her past. If she stayed long enough, the contempt in his eyes would shatter her.

As for Joey, she couldn't let the boy form an attachment that would break his tender heart. For his sake, even more than her own, she had to move on.

She would allow herself one more day to give Joey a good Christmas. Then she would have Hunter take her into South Pass City. If he learned about her there, at least she'd be out from under his roof.

Hunter opened the Bible and thumbed through the pages. Finding the familiar passage from Luke he began to read. Joey nestled against him, dreaming of angels and shepherds and a shining star. But it was Hunter's voice that Della heard, low and tender, caressing every syllable.

By the time he'd finished reading, Joey was fast asleep.

Balancing the boy against his shoulder, Hunter carried him across the room and up the ladder to the loft. When he returned, Della was back in the kitchen, measuring flour and sugar into a small bowl.

"I thought I'd make some sugar cookies for Joey's stocking," she said in answer to his questioning look. "I've nothing else to give him. If there's some little thing you could add yourself…"

For the space of a long breath, Hunter was silent. "There is," he said at last. "I thought of it as I was carrying him up to the loft. I'll work on it while you're making the cookies. After that, you're to put your feet up and rest." He scowled at her. "That's an order. You fainted last night, and you're still not as strong as you should be."

"I'll be fine." Della stirred the ingredients for the cookies, watching Hunter as he selected a chunk of dried pine wood from the bin by the stove. Taking a pocketknife out of his trousers, he sat down at the kitchen table and began to whittle.

Della rolled out the cookie dough and began cutting it into stars and trees that would fit inside Joey's stocking. Her eyes followed the movements of Hunter's big, brown hands as he shaved long, blond curls of wood from the chunk of kindling. The emerging shape looked like some kind of animal—a horse, she decided.

"After tomorrow, I'll be needing to move on," she said, avoiding his eyes. "If the weather's clear, would you mind taking me into South Pass City?"

Hunter's blade trimmed the curve of the miniature horse's neck. An eternity seemed to pass before he spoke. "That would be fine," he said. "I could use a few supplies, and Joey would enjoy the outing."

Della laid a small star onto the bottom of the flat cookie pan, wondering if she should say more. Should she thank Hunter for saving her life? Should she tell him how much she was going to miss him and Joey?

Should she tell him—heaven forbid—the truth?

"I'm hoping it won't be too late to catch the wagon train," she said. "The trip won't be pleasant, but it's already paid for, and it's still the fastest way to get me to Oregon."

"But not the safest. Not in the winter. The fools could bog down in the snow and freeze, or maybe starve. It could be the Donner party horror all over again."

"Maybe. But that's my chance to take." Della cut out another small star and laid it on the greased metal surface. Part of her wanted him to seize her in his arms, hold her close and forbid her to go. But that would only make matters worse, she reminded herself. As things stood, the best she could hope for was a clean getaway with no ugly confrontation to spoil their parting.

He had fallen silent. The cabin was so quiet that Della could hear the sound of his blade smoothing the wood. By the time she'd cut the last cookie, sprinkled the batch with cinnamon sugar and slid the pan into the oven, the miniature horse stood finished on the table. Hunter hadn't taken the time to add much detail, but the graceful little figure was so lifelike that it looked as if it might toss its head and break into a gallop.

"It's beautiful," Della said, clearing away the bowl and utensils she'd used to make the cookies. "Joey should be very happy with it."

"I hope so. Something tells me he will." Hunter's eyes twinkled mysteriously as he rose to his feet, swept the wood shavings into his open hand and tossed them into the fireplace. They burst into a crackling blaze that swiftly died away.

Della stacked the bowl and utensils in the tin dishpan, then added some soap shavings and hot water from the steaming kettle on the stove. Her eyes watched Hunter as he gazed into the fire. She'd done the right thing, making it clear that she planned to leave, she thought. Now he could relax, knowing she hadn't set her cap for him. And he could prepare Joey for what was bound to be a sad farewell.

Still, Hunter's obvious relief had stung her. He could have argued, at least, or invited her to stay a few more days. Instead, his quick reply had let her know how anxious he was to have her gone.

Never mind that, Della told herself. Hunter had awakened long-buried yearnings, making her more vulnerable than she ever wanted to be again. The sooner she got away from him, the better.

But what she wouldn't give for just one more of those delicious foot rubs….

"I'll finish cleaning up," he said, turning away from the fire and walking toward her. "You sit down and rest. I don't want you fainting again."

"No—don't bother. I'm almost finished." Della reached into the dishpan for the spoon she'd used to mix the cookies. Too late, she remembered that she'd just poured the dishwater from a simmering kettle without adding anything to cool it. The sudsy water was scalding hot.

Della gasped and jerked her hand away. Hunter reached her in two long strides, seizing her wrist, inspecting her reddened skin.

"I-I'm all right," Della stammered. "See, it's not even blist—"

"Be still," he growled. "Thank heaven it wasn't worse."
Dipping cold water from the bucket on the counter, he
poured it slowly over her hand. Della closed her eyes. The
pain was receding but she felt dizzy. She swayed and felt
his big, steadying hand slide around her waist.

She forced her eyes to open. Hunter was looking at her
intently, his eyes so deep and dark that she felt as if she
were tumbling into them. Strangely, she wanted nothing
more than to let go and fall.

"I'm not going to faint," she murmured. "I'm absolutely…fine."

He kissed her. For the first few seconds his rough lips
tasted hers, nipping and nuzzling. Then, as Della re-
sponded, her eyes closing, her body softening in his arms,
he groaned and took full possession. His lips molded her
mouth to his with hot, hungry kisses, tender kisses, brutal
kisses. Kisses that ignited blazing bonfires of need.

Della's arms slid around his neck. Her hands tangled in
his thick brown hair, pulling him closer, deeper. She'd
been aching for this, she realized, aching to hold him, to
feel his hunger, to know that whatever she gave him would
be given freely. She wanted Hunter McCall as she had
never wanted any man in her life.

Sweeping her off her feet, he strode toward the fireplace
and sank into the big armchair. Cradling her across his
knees, he kissed her again, his tongue penetrating and
thrusting in urgent pantomime of what they both craved so
desperately. Della's mouth answered him, her lips parting,
her tongue meeting his. Her body blazed with bittersweet
urges and sensations she thought she'd buried forever.

His lips moved lower, to her chin, her throat, the ridge of
her collarbone. His fingers fumbled with the front of her dress

before she could help him. Her own hand tore eagerly at the buttons, almost ripping them open. She wanted to feel his hands, his mouth on her body. She wanted his loving to burn away the memory of every man who'd ever touched her.

She whimpered softly as he buried his face between her breasts. "Della…" he murmured. "Lord, woman, how I've wanted you. Every time I've looked at you…"

She pressed him closer. Her breath eased out in a long sigh as his tongue found her nipple and began an exquisitely gentle caress. Deep inside her body a flower seemed to open, its petals moist and quivering. Wetness seeped between her thighs, ready to welcome him home.

His hand slid beneath her petticoat, moving upward to find the opening in her drawers. Now he would touch her, as she'd ached to be touched, yearned to be touched…

A stirring sound from the loft flung them apart like an electric jolt. Della scrambled off Hunter's lap, hastily fastening the buttons on her dress.

"Papa?" Joey's sleepy voice floated down through the opening. "Is it Christmas yet?"

"Not yet, son." Hunter pushed himself upright in the chair, his voice thick and husky. "Go back to sleep. It'll come soon enough."

Della was still catching her breath when she became aware of a spicy, slightly smoky smell emanating from the kitchen. The cookies! She dashed to the stove, yanked open the oven door and used a towel to snatch her treasures from the heat. The little stars around the edge of the pan were burned a dark brown, but a precious few in the middle were all right. She sighed. Her gift to Joey would just have to be smaller.

Behind her, she could hear Hunter moving the chair that held his coat near the stove. When she forced herself to turn around, she saw that he was getting ready to go outside.

"I'm going to check the barn," he said. "Maybe it'll cool me off a little." His eyes narrowed. "If you're waiting for me to apologize, Della, it's not going to happen. Having you in my arms felt damned good. Anytime you want to pick up where we left off…" He turned toward the door, leaving the sentence unfinished.

"You don't know me, Hunter. You don't know anything about me." Della blurted out the words.

"No? Maybe you'll tell me sometime. For now, you'd better get some rest." He strode out into the night, closing the door behind him.

With unsteady hands, Della filled Joey's stocking, putting the little horse in the toe and filling the rest of the space with paper-wrapped star cookies. She owed the child a debt of gratitude. His interruption had saved her from the worst mistake she could have made.

But she'd already compromised herself with Hunter. When he learned the truth about her, he would feel betrayed. He would hate her to the depths of his bitter, wounded heart. And Joey would be too young and innocent to understand why.

Drained and exhausted, she pressed her hands to her face. She would leave tomorrow if she could. But tomorrow was Christmas, and she would not spoil it for a little boy who'd known too much sadness in his life.

She would make the best of the day, Della resolved. But she would guard her heart, keeping Joey with her to avoid any awkward moments with Hunter. After that she would put the man and boy behind her and move on with her life. There was nothing else she could do.

Chapter Five

Hunter stood in the moonlit snow, staring up at the silver pinpoints of the stars. It was by no means the first time he'd looked into the night sky and tried to send his thoughts to Rachel. He did it often, in spite of his doubts that he could reach her. It helped him sort things out in his own mind. Sometimes it even helped ease the loneliness.

Mostly he told her about Joey, what a fine boy he was and how they both missed her. But what should he tell her tonight, a year from the date of her death?

Should he tell her that he'd met a wonderful but mysterious woman—a woman who'd made Joey smile and brought the magic of Christmas into their home?

Would Rachel understand if he told her how deeply he yearned to have a family around him, with more children and a good woman who could fill his life, and Joey's, with warmth and laughter?

What if he told her that, for all his undying love, he'd discovered there was room in his heart for someone else? Would Rachel bless him and set him free, or would she curse him with a lifetime of guilt and misery?

The dog nuzzled his hand with a cool, wet nose. Hunter scratched the shaggy head, knowing there would be no answers tonight. He was weary, befuddled and still burning with desire for Della's body.

Gazing toward the cabin, he saw the lamp in the bedroom flicker out. Della was exhausted and would soon be asleep. He could go back inside and climb up to the loft, safe from a confrontation that could make them both uncomfortable. It wasn't what he wanted to do. But for now, it was the choice of wisdom.

Did he love her? Only time would tell. But he wanted to take that time. He wanted to learn all about her, to build bridges of trust and intimacy between them. And yes, damn it, he wanted to make love to her. He wanted her beneath him in his bed, her slim white legs wrapping his hips as he drove into her, filling her with his seed, giving her his babies…

Was it too soon for such thoughts? He'd only known the woman for two days. But he was certain of one thing—he was not ready to let her walk away. Not, at least, until he knew more about her.

Tomorrow he would keep his distance, Hunter resolved. He would allow Della to give Joey a good Christmas without putting any pressure on her. When the boy was tucked into bed and the two of them were alone by the fire, then he would speak his piece.

Della was a headstrong woman and she'd made her decision to leave. He could only hope that one more day would change her mind.

By the time the sun was up, Della had the turkey stuffed and ready to go into the oven. The huge bird wouldn't be fully cooked until midafternoon, when they would eat their

Christmas dinner. Meanwhile there would be breakfast and the opening of Joey's stocking.

Joey had bounded out of bed at first light. He'd been wild to take down the lumpy stocking and open it right away. But Della, wanting to prolong the excitement, had insisted that he wait until after breakfast.

Hunter had taken his son out to the barn to help with the chores. He had made it clear that, even on Christmas morning, the animals had to come first. Welcoming the peace, Della hurried to have bacon and flapjacks with blackberry jam ready for a festive breakfast. Whatever else happened, she was going to make the best of the day.

She could see the two of them now through the kitchen window. They were throwing a stick for the dog to catch, laughing as the big, shaggy creature plowed through snow. Hunter was hatless, his hair tousled by the wind. Soon he would fling open the door and stride across the threshold, letting in a gust of cold, clean winter air. The sight of him would break her heart.

Della had come to realize that she was falling in love with him. It had surprised her at first that she was capable of loving a man. But Hunter's gentle strength had awakened long-buried emotions, making her feel alive for the first time in years. Not that it changed anything. She still needed to leave. But he'd given her hope that someday she might find happiness. For that, she would always be grateful.

Even so, Della knew there'd be nights when she would lie awake, cursing the memory of his kisses and aching for what she could never have.

She could hear Hunter and Joey on the porch now, stamping the snow off their boots. By the time they opened the door, Della had hot flapjacks on the table and a cheery smile on her face. She felt Hunter watching her as they sat down to eat, but she could not trust herself to meet his gaze. She was too raw, too vulnerable to face what she might see in his eyes.

Joey chattered his way through breakfast, so excited that Hunter had to remind him to eat. All this for a few overdone cookies and a small wooden horse. Della was sorry the boy wouldn't be opening a mountain of wonderful gifts. Hunter, however, didn't appear the least troubled. His face shone with a subtle anticipation that almost equaled his son's.

When breakfast was done and the dishes cleared away, Hunter lit the logs he'd stacked in the fireplace. Della watched the flickering light play across the rugged planes of his face. She had never known a man who took such tender care of others. His son, his animals, even the strangers who crossed his path, all received the best he could give. She could only hope that someday soon, for Joey's sake, he would find a woman worthy of his love.

With the three of them sitting around the fire, Hunter handed Joey his stocking. Joey's small face glowed as he reached into the top and pulled out Della's cookies, one by one. "Thank you, Miss Della," he said. "I've never had cookies like stars before."

"I made them just for you," Della said, thinking how she had almost burned the poor things to a cinder. "The other gift is from your father."

Joey reached deep into the foot of the stocking and pulled out the little horse. He grinned as he moved it through the air in a galloping motion. "Thanks, Pa," he said cheerfully. "It's almost like having a real horse!"

"It *is* a real horse," Hunter said.

Joey and Della stared at him, uncomprehending, as his smile broadened.

"I can't give you your real Christmas present yet," he said. "Until it's born, this little wooden horse will have to do."

Joey's blue eyes went saucer-wide. His mouth dropped open. "Sadie's foal? You're giving me Sadie's foal?"

"I've been thinking, it's time you had a horse of your own," Hunter said. "You can start out by learning to take care of it. It'll be hard work, mind you. But by the time the colt's old enough to be ridden you should be big enough to ride it."

Joey shook his head, as if he were still afraid to believe what he'd heard. "But the new wagon, Pa. You said—"

"I know what I said. But the wagon can wait. We'll get by with the buckboard for now."

"Pa!" Joey exploded across the space that separated them, flinging his arms around his father's neck. "This is the best—the best Christmas ever!"

Hunter held his son close. Watching them from the rocker, Della swallowed the tightness in her throat. Leaving these two would be one of the hardest things she'd even done. But the sooner she did it, the less hurt it would cause.

"What do you want to do between now and dinnertime?" Hunter asked. "No work. It's a holiday!"

"I know!" Joey said. "Miss Della told me how she used to go out and play games in the snow on Christmas Day. That's what I want to do!"

"And what kinds of games did Miss Della play in the snow?" Hunter met Della's eyes above Joey's fair head. "Maybe she can teach us."

"We usually built a snowman," Della said. "Sometimes we had snowball fights or played fox and geese. And the very last thing, before we went inside, we always made snow angels."

Hunter nodded. "Then what do you say we help Miss Della wash the breakfast dishes and set the table for dinner? Then she can come outside and play in the snow with us."

Hunter had almost forgotten how to play. He'd done far too little of it in his growing-up years. Then, not long after his marriage to Rachel, there'd been the war. By the time he'd returned, she was already ill. Life, it seemed, had drained all the play out of him.

But in the sunshine of this sparkling day, with Della and Joey laughing as they pelted him with snowballs, he felt young and free and light of heart.

They had started by building a snowman with twigs for arms and an old straw hat on its head. After that, Della had taught them how to play fox and geese, a kind of tag played on a wheel-shaped track in the snow. The game had degenerated into a wild snowball fight, with Joey and Della ganging up on Hunter until he looked like a snowman himself.

Della was beautiful, he thought, with snowflakes sparkling like jewels in her damp hair. The cold had reddened her cheeks and lips, and her hazel eyes danced with laughter. How could he not love this woman? How could he not want to spend the rest of his life with her, waking up to the sight of her face every morning, knowing that whatever the day brought she would be there beside him—and that, at its end, they would drift off to sleep in each other's arms?

Joey had run himself to the point of happy exhaustion. He was clearly getting cold and tired.

"That turkey should be just about cooked by now,"

Della said, glancing at Hunter above the boy's drooping head. "What do you say we go inside and warm up while I finish getting dinner ready?"

"But we haven't made snow angels!" Joey protested. "You said you'd show us how!"

"All right, it won't take long." Della looked around at the trampled snow. "First we need a nice, smooth patch of snow with no tracks," she said. "Can you help me find one, Joey?"

"Up there!" He pointed to a strip of pristine slope between the barn and the trees. It took only minutes for the three of them to reach it.

"I'll make the first angel," Della said, standing with her back to the snowy slope. "Watch me."

Raising her arms, she fell straight backward, into the soft snow. As Hunter and Joey watched, she moved her legs in and out to make a skirt. Then she moved her arms up and down to make wings. "Now help me up!" she said.

Laughing, they seized her hands and pulled her to her feet. There in the snow was a perfect angel shape.

"My turn!" Joey fell over backward in the snow, giggling as he fanned his arms and legs. When Hunter lifted him up there was a small angel next to the one Della had made.

Joey clapped his hands. "Now you, Papa!"

Hunter turned around. "Timber…" he called as he toppled into the snow. After he'd made the skirt and wings on his very tall angel, Della and Joey grabbed his hands and heaved him upright again.

"Look!" Joey said, pointing. "One little angel, one middle-sized angel and one great big angel. It's an angel family!"

The words clenched around Hunter's heart, but he forced himself to grin. "Come on," he said, ruffling Joey's hair. "I'll race you to the porch!"

The smell of roast turkey greeted them as they stomped off the snow and tumbled breathlessly into the kitchen. While Joey warmed himself by the fire and played with his little horse, Della made the gravy and took the rolls from the warmer above the stove. When all was ready, Hunter carved tender, succulent slices from the turkey and the three of them sat down at the table.

Joey murmured a few words of grace when asked, and the meal began. After the long romp in the snow, all of them were ravenous. "This is the best dinner I ever had!" Joey declared, filling his plate a second time. "Ma was too sick to cook much. And Pa, well…" His gaze shifted toward his father. "He cooks, but not like you do, Miss Della."

"Are you saying I'm not a good cook?" Hunter scowled at the boy in mock severity.

"You're not a bad cook," Joey said. "But we need a lady to cook for us. Miss Della can cook just fine. She's pretty, too. Why don't you ask her to get married, Pa? I bet she'd say yes."

Hunter's ears actually reddened. "I'm afraid Miss Della has other plans," he said. "She wants us to take her into town tomorrow and leave her there."

Joey's stricken expression tore at Della's heart. "But I want her to stay!" he cried. "So do you, don't you, Pa?"

Hunter looked pained. "Sorry, son, but Miss Della is her own boss. We can't make her stay if she has someplace else to go."

Joey turned to Della, his eyes brimming with tears. "Please stay, Miss Della," he begged. "I want you to stay. Pa wants you to stay. I'll bet Ma would even want you to stay if she knew how much we needed you!"

Della averted her eyes to hide the rush of emotion. Everything she'd ever wanted—love, warmth and safety—was here within these four log walls. But her ugly past stood before her like a barred gate, allowing her to see but not to touch. Too overcome to reply, she simply shook her head.

"Miss Della—"

"That's enough, son." Hunter's voice was low and taut. "It's Christmas Day. Don't spoil it."

Joey lowered his face and finished the meal in silence. Even a slice of warm apple pie for dessert failed to rouse a smile from him.

Della's heart ached for the boy. She had wanted to give him one shining, perfect Christmas to remember. Now that day had been tarnished by disappointment. And there was nothing she could do to ease the hurt.

After dinner they cleared the table and washed the dishes, then settled themselves in the chairs by the fire to sing the Christmas songs Della had taught Joey. But the brightness had gone out of the day. Joey was so tired and dispirited that he fell asleep in Hunter's arms halfway through "O Little Town of Bethlehem."

Della lit the lamp as Hunter carried his son up to the loft and put him to bed. The short winter day was darkening into twilight. Soon Christmas, with all its magic, would be over.

Leaning back into the rocking chair, she watched the

flames cast dancing shadows on the cabin walls. Except for the last hour, it had been a wonderful day—a day to keep in her heart like a flower pressed between the pages of a book. But it was time to put the day behind her and move on. To stay would be to risk hurting two people she'd come to love deeply.

Overhead, she could hear Hunter walking toward the ladder. Seconds later his long legs emerged from the loft. This would be a smart time to excuse herself and go to bed, Della thought. She was certainly tired enough.

But no, Hunter deserved better than that. She would sit with him awhile, enjoying their time alone and giving herself a few more memories. He had already made it clear that he didn't mind her leaving. A bit of pleasant conversation would be harmless enough.

He came down the ladder and walked to the fireplace, where he stood for a moment, warming himself and staring into the flames. When he turned around to face her, the storm in his eyes told Della she'd been wrong. She was in trouble, and now it was too late to run.

He sank into the chair, leaning forward with his elbows on his knees, a gentle giant of a man without a devious bone in his body. Whatever he wanted, Della knew she could not lie to him.

"Joey doesn't want you to go, Della," he said. "Neither do I. Why not stay for a while, at least until it's safe to travel. Maybe you'll get to like it here."

Maybe you'll get to like me. The unspoken words hung in the air between them. A lump of dread congealed in the pit of Della's stomach. She shook her head vigorously.

"I can't," she said, choking out the words.

He sighed and settled back into the chair. "What is it?

Another man? One who's waiting for you in Oregon? Is that why you're so anxious to leave?"

Again she shook her head. "There's no man." *Only you,* she thought.

"If you're worried about what happened last night, I can promise not to lay a hand on you," he said. "You're a lovely, desirable woman, Della, and I've come to care for you. But I won't force myself on you. That's the last thing I'd want to do."

She was trembling. "No—stop it, please, Hunter. I can't stay. I have my reasons! That's all there is to it!"

He moved forward to crouch in front of her, his big, powerful hands gripping her shoulders, his eyes drilling into hers. "We've come too far for me to let this go without a word, Della. Whether you leave or stay, I need to know what you're hiding."

Like a cornered animal, Della tried to shrink away, but his hands and eyes held her, refusing to let her go. Tears welled up in her eyes. She blinked them furiously away. The last thing she deserved or wanted from him was sympathy.

"All right, I'll tell you," she said in a cold voice. "When you know the truth, you won't have any argument against my leaving."

He released her and eased back into the chair, his expression guarded. Della licked her lips. Her hands clenched and unclenched in her lap as she groped for a way to begin.

"I told you I had a happy childhood, and I did," she said. "All that changed when I was seventeen, and a sweet-talking drifter named Brock Haddon came to town. My father said he was no good and forbade me to see him, but I thought I was in love. We ran away. You can guess the rest, or some of it. We moved from place to place, living in cheap rooms, running out in the middle of the night because we couldn't pay the rent. The work I got scrubbing floors and doing laundry put food in our mouths, but not much more. He kept saying he'd marry me when he made his pile, but it never happened. He spent his nights playing cards and most of his days sleeping."

She glanced at Hunter. He was leaning forward again, his face expressionless except for the lines of tension around his mouth. Della ached to spare him the rest of her story but it was already too late. Hunter, she knew, would not settle for anything less than the whole, ugly truth.

"I should have left him," she said. "But I was young and foolish, and I thought I could make him go straight. By the time I came to my senses, I was carrying a child. I was too sick to work, and I had no place to go."

Della fought to keep the emotion out of her voice. "There was this man—an awful man, big and mean. Brock owed him money, about five hundred dollars, and he was pushing to be paid. One night I came home, and the man was in my room. He told me I was his now, that Brock had offered his woman to pay the debt, and he meant to get his money's worth...."

Hunter muttered an oath under his breath. Oh, yes, he felt pity for her now. But he'd change his mind once he heard the whole story.

"By the time he finished with me, I was bruised and bleeding. Later that night I lost the baby. I was wandering the streets, covered in blood and out of my mind with shock and grief, when a woman found me. She took me to her...house."

Della hesitated, then plunged ahead. "I knew what kind of place it was, but I was long past caring. I was just grateful to have a roof over my head. She cleaned me up, fed me and brought a doctor in to make sure I was all right. A few weeks later, after I'd recovered, she bought me some pretty clothes and put me to work with her other girls. By then I didn't care what became of me. I stayed in that house for three years."

Della had been staring down at her hands, but now she looked up at Hunter to make certain he'd understood her meaning. Clearly he had. His face was so pale and cold and rigid that the features could have been sculpted from ice.

Why didn't he curse her, rail at her, call her all the vile names she'd called herself? Anything, she thought, would be easier to bear than this grim silence.

"A year ago I walked out of that place, determined to make a new life for myself," she said. "But so far, I haven't been able to walk far enough or fast enough to get away from my past. The people in the wagon train—they found out about me. That's why the wagon master thought he was entitled to—" She shook her head. "That's why I ran away. And that's why I have to leave now—before word gets around that Hunter McCall has taken in a...a whore!"

Hunter stared at her in numb anguish. He knew what he ought to say, that her past didn't matter, that he still wanted her to stay. But his own memories—his mother, walking through the door with her arms full of presents, and the look of wretched resignation in his father's eyes—loomed like a towering wall, blocking his thoughts and words.

Outside he was as calm as ice. Inside a battle raged between his head and heart.

How can I judge Della now? his heart argued. She was gentle and kind and loving. She'd been through some hellish years and had found the courage to change. Shouldn't that count for something?

She's a whore, his head countered shrilly. *Whores never change. Your mother didn't. Think of Joey. Think of what people will say if she stays!*

Della rose to her feet, her face an impassive mask. "I'll be going to bed now," she said. "Maybe you should, too. You'll be wanting to get an early start tomorrow morning."

As she turned away, he found his voice. "Della—"

She vanished into the bedroom and closed the door behind her.

For a long time Hunter sat staring into the flames. He loved Della—he was as certain of that as he was of anything in his life. She had come to him out of nowhere, like a sweet gift from heaven, bringing warmth, light and laughter into his gloomy heart. He could easily be content to spend the rest of his days with her, holding her in the night, raising their children, growing old together.

If it was just the two of them and they could go anywhere they wished, there would be no question of what to do. But this was his home. He had Rachel's memory to consider. And he had Joey.

Della had said that the people on the wagon train knew about her. If they'd made it to South Pass City, they were bound to talk. Sooner or later, everyone in town would know.

Joey was young and innocent now. But next year he'd be starting school. Children heard things, and they could be cruel. Hunter knew just how cruel they could be. The last thing he wanted was for Joey to feel the kind of pain he'd felt when someone shouted, for all to hear, that his mother was a whore.

But there was so much more to Della than her past. She was courageous, passionate and giving. She had all the qualities of a wonderful wife, mother and neighbor. Surely, once people got to know her, the rest wouldn't matter.

Putting on his coat, he went outside to check on the animals. A breathy chinook wind had sprung up from the south. Warm and moist, it sighed through the trees, blowing the snow from the limbs and sending it in showers to the ground.

Hunter felt the wetness on his face as he walked back to the house. Sinking onto the porch steps, he gazed across the yard at the snowman. By tomorrow it would already be melting.

Windblown clouds swept across the sky, etching moon shadows on the snow. Hunter gazed up at the half-veiled stars, wondering what Rachel would say if she could speak to him. What would she think if he told her he'd fallen in love with a reformed prostitute and wanted to make her his wife?

But that no longer mattered, Hunter realized. His shocked, silent reaction to Della's story had resolved the question for him. He had hurt her so deeply that nothing could persuade her to stay.

He had already lost her.

Chapter Six

The wind was still blowing in the morning when Hunter went out to saddle the horses. Gloomy clouds scudded across the sky. Long fingers of ice dripped from the eaves of the cabin.

Breakfast had been a grim affair. Joey had sulked his way through the hasty meal of Christmas leftovers. Della had been pale and distant, saying no more than what was necessary. Hunter had kept his silence, knowing that to open his heart would only make matters worse. The two-hour ride into town was going be a strain on them all.

He bridled Buck and the mare and laid the saddles over their blankets, going through the motions like a sleep-walker. Last night he'd scarcely closed his eyes, and, judging from the look of her, neither had Della. He felt sore and gritty and plain, damned miserable, and he was guessing that she felt the same.

Lord, what was he going to do? He would crawl on his knees if it would convince her to stay. But what was the use? Della was a proud woman, and last night's silence had wounded her deeply. She would not forgive him.

The dog pawed Hunter's leg in an unspoken request to go along. "Not this time, boy," Hunter said. "You stay and watch the place. We'll be back home before dark."

Sam trotted obediently into a corner and curled up on a pile of empty feed sacks. Hunter sighed as he tightened the cinch around the mare's rounding belly. Maybe the dog had the right idea, just accept what couldn't be and get on with life.

But how could he do that when losing Della felt like having his heart ripped out?

As he led the horses out of the barn, he saw that Della had come out onto the porch with Joey. She was wrapped in her shawl and carrying a sack with some turkey sandwiches she'd made for their lunch. Both she and the boy looked as though they were on their way to a funeral.

Joey trailed her down the steps. "Can I ride on Sadie with Miss Della?" he asked.

"Fine," Hunter said. "Just give me a minute to check the place and lock up."

He closed the barn door and then made a quick sweep of the cabin as he always did before he left, making sure the lamps were out, the fire was banked and nothing had been left to burn on the stove. When he came back outside, he saw Della standing with the horses. There was no sign of Joey.

Hunter strode down the steps. "Now, where's that blasted boy? He knows it's time to leave. If this is some kind of game—"

"No, it's all right," Della said. "He just wanted to see the snow angels again before they melted. He'll be right back."

Hunter scuffed his boots in the snow, knowing this would likely be his last moment alone with her. "Della," he said, groping for words. "I just want to say—"

"No." Her voice cut him off. "Don't say anything. I know what you think of me, so don't try to smooth things over. It won't help."

She lifted her boot to the stirrup, preparing to mount. Desperate now, Hunter seized her arm. "Damn it, Della, if you'd just—"

"No." She caught her balance as the startled mare danced away. "Leave me alone, Hunter. It was a bad idea, your asking me to stay. I'd wager your poor, sweet wife would turn over in her grave if you took up with the likes of—"

"Pa! Miss Della!" Joey came tearing around the barn, flushed and out of breath. "Come see—" he gasped. "The snow angels—"

Wheeling, he dashed back the way he'd come. Left with little choice, Hunter and Della plunged after him.

The snowy slope where they'd made their angels lay in the sheltered lee of the barn. Even after the night's warm wind, Hunter could see the tall angel, the middle-sized angel and the small angel standing side by side, like a family—a family that, by day's end, would be no more.

"Look," Joey said, pointing. "Higher up. Can you see it?"

Hunter heard Della's breath catch, and then he saw it, too.

On the slope, just above the three angels, was a delicate indentation in the snow, so perfectly formed that no one could have mistaken it for a trick of the wind. Hunter, Della and Joey gazed at it in rapt silence.

It was the figure of a fourth angel.

The tightness in Hunter's chest dissolved in a burst of wonder. What was he seeing? Was it an accident of some kind? An unspoken message? A miracle?

"It's Ma!" Joey, in his innocence, spoke the words that

Hunter dared not voice. "She made a snow angel so we'd know she was here!"

Hunter had never believed in angels. But Joey's simple explanation was the only one that made sense. He gazed at the images in the snow—the family standing together and the beautiful angel floating above them, blessing them. Suddenly everything became clear.

He turned toward Della. Tears were glittering in her eyes. "Stay, Della," he said, opening his arms. "Please stay and be part of our family."

She made a little broken sound. In the next instant he was clasping her close.

Joey squirmed his way between them. They stood together in the snow, holding each other in a circle of love.

Epilogue

December 24, 1869

Della stood wrapped in her husband's arms, watching the moonlight steal across the newly fallen snow. Behind them, firelight glowed on a lovingly decorated Christmas tree and the gifts piled beneath it. The aromas of pine, ginger, apples and cinnamon lingered in the air.

The past three years had been good to them. Hunter had built two more rooms onto the cabin to accommodate their growing family. This year there were two small stockings hanging from the mantle—eight-year-old Joey's and little sister Emma's. Next year there would be three.

The cabin also had a fine new front window, where Della could look out at the barn and the new paddock for the horses Hunter raised and trained. Beyond the log fences, forests of pine, aspen and maple swept upward like robes of living tapestry, crowned by snowcapped mountain peaks. The view was more splendid than any painting she could imagine.

These days she seldom thought of her old life. The past was behind her, and if the townspeople ever mentioned it, it was not within her hearing or Hunter's. Still, Della's thoughts often drifted back to the day when she and Hunter had nearly thrown away their future together—the day of the fourth angel.

They had kept the story as a precious family secret, how the snow angel had miraculously appeared in time to stop Della from leaving. No one could explain how it came to be. The slight impression in the snow was too perfect to be an accident, and the absence of tracks around it ruled out any human cause. They only knew that the sight of the fourth snow angel had opened two proud hearts, and in the end Della had stayed.

"What are you thinking?" Hunter nuzzled his wife's temple. His hand slipped downward to cradle her rounding belly.

"Nothing, really. Just counting blessings." Della closed her eyes and leaned back into the hollow of his shoulder. Tomorrow, toward the end of a festive Christmas Day, they would troop out to the smooth slope on the far side of the barn. There in the untouched snow they would make their angels—one tall, one middle-sized, one gangly and growing, one small and plump. Then Joey would draw another tiny angel in the snow to represent the baby who would join their family in the spring.

* * * * *

nocturne™

USA TODAY bestselling author

MAUREEN CHILD

ETERNALLY

He was a guardian. An immortal fighter of evil,
out to destroy a demon, and she was his next
target. He knew joining with her would make
him strong enough to defeat any demon.
But the cost might be losing the woman
who was his true salvation.

On sale November, wherever books are sold.

REQUEST YOUR FREE BOOKS!

 Harlequin® Historical
Historical Romantic Adventure!

2 FREE NOVELS PLUS 2
FREE GIFTS!

YES! Please send me 2 FREE Harlequin® Historical novels and my 2 FREE gifts. After receiving them, if I don't wish to receive any more books, I can return the shipping statement marked "cancel." If I don't cancel, I will receive 6 brand-new novels every month and be billed just $4.69 per book in the U.S., or $5.24 per book in Canada, plus 25¢ shipping and handling per book and applicable taxes, if any*. That's a savings of close to 15% off the cover price! I understand that accepting the 2 free books and gifts places me under no obligation to buy anything. I can always return a shipment and cancel at any time. Even if I never buy another book from Harlequin, the two free books and gifts are mine to keep forever.

246 HDN EEWW   349 HDN EEW9

Name	(PLEASE PRINT)
Address	Apt. #
City	State/Prov. Zip/Postal Code

Signature (if under 18, a parent or guardian must sign)

Mail to the Harlequin Reader Service®:

IN U.S.A.	**IN CANADA**
P.O. Box 1867	P.O. Box 609
Buffalo, NY	Fort Erie, Ontario
14240-1867	L2A 5X3

Not valid to current Harlequin Historical subscribers.

Want to try two free books from another line?
Call 1-800-873-8635 or visit www.morefreebooks.com.

* Terms and prices subject to change without notice. NY residents add applicable sales tax. Canadian residents will be charged applicable provincial taxes and GST. This offer is limited to one order per household. All orders subject to approval. Credit or debit balances in a customer's account(s) may be offset by any other outstanding balance owed by or to the customer. Please allow 4 to 6 weeks for delivery.

This holiday season, cozy up with

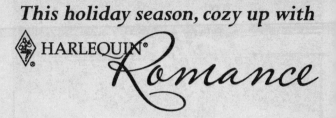

HARLEQUIN® *Romance*

**In November
we're proud to present**

JUDY CHRISTENBERRY
Her Christmas Wedding Wish

A beautiful story of love and family found.

And

LINDA GOODNIGHT
Married Under The Mistletoe

Don't miss this installment of

The Brides of Bella Lucia

From the Heart. For the Heart.

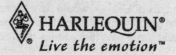

COMING NEXT MONTH FROM

HARLEQUIN®
HISTORICAL

- **MISTLETOE KISSES**
  (Regency Anthology)
  A Soldier's Tale by **Elizabeth Rolls**
  A Winter Night's Tale by **Deborah Hale**
  A Twelfth Night Tale by **Diane Gaston**
  Share the warmth and delight of a traditional Regency
  Christmas with award-winning authors **Elizabeth Rolls,
  Deborah Hale** and **Diane Gaston!**

- **INDISCRETIONS**
  by **Gail Ranstrom**
  (Regency)
  Her impulsive act had forced Lady Elise to run away from
  everything she had ever known...and it would surely come
  between her and the honorable man she had begun to love.

- **THE RASCAL**
  by **Lisa Plumley**
  (Western)
  No man would ever trap Grace Crabtree into wedlock—so
  why did the rugged, laconic, *infuriating* Jack Murphy keep
  flirting with her?

- **THE DEFIANT MISTRESS**
  by **Claire Thornton**
  (Restoration)
  *City of Flames—Smoldering desire at the heart of a
  burning London!*
  Gabriel, Marquis of Halross, would have his revenge. When
  before he had proudly intended to claim Athena as his wife,
  now she would travel with him...as his mistress!